Dying
to Score

Judith Cutler

HEADLINE

ucc 2/2000

First published in 1999
by HEADLINE BOOK PUBLISHING

First published in paperback in 1999
by HEADLINE BOOK PUBLISHING

10 9 8 7 6 5 4 3 2 1

ISBN 0 7472 6210 1

Printed and bound in Great Britain by
Clays Ltd, St Ives plc

HEADLINE BOOK PUBLISHING
A division of Hodder Headline PLC
338 Euston Road
London NW1 3BH
www.headline.co.uk
www.hodderheadline.com

To the memory of my father, Reg Cutler, 1907–1998

ACKNOWLEDGEMENTS

I would like to thank the following for their invaluable help with the allergies mentioned in the novel: Graham Pritchard, whose reaction to wasps gave me the idea for the novel; Mr P. Sherwood Burge; the Anaphylaxis Campaign. Warwickshire County Cricket Club gave me enormous help and encouragement during a cold, wet summer: thank you. West Midlands Police Officers, especially Superintendent Bob Baxter, were as usual endlessly patient when helping me with my inquiries, and bear no relationship to their fictional counterparts except in their hard work and dedication. Finally, thank you, Edwina Van Boolen, Frances Lally and Maureen Carter for your ongoing support and criticism.

Chapter One

The last thing I'd expected to do on the day I'd planned
a grand farewell to William Murdock College was go to
a funeral. What I'd meant to do was go out in style. Not
exactly a leaving party, because the official idea was that
I'd be coming back after a year's postgraduate course at
university, bubbling with new, improved ways of teaching
English to anyone who wanted to be taught. But I'd hired
a narrow boat to party us down a local cut: what other,
non-Birmingham, people might call a barge on a canal. I'd
organised booze and balloons, and everyone who knew me
was bidden. One or two old Murdock lags had promised
to turn up – Philomena, a senior nurse now, who'd never
let herself be demeaned when she'd had to take on a
college cleaning job, any more than her son, Winston,
nearly qualified as a medic, had by his stint as a security
guard in our foyer. He couldn't come, however – he would
be making one of his rare but invaluable appearances as a
left-arm fast bowler for Middlesex in the County Cricket
Championship and would probably be running up to destroy
the opposition's batsmen even as I popped the first bottle
of Cava – well, it wasn't meant to be a leaving party, so I
hadn't splashed out, as it were, on proper champagne.

And then there wasn't a party any more.

1

*   *   *

We all knew that Halima, one of our very brightest students, had a peanut allergy. She never went into the canteen these days, and everyone knew they mustn't eat peanuts anywhere near her. We all assumed it was because they gave her rhinitis or something. Just an inconvenience, like the asthma I get if I disturb too much dust, or run without my spray. But it was worse.

'Sophie!' A frantic voice interrupted a tedious planning meeting there was no point my being at anyway. 'You've got to come! We can't find the duty first-aider. And we couldn't find you! It may be too late!'

I moved faster than I knew how, pounding down the stairs. The kids had stationed themselves at each bend to make sure I got there.

'This floor. The history room!'

And then I took in the scene. Halima was waxen pale, drooping over a desk, her face drawn into a mask of total despair. Her hands were hideously swollen: it was as if someone had pumped her full of water. Huge white lumps bubbled under the transparent skin. A bit of chocolate complete with tooth-marks lay beside her – she must have realised too late what she'd done and spat it out – and her hand clutched what looked like a pen. Guessing it must be important and praying I wasn't too late, I jabbed it into her thigh.

'Help me get her on to the floor with her!' There was no blood pressure – I'd got to get blood to her brain.

But neither that nor the heart-thumping nor the mouth-to-mouth worked – her tongue was so swollen it was impossible to find an airway.

The family said she'd loved college so much they'd like the staff to be at her funeral, which had to be held immediately, according to Islam. So there we were on *my* last day at college in a sad corner of a municipal graveyard, saying farewell and not even thinking about a wake.

By common consent we trailed back to college, numb with grief and shock. All I had to do was sit and look at my unnaturally tidy desk. Tidy! Abandoned, more like. The contents were stowed in cardboard boxes stored for safe-keeping at the back of one of the language labs. My files were all in their cabinet, rigid with the shock of being organised at last.

I suppose I could have gone round one last time to say *au revoir*, but I'd hugged and kissed so many of my colleagues in the last two days that it was as if I was mourning them, too. So, holding in tears and with a crushing sense of anti-climax, I set off for home.

One of the things I do to cheer myself up is to cook and then eat wonderful food. I'd plundered the coriander in my garden so much recently that there wasn't enough left for the curry I had in mind, so I took myself the long way round, via Smethwick. The high street is now bypassed, so it wasn't difficult to park and wander from shop to shop, acquiring the best ginger, the plumpest aubergines, the freshest coriander. I even treated myself to some of those teeth-wrenching sweets.

I should have known better than to head for a main road to get me back to Harborne. A combination of road works and afternoon traffic had bunged things up nicely. Cutting my engine, I sat with the sun roof open, hoping I got fewer noxious fumes that way, and listening to Radio Three.

Before I realised properly what was happening, a woman erupted from a car ahead of me in the queue. She hurtled along the pavement away from me, out of my sight. The driver, not caring that the queue was now moving, gave chase. Every instinct of sisterhood told me to join in, but an even stronger imperative, the chorus of car horns behind me, told me at least to pull in before I did so.

Too late. All I could see was the man dragging the woman

back to his car. She didn't go quietly, kicking hard at the passenger door before he opened it and forced her in.

I didn't even get the registration number. And what would the police have said if I went trotting along with a description of the incident? 'A domestic,' in all probability.

There were times when even I had to shrug and walk away.

The house was quiet. Unnaturally quiet. Well, to be honest, it was probably a lot less quiet than on an ordinary day, because the council were mowing the grass verges and I added to their clatter a chorus of sneezes until I'd located and used my hay-fever spray. But it was quiet. The sort of quiet that makes people turn on day-time TV.

I spoke firmly to myself. *OK, Sophie – go and sit in the garden: there's a mound of reading to be done. Next year may be a sabbatical (unpaid), but it's not a holiday. How long is it since you studied? Well, you're going to find it tough. So the best thing you can do is start on those books now.*

OK, I conceded. So long as it's in the garden. In a deckchair. I'll get the sun-block and a floppy hat.

I fell asleep over the first page of the first chapter of the first book.

Stretching awake with a crick in my neck and a mouth like a compost heap, I staggered inside for some fruit juice. As I leaned on the fridge it dawned on me with excruciating slowness. End-of-termitis, that was what I'd got. A bad case. The only cure, as all teachers know, is to let it happen: switch the mind off with the cleaning that everyone else does in spring, and let the body get back to a normal human rhythm. And rest and indulge – just for a week. Everyone knew the first week of the holidays was dead time. You went away in weeks two or three, when you were sane. Any earlier, and all you'd do was snarl and sleep.

Finding I didn't even seem to have the energy to do anything with that coriander after all, I skipped tea and toddled off to Safeway, laid in supplies of every household cleaner under the sun, and put them ready for the next day.

That was better. Conscience assuaged. Now all I had to do was work out how to pass the rest of the evening. Except I wasn't sure I was even up to that.

Chris watched the waiter pouring water with as much care as if it were a grand cru. We were at my favourite Indian restaurant, for no particular reason except that he'd phoned me out of the blue and suggested a meal. I'd leapt at the idea. Chris and I went back years, in an on-off relationship, and catching up with him and his news was much better than contemplating the curtains I ought to take down. If I could only deliver them early enough next morning, the cleaners would have them ready for collection by late afternoon, so I could hang them and put a full stop to the first clean room.

'Penny for them,' he said.

I drew myself upright in my chair. 'Superintendent Groom, sir, I have to report that I was just considering my spring-cleaning,' I said. 'And, since fair exchange is no robbery, what about your thoughts? You've been very quiet too, you know.'

'Wondering if I shall ever get on top of this job,' he said, pushing his fingers through his hair. Not that there was much left to push through. 'There just aren't enough hours in the day. I was in at seven this morning, and – well, what time did we get here?'

'Half-eight. And you came straight from work?'

He nodded. 'Good job I can shower and change at the nick. When are you coming to see my new abode?'

'When you've got time to invite me!'

'Oh, don't wait that long.' He ran a finger around where a stiff white collar would have been half an hour ago. 'I still can't get used to the uniform. Not after all those years in CID.'

'You look very good in it, anyway. Though,' I added, retrieving an errant prawn, 'I could have wished you'd moved to traffic. Then you'd have got to wear all that sexy leather gear.' I was taking a risk. Chris and I had been in strictly friendship mode for months now, and had, as a consequence, got on much better.

But it was OK. 'I always think those white paper overalls would be sexier,' he grinned.

'OK in this weather,' I agreed. 'Anyway, this here job. What's the problem?'

He pulled a face. 'Where do I start? I mean, it was a huge promotion. OCU.'

This time I wouldn't pull him up for using an acronym. In any case I'd heard him use it often enough to know it meant Operational Command Unit. 'Go on.'

'Well, there's so much insecurity throughout the police service with all the financial pressure we're under. Moving people here, shifting responsibility there. Delegation! If only they'd delegate us the staff and the money as well as the work and the responsibility. Jesus, those budgets!' He wiped his hands over his face, as if to push away the memory. 'On top of it all, we've got a couple of drug-related deaths – someone new's started to push the stuff on my patch, and the bugger of it is, I can't be out there looking!'

'You mean you've got to leave it to someone else?' No, he wouldn't be enjoying that.

'I can authorise budgets, that's all. And talk to the investigating officers.'

'Talk to?'

'I make a space each day where I can talk to the DCIs – find out about progress. Toss a few ideas around.' His lip curled on the management cliché.

'Treading a fine line between *laissez-faire* and sticking the nose in?'

His nod was extremely glum.

'It'll get easier as you settle in,' I said. 'It's a skill. Come on, Chris. A new job, a new nick, a new patch. You're bound to find it tough. And you've got to come up for air occasionally. No one can work twelve- or thirteen-hour days without some breaks. Weekends too, if I know you.'

He nodded. 'I'm the one on twenty-four-hour call this weekend. So I won't be piling into my in-tray as I ought.'

I looked at him. 'Get what's-her-name – Helena – to help.'

He looked outraged. 'She's just a secretary!'

'In my experience, anyone who's a secretary as opposed to a typist is never *just* a secretary. She sounds mature, hard-working and very bright.' I'd taken a strong liking to her during our brief phone conversations while she was trying to connect me to Chris. 'She sorts out all your post every morning. Get her to colour-code it for priority.'

He was shaking his head.

'How long has she been working for the police? Five years? Didn't she even have a stint with Bob before his promotion? Well then, she knows every onion going.'

He looked stubborn.

'What are they saying? That Bob never did things the way you're doing them? Well, of course you won't tackle everything the same way. But why not stick to his routines until you know exactly what to keep, what to ditch.'

He put his fork down. 'He's such an act to follow.'

'I bet young Sheila down at Rose Road is saying exactly the same thing. "Hell, Chris's desk was so tidy; his coffee was so good." And she's a woman. Imagine, fighting her way up to be DCI and then wondering why. She'll have twice the difficulties you've got . . .'

'She's got Ian,' he said.

I acknowledged the point. Ian had taken Sheila under his wing like a favourite niece, and would pass on every dodge and wrinkle before he retired. 'Make Helena your Ian,' I said.

'But she's a civilian!'

And a woman, I added under my breath.

By common consent we let the topic drop. We'd enough friends and acquaintances to keep us going through the rest of the meal, and drifted inconsequentially from one to the next. Although we headed home in separate cars, he pulled in behind mine when we reached Balden Road.

'Why don't you pop in next door and see Aggie,' I suggested, 'while I brew coffee. Decaffeinated?'

Maybe it should have been real coffee, black. As we talked, his head slumped and I had to retrieve the cup. Well, I'd done it before and I dare say I'd do it again. I slipped off his shoes, tipped him over on to the sofa, and left a blanket within reach. For such a tall, spare man, he slept remarkably like a baby.

When I woke in the night wanting the loo, it was much cooler. I slipped down and covered him gently: he hadn't stirred in four hours.

Chapter Two

Perhaps it wasn't a good idea to be jogging through the leafy streets of Harborne in quite such a brief vest and shorts. Although the sun promised to be hot later, at this hour in the morning there was still a distinct chill in the air. Worse, the outfit exposed foolish amounts of the Rivers anatomy to the appraising glances of the Newish Men dropping their children off unnaturally early for school – presumably so they could park on the zigzag lines without being chastised by the crossing-warden. But if I was embarrassed on the side roads, they were nothing compared with Court Oak Road, which I had eventually to join: the rush-hour traffic heading towards the city centre was beautifully set, giving far too many opportunities for lecherous observations. I gazed resolutely away from the traffic. In one of the side roads opposite the park, someone's bonnet was up. Either the battery or the starter motor had expired. I was hardly dressed to be a Good Samaritan, but that had never stopped me, had it?

'If you can hang on for ten minutes, I can provide jump leads or a hammer,' I said to the pair of jeans bent over the entrails.

The occupier straightened slowly. The jeans were topped with a T-shirt. The owner was an Asian man in his twenties, his face vaguely familiar. An ex-William Murdock student, perhaps.

'I think it's the battery, love,' he said. 'Me electrics are all down. I've called the RAC but they say it could be two hours.' He glanced at an elaborate watch.

Love! They never learned, did they! 'OK. I'll be about ten minutes, like I said.' I nodded, and set off.

There were a couple of phone messages waiting, but I'd leave them till I got back. I pulled on a T-shirt and replaced the shorts with jeans before setting off in my car, which obligingly started first turn of the ignition key.

I got stuck in the traffic, of course, but pulled off the main road as soon as I could. Damn. It meant I'd end up pointing the same way as the sick car. But the Renault never objected to three-point turns, and I pulled up niftily nose-to-nose with him. He smiled warmly, maintaining his grin even when I removed the jump-lead clip from the terminal he'd attached it to and replaced it on the correct one.

He positively beamed when his car responded.

As I coiled the leads I pointed him in the direction of a battery depot and waved an affable goodbye. It was only when I'd dropped in at the newsagent's to buy a *Guardian* and caught a sports headline, that I realised who I'd been helping. One of Warwickshire's brightest hopes: a batsman who could bowl remarkably quickly when asked but hadn't yet become a true all-rounder.

Cricket! Yes, I could spend a day basking at the county ground! A miracle! But I'd better check the answerphone first.

The first message was from Ian Dale, Chris's colleague, who wanted me to clear my palate and my diary for a wine-tasting competition in a couple of weeks' time. The second was from Afzal, a solicitor friend of mine, who said he'd like to invite me to lunch. Since Afzal usually regarded lunch in the same way as I did – an opportunity to cram in mouthfuls of food between agenda items – I decided to phone him to accept before he changed his mind.

'How about today?' he asked.

'Today!'

'I shall be in court most of next week. And then – well, today would be best.'

I was intrigued: there was an unusual note of urgency in his voice. OK, it would mean shelving the cricket, but I had the whole weekend for that.

Right! All that sorted – and the clock insisted it was only ten past nine. Well, not much more than five past, to be honest. Any moment now the post might occupy another five minutes of my day.

Although I would have been early for lunch with Afzal, some idiot had parked a Toyota so badly in the minuscule car park of his new office that it took me five minutes of patient inching to get in. I greeted the receptionist cordially: Afzal had taken on a William Murdock work experience student during the year and had been so impressed that he'd offered her holiday cover work. It was nice when one of my students did so well.

Except they weren't mine any more, of course.

We were engaged in Murdock gossip, however, when Afzal showed his client out – a client who turned up his collar and hunched his back towards me as he scuttled out. If he was that furtive, I was surprised he'd chosen Afzal: his work centred almost exclusively on industrial law, unlike my own solicitor's, whose practice was decidedly eclectic. When I'd popped in to sign my will, I found myself sharing a waiting room with a man later sent down for fifteen years for dealing drugs. He'd had a big, badly parked car, too, come to think of it.

Afzal greeted me with his usual cool kiss, and spread his hands. 'Where would you like to eat?'

I shrugged. I didn't associate Golden Hillock Road with *haute cuisine*, though the cheapo balti restaurants took some beating. After last night's huge curry, however, I wasn't sure about cheapo baltis – today I'd have liked a little more refinement, even if it meant one of us driving and staying on the wagon. His turn, I rather thought, though I offered.

'No. I'll drive,' he said obligingly. 'I'm not drinking these days.'

Something in his intonation made me look at him sharply: for a Muslim he was usually very relaxed about alcohol, though I'd never seen him drink more than one glass. He spent a few moments giving detailed instructions covering every conceivable emergency to Inderjit, who smiled gently back. She was sure she could cope for an hour or two, especially since he took his mobile phone with him.

The place we finally fetched up in was a pub, unappealing enough; presumably he'd chosen it because it had a garden at the back. We sat sipping our drinks – mineral water for us both, when it came to it: the day was becoming too sticky for me to risk alcohol. After all, I had a car to get back across Birmingham.

'Sophie,' he began. 'I need to talk to you.'

This was so unlike his usual approach that I stared.

'A personal matter.' He dropped his eyes, almost as if he were feeling guilty. 'I'm thinking of getting married,' he said. 'Well, I'm forty,' he added as if in explanation.

'That's wonderful. Oh, I'm very pleased,' I said, hoping the exclamation and question marks didn't buzz out of my head. Afzal had been widowed in most tragic circumstances a few years back. He'd left London to try to bury himself in work up here, and then, a few months ago, we'd seemed to be starting a relationship. He'd been right to break it off – it wouldn't have worked for a number of reasons, including the fact that he was still in love with his dead wife and children. So his announcement took me by surprise, to say the least. It was time for me to say something else, wasn't it? And to get the voice natural. 'Do I know her?'

He shook his head.

A waitress appeared with plates of salad and flan. A wasp took an immediate but fleeting interest.

'I hardly know her myself. It's almost an arranged marriage, Sophie, but not quite. My aunt knows her aunt: you know how it is. She's a widow. She's got two children. Here.' He produced a photograph from his wallet.

The children were certainly lovely – bright-eyed, laughing babies. But I felt anxious.

'What about her? And what's her name?' I hoped the questions weren't too pointed.

To my relief he grinned. 'Fozia. And she doesn't photograph well. She's very nice-looking, though. And well-educated. A dentist, actually. That's how we met. Oh, Sophie – I wondered, but, you see, I was so shy—'

'Hence the aunties,' I said. 'I'm very happy for you, Afzal.'

I was.

'I wanted to be the first to tell you. Shahida – she was afraid—'

'I'd be hurt? Come on, Afzal – surely you and I have been just friends long enough for Shahida to have got it into her head that any item-ness between us was purely temporary! Not that I haven't reminded her practically every day at college.' Shahida was one of my closest friends but indefatigably romantic. 'And now she'll have the pleasure of matchmaking for me all over again! But I'm glad you told me yourself. Now, when am I going to meet your Fozia?'

We were in his baking-hot car when I said, 'The guy I saw in your office didn't seem your usual sort of client, Afzal. Are you branching out?'

He shook his head. I knew better than to prompt him. We spoke about traffic, the pollution that was turning the city

13

air into a hot golden blanket. He talked about his fiancée's children and his hopes for them. He asked, as we watched a taxi pumping out black fumes, 'Sophie, what would you do if someone were blackmailing you?'

'That rather presupposes I've got something to hide,' I retorted.

'Oh, most people have something in their past they'd rather wasn't generally known. Just suppose, anyway – what would you do?'

'Call the police,' I said promptly. Then I wondered if I should have done. Could it possibly be that Afzal . . . ? Surely not! I added, 'And talk to my solicitor, maybe. It must depend, surely, on what it is I want to hide.'

He nodded. 'You're right, of course. But it must take so much effort to talk to the guardians of law and order when what you've done is against the law, and if it were widely known could disgrace you. You wouldn't just pay up?'

'Meet someone under the station clock with a bag of used fivers? Assuming I had enough fivers to fill the bag, of course!'

'Would you confront – confess to – someone like Chris? Would you have the courage?'

His persistence was worrying. Surely no one could be trying to blackmail him! Much as I wanted to offer support, I couldn't ask him outright – not Afzal, who was always cagey about his past, which had involved dealings with some very unlovely people. 'The day I have anything to confess to Chris I'll ask you to be present,' I said gaily. But I wished he'd change the subject. There were just a couple of things I'd rather Chris didn't know about. Ever.

And, come to think of it, there was part of my past I desperately hoped would catch up with me – but Chris wouldn't like that either. Or did I mean especially?

*　　*　　*

The more I slowed down, the more miserable I became. Classic end-of-termitis symptoms, actually. So I started washing paint. But I was growing more and more ratty. How on earth would I get through the next year without the Murdock crowd and our shared Dutch-boy-thumb-in-the-dike-wall camaraderie? I scratched my head irritably. And then turned to the rest of my skin. That needed a good scratch too.

Hell! Something had brought me out in nettle-rash – the detergent, maybe, or even the rubber gloves. Emptying the bucket in the outside drain, I slung the gloves down beside it, for good measure. Blast it all. I'd have to try a different detergent the next day – I was too itchy to persist any more. I took an anti-histamine tablet, popped under the shower, and pondered my next move. It wouldn't be to choir rehearsal, that was for sure.

The rash went down quickly enough but allergic reactions like that always leave me feeling depressed and washed out. In this case, even more depressed and washed out. Maybe I needed a proper break after all. I'd certainly take one tomorrow. And perhaps I'd better check into the doctor's some time – a sudden vision of Halima made me shiver, despite the heat. No, all I had was an allergy, surely.

I would start indulging myself. I really would. I'd start now, in fact. A crisp salad picked from my garden, a little cold chicken, a baguette from the freezer newly baked and a very little white wine – not enough to foul up the anti-histamine. And then I retired to bed with a battered Georgette Heyer romance, complete with handsome clean-jawed hero, some chocolate I'd saved for just such an occasion and the Brahms concert on Radio Three.

It was already *CD Review* when I woke up.

Chapter Three

A fine morning, the last day of a county championship match, and the excuse that, though my nettle-rash had almost gone, it would be foolish to risk irritating my skin with further spring-cleaning – the obvious place for me was Edgbaston cricket ground. Somehow the fact that it was a Saturday, not a proper working day, helped. I packed lunch, plenty of fruit juice and water, sun-block, big floppy hat, long-sleeved blouse. I'd take my binoculars, too. A book as a barricade against unwanted lunch-time conversations. And my skirt – yes, that was long enough to pull down over my bare legs to protect them when the sun shifted round. Whatever the forecast said, I'd better take a cagoule, too.

The whole lot fitted neatly into a raffia picnic basket I'd picked up at the Oxfam shop with just such a jaunt in mind, but had never got round to using before.

I ran into Aggie, my next door neighbour, as I set out. She looked with interest at my basket, but her face puckered disparagingly when I explained.

'Thought all that grass'd give you hay-fever,' she said.

'It's already cut nice and short. And I've got my nose spray.' No need to explain about the chemical allergy – if I wasn't careful, I'd come home to find she'd cleaned the whole house for me, despite her seventy-plus summers.

'I don't know what you see in it all, anyway.'

One Christmas I'd given her a tea towel printed with a jokey explanation of the game. At least she now knew it was a good thing to take a wicket, but not to lose it, and that bowlers could run up, but it was batsmen who were run out. A lot of runs were good if you were batting, bad if you were trying to bowl out a side. She also knew there were fast bowlers, who could propel the ball at ninety miles an hour, and slow bowlers, who relied on spinning the ball in rough ground to make it deceive the batsman.

So she was well-informed, but far from impressed.

'Anyway, there's no football,' I said.

She nodded, and went in.

Dropped by the bus – using a car is sheer folly on match days – a couple of yards from the ground, I was just about to go through a turnstile when I heard the pounding of mammoth feet and my name being bellowed. I just had time to put down the basket before I was picked up and swung off my feet by a big pair of African-Caribbean hands.

'Winston,' I said with as much dignity as I could be bothered to muster, 'put me down, damn you.'

On *terra firma* again, slightly breathless, I smoothed my skirt and retrieved the basket. I pushed my sunglasses further up my nose. 'What are you doing here? I thought you were at Lord's.'

He looked embarrassed. 'We won by an innings.'

I knew from his face that he must have returned good figures. 'And how many wickets did you take – come on, Winston: I didn't pick up the scores last night. What were your figures? Come on, give!'

He was trying so hard to look modest! 'You know about my hat-trick in the first innings?'

A hat-trick! Three wickets in three balls! I didn't know, of course, but I beamed as if I knew that must be a mere prelude to something even grander.

'Well – Sophie, I took all ten wickets in the second innings!'

This was truly exceptional. Normally a bowler is pleased to take three or four. I grabbed him and hugged him hard. 'Oh, Winston! That's magnificent! Congratulations! What does your mum say?'

'She say' – he dropped into the sort of patois Philomena occasionally favoured – '"Why doan you take all dem udder wickets in dey first innin's? Why only de t'ree, boy?"'

'She must be bursting with pride. I know I am.' I hoped my face showed just how pleased I was. Winston and I went back a long time: OK, he may have owed some of his exam success to me, but I owed my life to him, a fact to which he'd never once alluded.

He peered at my neck. 'What have you been doing, Sophie? Looks as if it didn't agree with you, whatever it is.'

Not used to having a medical consultation under the interested gaze of a rapidly growing knot of middle-aged men and schoolboys, all with the same paraphernalia as I had – if in less stylish bags – I tried to shrug him away.

But he wasn't to be shrugged. 'Come on – what are you doing about it, Sophie?'

At last the embarrassed exasperation on my face must have registered and he started to walk to the main gates, drawing me with him. Well, making me scuttle after him, to be more accurate. Not that he meant to. But he was six foot plus, with legs in proportion. I like to think my legs are in proportion too, of course, but then I'm only five foot one.

We stopped midway between an ice-cream vendor and a hot-dog stall.

'Let's look.'

Which is how the first time I set eyes on Mike Lowden I had another young man busily stroking my neck.

19

Perhaps it was simply last night's surfeit of romantic fiction. But I'll swear my heart missed a beat. And I'm equally sure an embarrassing flush crawled up my neck. At least it would swamp the area Winston was inspecting. Certainly our eyes met – his were an exceptionally dark blue – and he halted in mid-stride. But he was talking to someone, and fell back into step with him.

Just like the love-sick teenagers who drooped around William Murdock's corridors, I gazed after him. But if I hadn't, I wouldn't have known he turned back to look at me.

I tried to drag my mind back to Winston's catechism. He deserved my attention – he was a friend trying to do me a service.

'Who was that?' I asked, forgetting all that.

'—could be serious – who? Where?'

I nodded – couldn't point in case by some miracle he turned back again. 'With dark hair. With the bulky guy in a tracksuit. Both carrying cricket bags.'

Now I came to look, there were a lot of big men in tracksuits all carrying cricket bags. Well, there would be, wouldn't there? And quite a lot of dark-haired men, too. All of them walking away from me.

Winston's turn to shrug. 'Tell you what, Sophie, I got this freebie ticket waiting for me on the gate. Where you planning to sit?'

I gestured – anywhere.

'You're not a member?'

'No. One of the things I've never quite got round to.'

'Tell you what, you go and get a couple of scorecards. I'll go and pick up my comp and then go and cadge another one for you from one of the lads in there.' He nodded in the direction of the dressing room. 'See you back here.' He pointed downwards as if to pinpoint the precise spot.

I didn't argue. A day in Winston's company would be

pleasant in itself. It'd be nice to meet some of his mates, too. I wouldn't even think about the remote possibility of a drink in the members' and players' bar at the end of the day and the tiny chance that the owner of those blue eyes might be—

No, I wouldn't.

It took Winston only about three minutes to accomplish both missions, and then a further five to extricate himself from the surge of small boys that engulfed us as soon as word had got around that Winston Rhodes was back in Birmingham. Winston signed and smiled and smiled and signed, with a careful word for each child. African-Caribbeans, Sikhs, Muslims, poor and middle-class white kids. A small sea of integration. There were girls, too – I saw myself as a child, and later as a teenager. I'd nearly been sacked from my supposedly co-educational school because I would insist on playing what the school authorities insisted was an exclusively male game. At last the bell sounded – play would begin in ten minutes – so Winston reminded them that they wouldn't wish to miss the start and ushered me up before him into the members' stand.

I'd forgotten how a ground buzzes with anticipation before the start of play. It's as characteristic as that big roar in a soccer ground or the sound of an orchestra tuning up. Why on earth had I deprived myself for so long? We settled in the middle of a row – perhaps Winston thought he'd be freer from interruption there. He was certainly recognised – his face, even behind wrap-around sunglasses, as distinctive as his figure, suggesting some handsome hidalgo in his ancestry. But apart from some appreciative nods, and a couple of people reaching across to shake hands, all was very calm. One woman – accompanied by a spouse and a teddy bear, though not necessarily in that order – offered him a sweet, and encouraged the bear to bow. Warwickshire's nickname is, after all, the Bears.

And then the umpires appeared.

We were all sure that Warwickshire would win, of course

– Rutland, new to the first-class game, were towards the bottom of the Championship table – but we hoped they'd have to struggle just long enough to give us a fullish day's play. For a while there was lip-chewing apprehension – the man who opened Rutland's bowling was an ex-international player, and although he was slower than in his heyday, he had the opening bat caught without adding to his overnight score. And then there was a brilliant run-out. The Bears' player was probably only an inch from the safety of his crease. I gestured the distance to Winston, unprovided with binoculars. And then passed mine over to him.

'Stupid bugger, taking a risk like that,' he muttered. 'Humph – Timpson's up to his usual tricks.'

All I could now see was the wicket-keeper exchanging a few words with the new batsman as he crossed to the other end for the start of the next over.

'Tricks?' I prompted.

'Sledging.'

'Sledging?'

'You know – talking at a player to disturb his concentration.'

'You mean reminding him how good the bowler is, how he got a duck in his first innings, that kind of thing?'

Winston grunted. 'Mostly. But there are blokes who use a more extreme form of psychological warfare. There was that Aussie a couple of years back – d'you remember? The batsman threatened to shove his bat down his throat. There was a disciplinary. Then it turned out the wicket-keeper kept describing a mole he claimed he'd seen on the batsman's wife.'

'Not on her arm or face, I take it?'

'Right. Ah, that's better!' He slammed his huge fists – the ones that had been so tenderly probing my neck a few minutes ago – together in enthusiastic applause.

To my chagrin I didn't know anything about that dark-haired

young man – not even which side he played for. Retrieving my binoculars as quickly as was decent, I scanned the field. Not Rutland, unless he was one of the fielders close enough to the batsman to be wearing a helmet. And, despite the helmets, I was sure he hadn't been either of the batsmen just dismissed. Or one of the men currently at the crease.

The play settled down to a dogged battle, the batsmen pinned down at one end by the wily old pro, Butler. The other bowler wasn't nearly so accurate, and they started to score more freely, so freely that the spectators around us were beginning to talk about it all being over by tea-time.

'Cliché of the week coming up,' Winston said. 'It's a funny game, cricket. It'd only take another wicket to make the Bears look dead ropy. Fancy a beer?'

'This one's on me.'

'This one's on *me*,' he said. 'My shout. OK?'

'OK, Winston. So long as mine's the next!'

While he was away – and he was gone long enough to suggest there'd been a heavy fall of snow – Rutland took another wicket. A huge roar of applause greeted the new batsman, a slender black boy.

'That's the new South African signing,' the teddy bear lady told me. 'Teddy Nkosi.'

Teddy didn't sound very ethnic to me.

'Well,' she smiled, 'none of us can pronounce his real name, and since he's playing for the Bears . . . He's lodging with one of my friends: such a sweet young man. Very religious. It was his church that sponsored his cricket training. If you have time to come to the bar at the end of play, I'll introduce you, if you like.'

'I'd love to meet him,' I said sincerely. 'I'll probably be going for a drink with Winston, though.'

'If it's in the Tom Dollery Bar, you'll find we all get mixed up together anyway,' she said. 'It's not like football, you know, where the players – well, you'd think they were young gods, they've got such bobs on themselves. They wouldn't be hobnobbing with the likes of you and me, oh dear no. But these lads—'

Teddy took guard. I watched through the binoculars. He flicked his head backwards and forwards a couple of times, as if trying to put something out of his thoughts. There was a murmur of what sounded like disapproval from the spectators. I moved the binoculars. The wicket-keeper – Timpson – was very close to the stumps, knees bent, back rounded, scratching exaggeratedly under his arms. From a stand the other side of the ground from us a couple of bananas were lobbed across the boundary rope. It was a matter of moments before the stewards stepped in, and lots of other binoculars followed their progress as they first remonstrated with, then removed a couple of youths.

'It's the drink talking,' the teddy bear lady said. 'You can see why they've banned people from bringing their own drink into the ground.'

'I hope they ban *them*,' I said.

'I'm sure they will. I'm sure they're not home supporters. Oh dear, such a nice young man.'

Meanwhile, one of the umpires, apparently going for a stroll while everyone's attention was elsewhere, had fetched up beside Timpson. His finger was bobbing in admonition. But Timpson – ostentatiously fiddling with his gloves – looked to me remarkably unrepentant.

Staying in our seats, Winston and I shared my lunch and one his mother had packed. He looked murderous. I waited until I hoped the edge was off both his hunger and his anger, then said mildly, 'You might as well tell me.'

He looked around, and shook his head. 'When we've eaten we'll go and get an ice-cream and I'll tell you then.' With an effort, he pulled himself together. 'What do you think of this new kid, then? Nkosi?'

'He's got admirable powers of concentration,' I said. 'I was afraid they'd have him in his first couple of overs – but he's played like a veteran since. The scoreboard says it all.' And I hadn't once wished him out, much as I wanted to see that young man with the blue eyes and dark hair.

The queue was frustratingly long, and had Winston tapping his foot as if waiting to start his run-up. We talked lightly about life at William Murdock until we reached the vendor.

Winston was halfway into a huge cone before he spoke again. 'I was talking to some of the lads,' he said, checking he couldn't be overheard. 'They told me what Teddy found when he went to unpack his gear today.'

'Don't tell me. Bananas? Hell, Winston. I know it used to happen in football – maybe it still does – but in *cricket*!'

'No, it's not cricket, is it, old bean,' he said in an Oxford accent as exaggerated as his mother's patois.

'Has anything like that ever happened to you?' I asked quietly. 'Or are people like that less likely to take on six foot whatever you are of fast bowler than a slip of a kid like that?'

'Probably. Nobody's given me bananas yet, anyway. But I've had the odd bit of lip. Funny, at William Murdock, being black or Asian was almost the norm. It's a bit different in medical school – it may have escaped your notice, Sophie, that while there are quite a lot of Asian doctors, there aren't all that many black ones.'

'You get hassled?'

'No, in a sense it's worse – it's just these public-school types are genuinely surprised you're training to be a medic, not resigned to your lot as an orderly sloshing bedpans. And I tell you, I'm quite anxious about the future, Sophie – there's not all that many black guys in the upper echelons.'

'Are you regretting going into medicine?'

'Enough to have made me decide not to go straight into practice when I qualify. I'm signing up to play full-time. It's quite a lucrative career while it lasts. And there's all those contacts you get. And then, when I get a bit old and creaky—'

'When you reach thirty, you mean?'

'—then I can pick up the medical career. If I want. But I'm going to qualify first. No need for you to look like my mum!'

Play after lunch staggered into the doldrums, and then the Bears lost a wicket. Teddy Nkosi held on, though, even when the incoming batsman did his best to get them both run out but settled for dollying an easy catch back to the bowler. And then a warm round of applause heralded the arrival of a young man with dark hair.

'Who's he?' I asked Winston, as he took guard.

'Mike Lowden,' he said, pointing to the scorecard. 'Good steady player. Never been quite lucky enough to get into the England squad. He's been an anchor man in the A side, of course. Trouble is, he's a bit like Gower. Bats like an angel on his day, but if he gets bored he gets out.'

'Doesn't look as if he's bored today,' I observed. He'd just hit the bowler back over his head into the crowd.

We all tutted. It's one thing to wallop the bowling when you've got your eye in. But in these circumstances it could be downright irresponsible. Perhaps he had second thoughts. He certainly didn't go for any more risky shots. In fact, he seemed to me to be giving as much of the bowling as he could to young Teddy.

Suddenly he rattled off four boundaries from as many deliveries. Under that helmet he'd got a nice grin, and I sensed he was enjoying being unpredictable. Then he went too far. When Teddy was only six from his fifty and the Bears ten from victory, he hit one into apparent infinity, only to be caught out.

If it was usual for players to head for the shower on dismissal, he broke that convention too: he went straight on to the players' balcony, and was the first to get to his feet to lead the applause for Teddy's half-century.

And then the game was over. The Bears had won again. More valuable championship points.

I started to gather my things.

'No sweat, man,' Winston said. 'Remember what my mum says.'

'"When de good Lord made time, He made plenty of it,"' I said. 'Only I think it's a Black Country saying too.'

'Black, schlack,' he grinned. 'Anyway, we're going for a drink, you and me. Tell you what, I'll hang on here.' He looked at me knowingly under his lashes. 'You'll want to powder your nose or whatever.'

I did. I completely redid my make-up, brushed my hair till it shone, even if the sun-hat had flattened it a bit. As a bonus, my rash had completely gone. I gave a quick squirt of the light perfume I favour in summer and set off, head high. But heart beating rather too hard.

Chapter Four

True to her promise, the teddy bear lady introduced me
to Teddy Nkosi. She fought her way to me, dragging him
behind her through the scrum round Winston. He was even
smaller than he'd seemed on the pitch – hardly more than
a boy, slight and no more than five foot five tall. When he
smiled, he looked even younger. I boiled to think anyone
could have behaved crassly towards him, and tried to put
him at his ease. As a conversationalist, however, he was
hard going – it was easy to see why even kind young men
like Winston should merely greet him with enthusiastic
congratulations and then turn to someone else. I worked
hard to establish common ground with him. I tried his
talent first of all.

He shook his head. 'There are others much better than me.
I was just lucky.' He spoke softly, with a very strong South
African accent.

Next I tried education. Again he dismissed it as good
fortune that he'd found someone to sponsor him, though
everyone hoped things would get better. I agreed. Equipped,
thanks to my cousin who was an expert on Third World
politics, with all sorts of little-known and outrageous facts
about the difference in expenditure under apartheid between
white and black children, I could have kept going far longer
than him on the iniquities of the old system. But I wanted to

bring him out, not smother him. I tried all the conversational gambits I'd ever used with tongue-tied students, and was about to give up when I struck gold: the name of Basil D'Oliveira, the great South African cricketer who'd played in England in the sixties and seventies. It turned out Teddy's middle name was Basil, so highly did his family revere him. I'd seen him when I was in my teens, playing on this very ground. Teddy's eyes lit up at the story – but again, it was I who was doing all the talking, not he.

And I felt eyes on me. I was desperate to look past him to see who was watching me so closely. Only the sternest application of good manners stopped me. At last came an interruption in the form of Winston, slinging his arm round me and shoving a glass into my hand.

'This was supposed to be my shout,' I objected.

'Lucky bastard picked up a cheque for a thousand quid yesterday,' another voice announced. 'Don't stop him putting his hand in his pocket. Not often he gives his wallet an airing.'

The speaker was the Rutland wicket-keeper, Guy Timpson. He was already halfway down a pint glass, which he waved in the air as a general greeting. If I'd been Teddy, and he'd slapped me on the shoulders with all that false bonhomie, I might have been tempted to elbow him in the solar plexus. Teddy, however, had better manners, but our discussion on cricketers past and present ground to a remarkably swift halt, and he toddled off in search of the teddy bear lady.

So I was left with Guy. Built like a classic coalminer – broad shoulders, deep chest, sturdy bottom and rather short legs – he might have been designed as a pace bowler, not a keeper.

'You're a new face round here,' he said. His smile was no doubt meant to be inviting.

I nodded. But I didn't want to flirt with someone who could behave as he'd done.

And then – full marks for timing! – the stranded motorist of yesterday shot over.

'Hey! It's my rescuer! Hey, lady!' He gripped my hand with fervour. 'You really saved my life yesterday!'

By now I was able to put a name to his face – Barkat Aslam – and grinned back. 'Glad I could help.'

'She knows about cars, this one!' he told anyone who might be interested.

'Saved your bacon, did she?' Guy enquired.

I might have thought the image inappropriate to use to a Muslim, but Barkat simply nodded. 'Flat battery, man. She went and got her car to help.'

'I thought,' said Guy, drawing on his pint, 'you Warwickshire men all had nice new shiny Peugeots – corporate sponsorship and all that. Not like us poor oiks from the sticks.'

'Don't you get a car, man?'

'Only the captain and vice-captain. The committee couldn't get sponsorship for the rest of us. Not famous enough, see.' It was all said with an ironic smile.

I couldn't place his accent.

The smile became even more ironic. 'But how come your nice new Peugeot packed up?'

Barkat waved a hand so airily I knew he was embarrassed. 'Oh, in for service, man. I was using my cousin's.'

'Service, eh? And no courtesy car?' Guy tutted.

A memory started to niggle at my brain, but stayed well below the surface. Clearly Barkat wanted to change the subject. I couldn't comment on his batting brilliance because he'd been out last night for an undistinguished five.

'Last courtesy car I had,' I put in, 'was so bottom-of-the-range that it had a little hole by the pedals.'

'Hole?' Barkat repeated.

31

'So you could put your foot through and help push,' I said. OK, pretty weak. But not as weak as the poor car's acceleration, come to think of it.

There was general, sympathetic laughter. Barkat excused himself. Winston rejoined me, adopting a rather protective stance. If a handsome young man nearly young enough to be my son wanted to protect me, in general I wouldn't have minded. But the body language was misleading. Winston and I were mates, and though I was delighted we were, that was all I was quite sure either of us wanted it to be. And what if someone else were watching, and got altogether the wrong impression? If only Guy would go away – I was sure, come to think of it, it was Winston's anger at some of the day's events that made him so stiff-legged.

Other players drifted into the group. Most wanted to congratulate Winston on his previous day's performance and ask, like his mother, why he hadn't taken a few more wickets. Timpson lapsed into comparative silence. He might have been bored; maybe plain sleepy. One or two newcomers looked at me a little sideways: it was clear I was somehow with Winston, but in no obvious capacity. At last it dawned on him that he ought to introduce me. Which he did. Simply as Sophie.

'I used to teach him,' I added, as if in extenuation.

Amidst all the derisory comments about Winston's general dimness and academic incompetence – I suspected most of them knew about his medical studies – I was aware that Timpson was now staring at me very hard. And then at Winston. But Barkat was now back with a brimming orange juice and the conversation sloshed in different directions.

Still no Mike Lowden. Every other cricketer in the Midlands seemed to have passed into our group except him. Ashamed of myself as I was, I still risked stepping back to scan the room. And looked once again straight into his eyes.

He was facing me, but deep in conversation with the teddy bear lady, her husband and Teddy Nkosi. Perhaps he was better at drawing him out than I'd been. Maybe a smile flickered between us. I don't know. What I did know, with absolute certainty, was that somehow or other we would be in the same group before it was time to drift back home.

Or would we? Suddenly the news went round that someone was hosting a charity barbecue, and we were all to go. Oh yes, all of us. The gesture included me, as Winston's adjunct. We were all herded out into the evening sun: plenty of cars for us to share!

To hell with worrying if Mike might be there! It felt like being young again. A spontaneous party. Most of my friends these days were too knackered for such frivolity, either that or needing to find baby-sitters. Or both. I'd worry later about all the sensible things, like how to get home from somewhere I didn't even know I was going.

'Come on, Teddy!' Winston yelled to the figure dawdling at the top of the steps. 'You're coming too, man!'

He shook his head.

'Come on, man, you'll enjoy it. You know Sophie here. And the lads. Come on – let your hair down!'

I smiled: 'Come on – just for a bit.' Poor kid, he'd been here three or four months and yet still seemed unsure of the ropes.

'But whose car . . . ?' He came hesitantly down and could see that Winston and I were standing round like spare dinners.

Two voices spoke at once. 'Mine.'

One of them was Guy Timpson's. The other – and Teddy turned to him with obvious relief – was Mike Lowden's.

'Haven't had a chance to say well done, yet, Dusky!' he said, gripping Winston's hand.

Dusky! That didn't sound very auspicious! My head must have jerked back in spite of myself.

It was enough of a movement to make Winston reassure me. 'Yeah, we all have nicknames. Some more flattering than others. There have been other Rhodes before me, see?'

'Including the more famous – oh, for the time being! – Dusty Rhodes,' I said, beginning to catch on.

'So he became Dusky. His own suggestion, I promise,' Mike said. His voice combined amusement with apology.

'Better than That Black Brummie Bastard, I suppose,' Winston mused.

Lowden unlocked his car. He looked at Guy. 'Now, you could imagine that we call Guy the Gorilla—'

'But that's been used before, too,' I said.

'So we call him something else,' said Winston. 'Hell, Mike, Sophie used to teach me – it'd be like swearing in front of my mum to use that sort of word in front of her!'

'I wouldn't soil my lips with it, then,' Mike said crisply. 'You and Teddy in the back, Sophie? You'll be a bit cramped – Dusky has to have the seat right back.'

And so would he. Not a small man, Mike.

'No room for me, then, Millie?' Guy asked. He turned to me. 'M.L. Millilitre. Get it?'

Mike shrugged. 'Look, your skipper's waving you over. He's got a map.'

I suspected the big Peugeot would accommodate us all, but didn't choose to argue. Guy slouched off.

Mike thrust a photocopied map at Winston. 'Will you navigate? No! Last time you tried we ended up going due south when we were supposed to be heading north. Sophie – could you help?'

'I should think so,' I said. And smiled back.

Chapter Five

My navigational skills were hardly needed, the target being a house in Warley, which was reached by simply heading for my house and then picking up the A4123. Although most of the area is – or, more accurately, was – industrial, there were still some pockets of attractive houses. This was certainly one such area, though this particular house was interesting rather than attractive: it had been added on to and modified in so many ways it would be hard to trace the original shape.

We went through the garden gate past the triple garage, occupied so far as I could see by children's cycles, into the garden – or, indeed, the grounds! – to be greeted by a miniskirted waitress proffering elegant tulip glasses. Winston winked broadly at me, and moved quite briskly away, drawing Teddy in his wake.

Just the two of us, then. Would this make for embarrassed silences? Somehow I wasn't expecting any.

Mike swirled his glass under his nose before quaffing. The nose, an elegant, straight one, wrinkled slightly. 'Hm. What do you think?'

'I think it's Chardonnay plus bubbles, but what the hell, Archie!'

'Well, cheerio, my deario!' He was smiling too. A silly sort of smile that matched mine. Lots of things about him matched mine. His body language, in short. We were mirroring away like illustrations from a textbook.

I ought to have been worrying about Teddy – making sure that he wasn't standing around like flat lemonade. With flat lemonade. I ought to have sought out our host. I ought to have done all sorts of good guest things, but this evening I was going to be selfish. And that – hell! – included tearing myself away from Mike to go in search of a loo.

I'd read about parties where the guests snorted coke, of course. But my sort of person can't afford that sort of pastime. And my nonconformist soul was rather shocked to find a razor blade and a mirror simply lying on the bathroom windowsill. I thought sensible thoughts about the kids who played with those bikes finding the blade.

From shock I went into curiosity mode. Who would be using the stuff? No one amongst the players, surely! People got banned from every sport for using cannabis, let alone something like cocaine. Well, I suppose I could keep an eye open for the sneezing and the high-spirited. But even with hay-fever you could be quite cheerful. And in any case, who was I to worry? Not my premises, not my friends, not my responsibility. 'None of your business, Sophie,' I said aloud.

Except for the naked razor blade and the children.

In the end, I simply wrapped the thing in toilet roll and slipped it under the mirror. I even left a little tuft of paper showing, so if the user wanted some more, he or she would be able to tell what I'd been up to.

Back outside, then.

Mike had his back to me. Absent-mindedly taking another glass of fizz and a canapé from a different waitress, I watched him as I sipped. He was as tall as Chris, about five foot ten. Whereas Chris was now almost bald, Mike still sported a full head of curly dark hair. Broad shoulders, narrow hips: the sort of shape for which jeans and a T-shirt were designed. Well, your quintessentially desirable man, I suppose. And then I thought of the other desirable men who'd garnished my life, and had soon ended up as undesirable as yesterday's sliced cucumber. It was time for me to think a bit. No. I didn't want to think. I wanted to know, this time, yes, I really did need to know whether this man was already sharing his life with someone. And I didn't want him to be no more than a handsome face and a striking body. I wanted him to have a mind.

Close enough to touch him now, I could have reached out and rearranged that little tendril of hair that wouldn't lie close to the nape of his neck.

He turned.

Surely his delight was too naked to be feigned? We fell into step, walking, pausing by banks of Technicolor flowers that might have sprung straight from the pages of a seed catalogue.

'Tell me about yourself,' he said. 'I want to know all about you.' When I shook my head, he added, 'All right, add to what all I already know. You taught Winston, I know that. And he says you helped him in a nasty racial prejudice case.'

I must have looked shocked. Winston and I have never mentioned that publicly.

'He rates you, does Winston. Very highly. As highly as I rate him. And I can see you're a generally nice type – spending all that time with young Teddy. And you're good with cars. And Guy makes your flesh creep. But apart from the obvious thing' – he swathed the whole of the visible me in his smile – 'I know nothing. And I want to know.'

'Thirty-seven. College lecturer on sabbatical. House in Harborne shared with elderly teddy bear. There you are. Oh, I sing a bit. For a hobby. Hell, it sounds like a *New Statesman* Heartsearch ad.'

Mike laughed. I did rather hope those splendid teeth were his own, but a number of my cricketer friends sported the odd denture – cricket balls hit hard, and the use of helmets was a relative innovation. While he wafted away a hover-fly, my mind took off on a crazy vision of his demanding a mug in which to overnight his top set.

'OK. Another one for the lonely hearts – Saturday *Guardian*. Thirty-three. Biology graduate. Passion for local history. Tired of rolling and having no moss. Interests: politics, good food. Prepared to open mind to any new experience.'

'Biology?' I wasn't sure why I picked on the thing I knew least about.

'Hmm. I suppose I was good at the sciences at school. And I liked biology better than the others. I knew I didn't want to do medicine. For a time I toyed with the idea of marine biology in the States: then I found out how many native-grown marine biologists there are in the States, and couldn't really rate my employment chances very high.'

'And they don't play cricket in the States.' Funny how the mouth says all these useful things when what you really want it to say is *how soon can I decently invite you into my bed?* 'And what about this local history?'

'One of those serendipitous things. We had to go to lectures that weren't part of our programme, of course. Lots of people skived. But I went along because I quite fancied this woman who was on the history course and I thought – well, you know how you do. But then the lecturer got talking about how it was advances in public health, not the sort of things you get from medicine, that do the most good to the majority.'

'Like that pump in Victorian London that gave everyone typhoid or cholera or whatever, and when they stopped people using it the incidence of disease dropped?'

'Right! So I started looking harder at the Black Country and Birmingham. It's become a sort of passion. And as long as I can play cricket, I have enough time and money to indulge it. When the joints and the timing go . . .' He shrugged. 'Decision time, I suppose. But I don't see myself teaching biology in an inner-city comp.'

'Oh, you'd manage something more prestigious than that. Birmingham's still got its famous grammar schools.' I couldn't keep a tiny note of derision from my voice.

He looked at me sideways. 'I wouldn't want that. You know the Bears have all sorts of links with schools: I'm involved with some of the most deprived kids you can imagine. Poor, as in poor.'

I nodded. I knew what it was like to feel you wanted to feed them before you could teach them. 'My college isn't a prestigious one, either. It's slap in the middle of underfunded Brum. Underfunded so long you don't even imagine after a while that things could be better. Should be better.'

By now we were level with a swimming pool, tucked in a corner where other gardeners might have put a compost heap. It was currently unoccupied, but a big, heavily shouldered man was standing peering into it. From the angle of his body I rather think he might have been peeing into it, but he'd already disposed of the evidence.

Mike stopped short. 'Can you hear anything?'

''Fraid so. *I hear music when there's no one there!*' I warbled. 'It's like Alton Towers, isn't it? Those must be the loudspeakers, there.'

'How on earth do the neighbours cope?'

'Perhaps they're all invited here.'

A vigorous argument was in progress over in the other corner, by what seemed to be an excellent sandpit. Barkat and another man. In the dusk, all you could see of him was his white hair. They weren't getting physical, but the language's blend of the profane with the obscene was so proficient it was almost artistic. Except it definitely wasn't.

'D'you think we ought to do anything?' I asked.

'Us! Why?'

'Oh,' I said, flushing at the disbelief in his voice. 'Put it down to all my years at William Murdock and the concomitant professional sorting-out of bickering kids.'

'You'd spend half your life sorting out Barkat, then. He's a stroppy little bastard.' He sounded as if he meant it.

'I should have left his car unmended, then?' I suggested, trying to return the conversation to something like its previous tone.

'What is it they put in petrol tanks to louse things up?'

'Sugar?'

'Right. A good half-pound of the stuff.'

'Do you need that much?'

'You're the expert!'

We turned, dawdling towards a pergola and rose walk. It was illuminated by candles in glass shields.

Mike sniffed. 'Scented? Why on earth?'

'Mosquitoes for the getting rid of, I'd say.'

'The bees like them, anyway. Come, let me take you away from this IKEA paradise—'

'IKEA! No, something much less good value. A heaven where all barbecues are built in with dear little chimneys and all garden furniture is stripy. What's that big tent thing for and why doesn't it have any sides?'

'Sophie, you're revealing your total ignorance of colour-supplement living. And I'd almost accuse you of aesthetic snobbery.'

'I'd almost plead guilty as charged.'

We headed back to the house and the food and the by now quite loud music and the men with their women in expensive dresses. At least I'd got some make-up on, thanks to Winston. But my outfit was so distinctly downmarket I felt quite uneasy. I certainly wished for Mike's sake I'd been smarter. But he made no sign – other than a low-key amusement – at being quite shamelessly vamped by a woman who'd clearly taken Liz Hurley as a role model for her couture. By now our hands had found each other's. Food? We pounced on deliciously spiced chicken joints, which our first simultaneous bites revealed as undercooked. We grimaced and rejected them as one.

'No Tom Jones and Mrs – what was that woman's name?' he said, touching my arm.

I shook my head. 'It's such a long time since I read it.'

He laughed. 'Anyone else would have said they didn't see it.'

'What, not see that wonderful Albert Finney film?'

'The TV version, Sophie.'

'Ah,' I said. 'You see, most evenings I have to mark or prepare. Had to. But not for another year!'

Unfortunately my triumphant gesture sprayed wine rather liberally over the lawn. Was I that tipsy? I noticed that since his first glass of fizz he'd stuck to water.

'I'm sure we can find some better wine somewhere else,' he said into my right ear.

'But there's Teddy – oh dear, I want to make sure he's got enough money to get home!'

'Wrapped in a hankie in his pocket!' He laughed mockingly. 'But you're right. He needs to know there's no lift in the offing, and that they won't mind if he calls a cab.'

'And Winston. Can't just walk away when we haven't seen each other for a couple of years. He'll be off to – where are they playing? Lord's? – tomorrow. And though I've not been introduced to our hosts, the least I can do is thank them.'

He nodded and we went inside, via a huge double-glazed conservatory, full of predatory-looking cacti and succulents. I shuddered.

'Cold?'

'Those things. Stand still long enough and they'd have you for supper. Do you know your way round here?'

'Sort of. They give loads of parties every season. But I don't think it'll get him on to the club committee,' he added, close to my ear. 'Through here.'

'Here' was a living room so heavily floral it was impossible to tell where sofa ended and carpet began.

We were prevented from making any observations at all by the arrival of another guest: a stringy, almost bald man still in a Rutland sweatshirt. He was sneezing explosively.

'No, it's not this room,' he said, as if reading my mind. 'I can take it for so long out there, but then the pollen gets to me. Tobacco plants. My God!'

Silently I waved my nose-spray at him. 'You tried this sort of thing?'

'Allergic, I'm afraid.' He sneezed again. 'The preservative. I use another one. And I can't find it!' He disappeared behind a wad of tissues, then thrust out a hand. 'Ken Griffiths. Rutland physio.'

I shook hands, and listened contentedly while he congratulated Mike on his innings.

If my eyes drifted they found cricket memorabilia on the walls and in china cabinets. Manly faces from my youth squinted into the sun from silver frames. Griffiths continued to punctuate his conversation with sneezes.

At last, Mike drew away. I followed him into the hall. It was seething with people, but, grabbing my hand, he pushed his way through to a beautifully dressed woman, sixty-five going on forty. Her skin was so deeply tanned – weathered, even – that she might have been an advert for the before stage of moisturiser. She sported gorgeous sapphires and a genuinely nice smile.

'Mike!' She reached up and kissed him affectionately. 'Hey – you're not going already!'

''Fraid so.' At least he remembered the part of the adage that says you shouldn't explain. 'Sal, this is Sophie. Sophie: Sal.'

We shook hands.

'Nice to meet you, Sophie. It's about time someone took Mike in hand – look at his hair! When did you last have that cut, Mike?' She reached up and grabbed a handful. The gesture was horribly intimate.

As if on cue, someone bounced in with a little camera and fired the flash-gun. Blinking, I discovered the perpetrator was Guy Timpson. He also caught Ken Griffiths in mid-sneeze. Funny taste in souvenirs some people had.

'Why don't you just go and play somewhere else?' Mike demanded. 'Like outside?'

'Nicer inside,' Guy retorted. And took another photo, of the woman in the half-dress.

'It's those wasps,' Sal said apologetically. 'You know he has to be careful—'

Griffiths sneezed.

I asked about Teddy and, as an afterthought, Winston.

Sal smiled. 'Teddy's in the grandchildren's room playing computer games. Don't worry – we'll sort out a lift for him.'

'We'll see him tomorrow,' Mike said. 'Apologise.'

'Nothing to apologise for. You wouldn't separate him from the joystick unless you cut his hand off. And Winston's in the kitchen, with the food. To look at him you'd never guess. I suppose you young men find ways to burn up the calories.' Nudge, nudge, wink, wink. 'But you're like a lath, Sophie. How do you manage to keep so slim?'

'I work in a fifteen-storey building where the lifts hardly ever function.' And, come to think of it, I was hungry myself. But there was enough in my freezer for an alfresco picnic if we went to my place.

Winston was in expansive mood, despite an attendant nymph wearing little more than the Hurley clone was, and hugged me hugely. Another flash photo for Guy's collection.

'The Jeremy Beadle of Oakham,' Mike muttered.

And with that we bowed our way out.

'Coffee?' I asked euphemistically, as we headed back towards Harborne and my house, with a packet of condoms in the bedside cabinet. I hoped a cloud of moths wouldn't erupt when we opened it.

'So long as it's at my place. Only just down the road. Bournville. I've got to take my contact lenses out, and I've forgotten the little goldfish bowl they live in.'

'Just contact lenses?' I asked, trying not to look at his teeth. A tiny touch of suspicion slipped into my voice.

He glanced sideways at me, beginning to laugh. 'Just lenses, I promise. My teeth are entirely my own.'

Chapter Six

'Here you are! My little Mrs Tiggy-winkle house!' Mike
said, stopping in front of the house at the end of a small
cul-de-sac. He opened the front door with a flourish and
stabbed the burglar alarm.

Not that it was particularly small: it had been extended –
though much more sympathetically than Sal's. It was tucked
into a corner of the vast estate of well-designed and built
houses Cadbury's had provided for their workers.

'But this,' he said, as he dug wine from a glory-hole and
slipped on to it one of those chiller jackets, 'this was actually
a council house a long time ago. They challenged a woman
architect to come up with the most houses she could fit on this
tiny patch. So they're all slightly different. Wait till you see
upstairs – all lovely sloping ceilings and dormer windows.'

Though the furniture was cottage Victorian, and therefore
about forty years too early, it all fitted. Above the grate was
a mirrored chimneypiece, complete with little twirly wooden
pillars supporting tiny shelves. A fire screen. Some lovely,
lovely watercolours, one of which claimed to be a David
Cox. It might have been too. Just. An alcove lined with
bookshelves was weighed down under what seemed from
the quickest of scans to be a catholic collection.

And knickknacks. Victorian china.

My stomach sank. Was I detecting a woman's influence

here? It wasn't a pretty-pretty room, but it certainly wasn't spartan and masculine, like Chris's, for instance. Poor Chris: I hoped he wasn't going to be dragged from his bed at all hours this weekend. Especially before midnight. Even a wrong number that side of the witching hour could keep him awake all night. Later, and he'd often drop off again. Still, Smethwick wasn't likely to be violent, surely?

'Penny for them,' Mike said, passing me an elegant glass of what smelt like – was! – a New Zealand Montana, a very good one too.

'I was thinking about a friend of mine. Chris. A police superintendent. He's just been promoted to run a big patch in the Black Country – if Barkat and whoever had come to blows, it would have been Chris's people who would have had to sort it out. And at weekends they shove three patches together with one superintendent in charge of everything. This is his first big weekend.'

He sat down on a sofa, and patted the cushion beside him. 'Don't worry. It's been resprung. What sort of a man goes in for that sort of work?'

'A man who believes in Duty with a capital D. Who believes in the mortification of the flesh. Who was, on and off, my significant other and is now a friend, full stop.'

He raised sober eyebrows in acknowledgement, pulling his lips into a downward arc. 'My ex – we were married a couple of years – had a raging romance with our friend Guy. He got her pregnant, paid for her to have an abortion, promised to marry her if we divorced, and then – didn't.'

'Did you try to get back together?' We seemed to be fingering each other's bruises remarkably quickly.

His mouth tightened.

I waited.

'I'd moved on from there. It wasn't a question of not

forgiving her, Sophie. If she hadn't had the abortion I could have coped with the kid.'

I looked at him.

'OK. Maybe not Guy's, to be strictly honest. We sold our house for the divorce – she was very fierce about money and her rights. The stress . . . For a whole season I was hardly worth a first-team place. The bastard. I could have – yes, there were times I could have killed him. One night – I've never, ever told anyone this.' He clutched my hand. I returned the pressure. There was nothing I could usefully say, but he had to know I was there for him. 'I wanted to die but I decided to take him with me. I was going to offer to buy him a drink and crash the car at speed. So I drove all the way to Oakham. I knew exactly where he lived. In a small executive housing development. And I drove round and round it. Five or six times. As if I was test-driving a car, or something. Then I decided – do you know, I couldn't bear even to die with the man. I wanted him dead. And me dead. But not together. And then I thought of the baby, and I thought maybe there'd been enough death anyway. And I wanted to live. That's why I don't even want to have the bastard in my car, Sophie!' He almost flung away my hand, as if the anger was driving out any other feeling.

He stood up.

'God, even talking about him leaves a foul taste.'

The David Cox might have been a millimetre out of line. He stalked over and adjusted it. At last, he smiled apologetically and sat down, turning half towards me. Our hands linked again. 'So I bought this place. It was almost derelict, and I spent the winter working on it. Got dermatitis from the plaster and a lot of satisfaction. My own place. No, she never lived here with me. Nor has anyone else.'

He reached for the wine, ready to top up my glass.

'No more, thanks. This last year at work I've been under

some pressure. I got what they call teacher's tum. Gastritis. It's almost better now, but sometimes it takes exception to wine.'

'Are you all right? You should have told me.' He brushed my hair back from my face.

'I could do with some food,' I said, reflecting equally on the half-raw chicken leg and the tenderness of his touch.

'Would bread and cheese do?'

No, I don't think cheese is usually an aphrodisiac. Not that we needed one. But sometimes it stops me sleeping, and in truth I didn't sleep much.

In the kitchen, before we went up, he said, 'You will stay, won't you? I want – I want you to stay.'

No quips about snoring. I just nodded.

A particularly vociferous batch of birds started yelling from the playing field at the back of his house at an unbelievable hour in the morning. I might have pointed out to them that it was still dark. Instead, I lay listening to his breathing. I felt this emotion buzzing around me that I couldn't pin down. Still puzzled, I slipped off to the bathroom. Hell, what was the etiquette of four o'clock loo-flushing in his house? Eventually I plumped for not waking him.

As I slipped back into bed, rolling on to my side, he rolled too, pulling me to him as if I were a large teddy bear. I snuggled into shape.

And suddenly I managed to identify that strange feeling. It was happiness.

It was still with me the following morning.

Such a cliché. The wind was blowing the curtains from the open window, letting sun stream in. Those birds, though they'd simmered down somewhat, were still carolling away.

A tray had appeared on the bedside table loaded with fruit juice and strawberries—

'Strawberries?' I squeaked, heaving myself on to one elbow.

'I've got a trough on the kitchen windowsill full of strawberry plants. I'd never expected they'd give me a decent crop, though. Hell, isn't this rather like *Tess of the D'Urbervilles*?' He was pressing a strawberry against my lips.

'But you're not the wicked Alec, are you?' I smiled, accepting it. And the offer behind it.

Mike was playing on the Sunday afternoon, a limited-over match against Rutland in the AXA League, so his morning had to run to a schedule, relaxed though that might be. It turned out he went in for stretches too, so I had company for my exercise routine. In the absence of my gear, I had to let him jog off on his own, of course.

'But tomorrow we'll do it together,' he said, kissing me extravagantly as he set off.

Tomorrow. Well, I couldn't see any problems with that.

He'd given me a spare set of keys, which made me even happier. An omen. No, a confirmation. I stowed the house set in my bag, and fingered the car keys. I had to nip home to change. I could have managed by bus, I suppose – and there was certainly no reason why I shouldn't cycle backwards and forwards in future – but I never turn down the chance to drive a different car. This one happened to be a big Peugeot, which announced to anyone wishing to know that Peugeot were sponsoring Warwickshire. It was a good job Mike and I had nothing to hide – this was clearly not a car with which to conduct discreet liaisons.

I'd never seen Edgbaston looking so pretty as it did that

afternoon. Oh, it was all in my head: there'd been no magic shower to perk everything up. But the tubs and hanging baskets were cornucopias, planted by someone with an eye for colour and texture. The buildings, not architectural gems by any stretch of the imagination, were clean and free from litter. It was a Sunday match so there were a lot of families, and the buzz was not just concentration and anticipation, but jolliness too. Pathetic fallacy, I'd have told my students. Except I didn't have any students to worry about for over a year. Funny, I'd never realised before that that was my main emotional response: students were to be worried about. And proud of. Substitute nephews and nieces – at least they went home at the end of the day. I'd go into college to see them when the A level and GCSE results came out – plenty of tissues and lots of praise. But just for the moment, I wouldn't worry.

In fact, I couldn't think of anything to worry about. I was happy. I'd sit and revel in the strange new emotion that was enveloping me and made me want to smile. As far as Mike's performance on the field this afternoon was concerned, I couldn't help a tiny frisson of anxiety – I hoped our nocturnal activities wouldn't have affected his concentration. Somehow I doubted it. As he left me near a little group of team wives and girlfriends his last words were, 'This match is for you. Anything I do well in it.' His kiss was socially acceptable, but emotionally right too.

Yes, I was happy.

I'd never actually seen myself as a lady with a knight wearing her favours. I'd have looked OK in those high-waisted gowns, come to think of it, and always rather fancied one of those floaty head-dresses. But any resemblance Mike bore to a knight was heavily disguised by the AXA League blue and yellow strip. Give me cricket whites any day. Still, aesthetics apart, we were in for a good match. The Bears had been sufficiently stung by Rutland's rude attempts to deny them victory yesterday to be very much on their toes, particularly when Rutland won the toss and chose to bat.

And didn't lose any early wickets. The opening batsmen were playing very well indeed. The fact that one of them was Guy Timpson didn't make things any better. In fact, he was on thirty-five when he lost his partner to a brilliant diving catch from the wicket-keeper. The next man in was soon bowled, and the next caught easily by Mike. At least he made it look easy: a skied ball against the background of a big crowd is always difficult.

Timpson was getting steadily closer to his fifty. There was a change of bowling – not a bad idea. No Barkat? There'd been an announcement over the PA system that he'd been replaced at the last moment. Whether now was the moment to try a bowler as young and inexperienced as Teddy was debatable – especially as he was a leg-spin bowler. With leg-spinners there's always some action: if they're as good as Shane Warne, they tend to take wickets; if they're not, the batsmen can get a lot of runs very quickly. As an ex-spin bowler myself, I prefer the former. Through the binoculars I could see Timpson say something which made Nkosi duck his head the way he'd done yesterday. Despite his elegant, classical action, his first few deliveries were so wild it seemed as if he was making Timpson a present of the runs.

Mike strolled over to hand Teddy the ball. Nothing unusual in that. A senior player will often come up with a strategy the bowler hasn't thought of, or simply a word of encouragement. I couldn't see what Mike said, but certainly Teddy grinned. The next ball was a different matter altogether. Timpson dabbed it down, watching it skirl past his stumps with an inch to spare. The next one fired off at an angle that had the wicket-keeper diving for it, despite Timpson's obvious intention to hit it straight into the pavilion. The last one seemed even to my eyes reasonably harmless, and Timpson played it into an unoccupied piece of field, stealing a single so he could have the batting in the next over. But a fielder was on it like a panther, picking it up and throwing to the bowler's end in one fluid movement. Run out!

The umpire wasn't sure. He asked his colleague. Yes, of course it was out! And the fielder was Mike. I couldn't lip-read what Timpson said as he left the field, but I'd bet it wasn't 'Have a nice day.'

For the rest of the innings – which closed at a respectable 180 for eight – nothing untoward occurred. Mike fielded tidily but took no brilliant catches, and wasn't asked to bowl. No fairy tales so far.

Not until the Bears' innings. Timpson and his captain were first down the pavilion steps, Timpson wearing only light inner gloves, and swinging and clapping together the huge outer keeper's gloves. He only pulled them on as the Warwickshire opener took guard – to little avail, I'm afraid. The pattern was uncannily like the previous day's, with a disconcerting tumble of early wickets. Butler, the old pro, had four for twenty at one point. Teddy was struggling. At last Mike strode in. I wouldn't fantasise that he looked in my direction as he ran down the pavilion steps. I wouldn't have wanted him to. I wanted him to go and do his job, which was to rescue his team from an unpleasant situation and maybe even to set them on a winning course. Timpson, of course, was busily sledging away.

Mike did what I'd have done: settled down to get used to the light and the pitch and not worry about scoring quickly at this stage. The Bears slipped further and further behind the required run rate. The spectators, made vociferous by beer, were getting quite free with their advice. And then they started to notice that the runs were beginning to come a little more often.

Teddy gained confidence and started to score more freely. But it was Mike who was doing the lion's share, now powering along to overtake Teddy's score, and indeed, the rest of the other players put together. His fifty came with a six; he might even be heading for a century. This is no mean achievement in a four-day country cricket match, but a rare enough occurrence in limited-over cricket, in which each side bats once only, against the clock. There was one tricky over. He snicked a catch to a fielder so surprised he dropped it. The next ball was horribly close to bowling him.

But he got himself together again. And the runs continued. He was on 98. And only six more were needed for the Bears to win.

From around the ground there was plenty of advice on how he should get them. In one big hit. But he went for an easy single, giving Teddy the bowling. He played out the over without scoring. Now for the last over.

He wasn't going to go for the big one, was he? He'd get two off this. But the return to the wicket-keeper was sharp enough for Timpson to sling the ball at the stumps in the hope of getting a run-out. He didn't aim at the stumps, though. He aimed at Mike's body. As he doubled up in pain, falling forward, everyone ran to him. Even Timpson. The Bears' physio sprinted on to the pitch.

I crammed my fingers against my mouth.

At last, at long last, he was on his feet. True, his wave of the bat looked pretty feeble, but all of us in the crowd were on our feet, cheering. The umpire had declared the second run completed, so that was Mike's century.

What would he do now? Retire hurt and let someone else get those last four runs? I didn't think so. Nor did he. Whatever the pain he was in, he lifted his bat in a great hoick – and the ball landed close enough to me for one of my neighbours to catch it.

* * *

So what would happen in the bar? My theory was that Timpson would come trotting up offering fulsome public apologies for what had *obviously* been an accident. The umpires hadn't treated it as anything else, as far as I knew. And Mike was all right, badly bruised, he'd said, with something magic from the physio to control the pain and his new colour scheme.

'A couple of inches higher and it could have stopped your heart,' I said quietly.

'A couple of inches to the left and it would have bounced off my chest pad and no harm done. Not a lot done anyway. Except you'll have to be careful how you hug me.'

'Who says I want to, anyway?'

'But Sophie, *everyone* wants to hug the Man of the Match.'

'Since when was I everyone?' To cool the conversation, I asked what no doubt everyone wanted to know. 'What happened to Barkat? Why wasn't he playing?'

His lips tightened in disapproval. 'Little bugger just didn't turn up, did he? I suppose he stayed on at the barbie and got so pissed he had to sleep it off. Not even a phone call, though. Oh, it's typical of the man – so bloody irresponsible!'

We stopped at his home to pick up his contact lens kit, razor and a change of clothes. While he gathered his things, I sat in his garden, basking in the late-evening sun. Although many of the plants were young enough to suggest he'd had to do the same resuscitation job on the garden as on the house, everything was growing well. He'd chosen old-fashioned varieties, and the borders were a-hum with bees. He might have been miles from the city centre, protected as he was by high neighbours' hedges and the school playing fields at the back.

'Erotic possibilities?' he asked, kissing me.

'Have you got a big enough airbed? I know it's better to have slabbed areas than lawns, according to the pundits—'

'But maybe the pundits have never tried it for alfresco sex. If only I'd known!'

We were on my much smaller patio, finishing our meal – pasta, crusty bread from the freezer, salad from the garden. He was topping up my glass with a fruity South African chenin blanc when he said, without looking at me, 'Guy was talking about you today when I was out in the middle.'

'Me? Why should he talk about me?'

'The bugger's no fool. He knows you're important to me.' This time he did turn to me, his smile lighting his face.

'It's mutual,' I said. 'More to the point, what was he saying? If it bears repeating, that is.'

'You and Winston.'

'But—'

'He was saying you were close.'

'I get close to a lot of students, and he was a special one, but that's all.' To my own ears I sounded defensive. I decided to push the matter further. 'Close as in lovers, you mean? Damn it, I'm old enough to be his mother. Just.'

'He didn't say. That's how it starts. Whispers, hints. Nothing you can pin down so nothing you can deny.'

You couldn't miss the anxiety in his face. I decided to tell him the whole story. 'You know about the racism episode. Well, there's another connection. While he was waiting to go to university, he became a college security guard.'

'I suppose you don't argue with someone his size!' He wanted to believe the best of me, didn't he?

'He took a lot of lip with more equanimity than most men his age. But he knew when to move in. And did so with great effect when I – hell!'

The phone. I suppose I could have let the answerphone take it, but I never manage to. It was Shahida, my college friend, wanting to know how I felt about Afzal's marriage. Not that she put it as crudely as that. She went all round the Wrekin – gossip from college, news about her daughter and her mother-in-law – but what she really wanted to know was if I had a broken heart.

'Shaz,' I said firmly, 'I like him very much. But we never were an item. Ever. The one night he spent here he was in the spare bed and absolutely alone. We are friends. OK? And I'm sorry to cut you short, but I've got a guest. I'll give you a buzz. OK?'

Perhaps I spoke loudly enough for Mike to overhear. If he did, he didn't give any indication of wanting to discuss the matter further – or indeed, the subject of Winston. There were other – more urgent – discoveries we wanted to make. And not in the spare bed.

Chapter Seven

It must be love. To find smoothing Lasonil on to someone's chest at seven-twenty in the morning an erotic experience confirmed it must be love. The little tube was oddly familiar: it was made by the same company that produced my thrush-killer. Not the song-bird – I haven't got Italian tendencies, despite my reservations about the previous day's dawn chorus – but *Candida albicans*.

'It's supposed to get rid of the bruising,' Mike said.

'Have you tried arnica? I've got some in the bathroom.'

He shook his head. 'Some of the lads swear by homoeo-pathic stuff but it's never quite convinced my scientific mind. Trouble is, you get lots of bruises in this game. There's a good one here.' He rolled over for me to treat one of his perfect buttocks, disfigured by a purple-brown stain. 'It's not the best thing to be found with, though. Some policemen see it as evidence you're doing drugs – injecting. This disperses the bruising round where the needle goes in.'

'You must have some on your thighs, too,' I said, hopefully. 'I could smooth some of this stuff on them.'

Half of his body was inclined to accept my sugges-tion; the other half reached for the watch on the bedside table.

'If we're to have that jog before I set off for Greet, then I think I'd better rub my own thighs,' he said, regretfully.

57

'But I'm sure you'd do it better. Perhaps you'd care to try this evening?'

'Your place or mine?'

'Turn and turn about suits me. Provided you don't mind having my not unobtrusive car outside your front door.'

'Does it look as if I mind?'

As he set off to talk to eleven-year-olds in one of Birmingham's less lovely districts, I set off to my dentist's, just three or four hundred yards away. I walked slowly. I didn't expect the encounter with Mr Swindale to be particularly pleasant, because I'd had to book an hour-long appointment, and that suggested a lot of drilling and filling to do, all on one poor molar.

The receptionist, who usually likes to give each patient an update on the state of her gerbils, stared at me this morning in a silence I could only feel was pointed. Nonplussed, but not, to be honest, too sorry to be spared an account of her rodent's cancer, I headed for the waiting room. At least no one treated me like a pariah there. We all exchanged glum nods, and stuck our noses in whatever reading matter came to hand.

Agreeing with Mr Swindale that neither of us wanted me to suffer, I gaped for the first injection. No pain – Mr Swindale was good at injections – but a sudden roaring in the ears. The second injection and I was afraid I was dying, my head whooshed so much. But I was back in the land of the living almost immediately, with a strongly beating heart. Indeed, a frantically beating heart.

'Adrenalin,' Swindale said tersely when I commented on it. 'To stop the local anaesthetic spilling into your bloodstream. OK now?'

I was fine until he dispatched me to the waiting room: he could deal with another patient while my face froze. And this time the other patients weren't glum, they were curious – stared so hard at me I thought I must have some blood on my face and withdrew to the loo. Expecting to peer at a female Dracula in the mirror, I saw just me. So I shrugged and went back. To another set of stares.

An hour and a half later, I staggered back home, wondering if I dared risk a cup of tea without dribbling. The answerphone pulsed redly. Bother it. Couldn't talk to anyone with my face like this anyway.

Sauntering into the garden, I waved to Aggie, my neighbour, who came to the fence as briskly as her stick would let her.

'This new young man of yours,' she said without preamble. 'I'm sorry to be the one to tell you, me love, but it says in me paper he's a killer. Killed a man.'

'What?' If my head had whirled with the adrenalin, the whole of me whirled now. Not Mike.

'You're in the paper too. Big photo of you.'

I held on to the fence so tightly I could feel splinters going in. Good. At least there was some other pain to think about when I'd dealt with this. She shuffled out again.

'Here you are – "Woman Winston Killed For". Though I can't say it's a very nice picture of you.'

Nor was it. The photographer had caught me agape. But to hell with that.

'Oh, Aggie,' I said, ready to weep with relief, 'that's not my young man.'

'It looks as if he ought to be,' she said. And then she relented. 'You'd better get yourself round here for a nice cup of tea. I've got some tweezers – you can start on them splinters while you tell me all about it.'

One of my memories of the time Winston saved my life was the A&E nurse counting splinters from my hands, 'Loves me.

Loves me not.' I did it myself today. But there were only three. He loved me.

'That's Winston Rhodes,' I said, through a biscuit my jaw wasn't up to chomping. 'He's a friend. He's not my young man.'

'I've seen his car,' Aggie said stubbornly. 'Yesterday morning and all last night. That big one with Warwickshire written all over it.'

'Winston doesn't play for Warwickshire,' I said, trying to be patient. After all, I had a couple of urgent phone calls to make, clogged up mouth or not. 'It was my new young man's car. Mike.'

'So who's this Winston, then?'

'Do you remember a long time ago when someone was chasing me up some scaffolding? He had a gun?'

'Never did know what you saw in that one.'

'Quite. Well, Winston saw what was happening and threw a stone at him to stop him shooting me. The trouble was' – and I swept my hand across her paper – 'he killed him. Didn't mean to. Just wanted to save me. Not like this suggests at all.'

Aggie shook her head. 'What you need to do is talk to that other nice young man of yours. Azfal.'

'Afzal,' I corrected her automatically.

'The solicitor,' she continued. 'Because people shouldn't be allowed to go round saying things like that.'

I didn't point out that newspapers wrote trash because even people like her bought papers that printed trash. I nodded, finished the tea, and got to my feet. 'You're right. I must go and phone him now. And Winston.' And Mike, I added under my breath. And he wouldn't be happy, either – because the man who'd taken and supplied the photo could have been none other than Guy Timpson. No prizes after this little lot for guessing what his nickname was.

*   *   *

The answerphone now flashed with several more messages. Winston had left three of them, getting more and more emphatic with each one. I wasn't surprised. Winston always kept his temper under the tightest control, but when he lost it, he was good at anger.

He had even more to be angry about than I could have imagined. 'They've bloody suspended me, Sophie. The uni *and* Middlesex. "Pending further information."'

'You can give them that easily enough,' I said. 'Phone Chris Groom. He was the officer in charge of the case. He'll tell them that you used no more than reasonable force, or whatever the phrase is. You were never charged with anything. Damn it, didn't they give you some sort of commendation for saving my neck?'

'That was then,' he wailed. 'God, if I get my hands on fucking Timpson he won't know what's hit him.'

'Why do you think it's Timpson?'

'He took the sodding photo, didn't he?'

'I wonder where he got the information from? I never talk about it, and I bet you don't!'

'He's got it from somewhere. I'm going to find that piece of shit, Sophie, and—'

'Cool it, Winston. There's nothing wrong that can't be put right.'

'You don't call suspension— I'll bloody kill him!'

'Stay by the phone,' I said, thinking that a bit of preventative action might be sensible. 'I'm phoning Chris right now.'

Or I would have done if the switchboard hadn't been asleep, or whatever it is that afflicts switchboards when you hang on for seven minutes without anyone answering. Then you slam the phone down and try again, and someone replies sweetly first ring.

Then there was the wait while they checked his number and tried to reach him. Helena – I got Helena, at least.

'Sophie – what on earth's the matter?'

'A big filling,' I said. 'And a big problem that Chris can solve in the twinkling of a word-processor.'

'Fire away.'

I fired.

Having reassured Winston that Chris would phone both his medical school and Middlesex, writing later to confirm that Winston had actually been a very good citizen, I turned my attention to the other messages. Nothing from Mike: I presumed that was simply because in general teachers wouldn't soil their hands with that sort of paper. But I needed to talk to him before someone else kindly drew his attention to it. I'd better phone Afzal as well – not that he was really my solicitor, but there are some occasions when a friendly voice offering legal advice is nicer than an impersonal one. And because we'd been talking about blackmail, which seemed to my still fuzzy brain to be not too far from what was happening to me and Winston.

'Say nothing,' he said tersely. 'It'll all blow over. Yesterday's news. Especially with that cricketer dying.'

'Cricketer? Dying?' My throat was so tight I could hardly get the words out. 'Dying?' That ball yesterday! All I could see was Mike's lovely, living body falling down lifeless.

'Yes, that Warwickshire player. It was on the lunchtime news.'

'Who? Afzal, for Christ's sake tell me who!' I was gripping the table trying to stay upright. 'Who?'

'What's his name? That young batsman. Barkat Aslam.'

Dimly, I could hear him asking if I was all right. I clawed back from the woozy depths I was sliding into. 'Sure,' I said. And wasn't.

*   *   *

I came to to find Aggie slapping me about the face with a wet tea-towel.

'That nice young Azfal told me to come round,' she said, sitting on the bottom step of the stairs to contemplate her handiwork. 'That's better. Got a bit of colour in your cheeks now. He rang and said your phone had gone dead. It's all this running about on an empty stomach as does it. And so I shall tell this Mark of yours.'

'Mike,' I said automatically.

As soon as I'd persuaded her it was safe to leave me, I grabbed the phone book. There couldn't be all that many schools in Greet, and I'd work my way through the lot if necessary. And no matter how far Mike might be from the secretary's office, she could go and find him while I hung on.

'You poor kid,' he said. 'Look, I shall be finished here in twenty minutes. I was supposed to let the physio check out my chest, but I'll come straight back.'

'No. Go and get inspected. There's nothing happening here, after all. It's Winston that's taking all the flack.'

'Want a bet? The press'll want to talk to you, you can bet your boots. Pack an overnight bag. We'll go to ground at my place.'

I liked *we*.

Spinning down Balden Road, my panniers loaded, I glanced back at my house. Yes, there was definitely a strange car driving up. And a little van with the name of a radio station blazoned over it. Coming to rest at the kerb, I took a better look. And for the first time managed a grin. Funny how everyone assumed anyone they were interested in would be driving a car. Mine sat reproachfully at the kerb where it lived. I pushed off, still grinning.

But there was someone who wouldn't be grinning again. Young Barkat. I'd sorted out his car only yards from here. A kid with a grin and a propensity for loud arguments. I'd drunk with him. No, I'd not known him well enough to shed tears – I hadn't particularly liked what I'd seen of him – but I felt chilled. A young life – another young life – cut short. What on earth could have happened to him?

I bowled up to my butcher's just as he was closing, rather late, for the half-day. With wonderful grace he opened up sufficiently for me to buy some steak, chicken and bacon, all of which could lodge at Mike's with me. The delicatessen. Some melting St Agur, amongst other cheeses, and some bread. The big Sainsbury's in Selly Oak could provide any basics. And leaving goodness knew what chaos behind, I pedalled on my way, stopping only at a newsagent's to see if there was any more news about Barkat. None, not till the evening edition, I supposed. Well, if there was nothing on TV, I could always make one or two phone calls – get the police to help me with my inquiries.

It made a change from my helping them, after all.

Chapter Eight

So much for my nasty suspicious mind. According to the evening news, Barkat had been killed in a car smash. He'd been driving very fast – 'like a bat out of hell', according to an eye witness in a car that he'd overtaken – and had lost control when he'd tried to brake for traffic lights. The only thing that struck me as odd was that anyone driving at that speed should try to stop at lights at three in the morning. If he'd careered to the far side of the junction, as seemed likely from the film footage, without hitting anyone, then presumably no one had been coming through it. But I was being logical, of course. When you're doing eighty in a built-up area at three in the morning, perhaps logic doesn't work like that. Not that it was something I wanted to put to the test. And not on the A4123 – the main road between Birmingham and Wolverhampton, the proud possessor of more black spots than the average adolescent. It was one road I always took at the regulation forty – encouraged, perhaps, by the presence, or at least warnings, of speed cameras. Come to think of it, they should have tracked him nicely.

It was good to have something to take my mind off the fact that it was now six-thirty and there was still no Mike.

I felt stranded. In my own territory I'd have found things to do – all too many. I could have had a drink or lounged or caught up on some of that reading. But close as I felt we were getting, I couldn't feel comfortable – couldn't feel at home, that was it. Letting myself out into the garden, I worried a few weeds, and, for want of knowing where he'd keep stakes and ties, inadequately propped the odd drooping branch up against another. At last, telling myself I was being foolish, I went and got a lager from his fridge and picked out a paperback from the shelves in his bedroom. I'd just installed myself outside when at last came the sound of Mike's key, and his voice calling.

'When I win the lottery,' he said at last, 'I shall donate a large dollop to Selly Oak A&E. Enough to buy them some new magazines and pictures at least. Preferably enough for new some staff. Maybe enough for a new X-ray machine. All that waiting! And I was rushed through because I'm a Celebrity, for God's sake!'

'X-ray?' I held him at arm's length.

'The physio wasn't entirely happy with my chest. Thought I might have cracked my sternum. Turns out there's nothing wrong that a bit more rubbing with Lasonil cream won't put right. Tell you what, I could do with some more now. And there's a very painful spot on my thigh . . .'

We didn't talk much about Guy. I didn't want to stoke further resentment. What Mike did want to know was how Winston came to have killed someone, and I filled him in while I washed the lettuce, and he made the dressing.

'It puzzles me,' he said. 'All this garlic? OK. How did he get all the information? The photo, that's easy. He does it wherever he goes. But the gen to back it up . . .' He shook his head.

'I've been wondering. I suppose he must have a contact somewhere to do his research,' I said. 'Or maybe he's just got a CD-ROM system with the *Guardian* on CD. I never made it to the front page, but, yes, I was in there. The man he killed was quite well-known, you see.'

He nodded. 'What are you going to do about it?'

I told him what I'd done so far. 'I've been a nine-days' wonder before. What worries me is that you'll be involved in all this.'

'Cricketers aren't known for being shy, retiring violets,' he said, risking his sternum again. 'We'll manage together, won't we?'

The next morning Mike set off for further physiotherapy. His house seemed even quieter than mine. A phone call to Aggie confirmed that there were still a couple of strange cars parked outside my house occupied by people with long lenses on their cameras.

'Been knocking on my front door,' she grumbled. 'Wanted to use my lav, first off. Then it was, "What about a cup of tea? Two sugars please." And then they started on about that Winston.'

'What did you say?'

'I told them as I'd known you for years, that you were a perfect neighbour who did my garden when I broke my hip and that who you kissed was your business and that you were going out with a nice young man called Mark.'

This time I didn't correct her. Nor did I ask her how she knew he was a nice young man.

She promised to keep an eye on things. 'And I'll get straight on to the police if there's any trouble. Talk to that nice man Ian.'

'You know he's retiring at the end of the month?'

'Course I do. He's sent me an invite to his party. This morning's post. I dare say you'll have one. D'you want me to check?'

'No. They'll only start hassling you again. Just give me a

buzz when the coast's clear, would you?' I gave her Mike's number. 'And I'll phone you for up-to-the-minute reports!'

I paged my answerphone: several newspapers, a radio station and a TV station were clogging it up, with numbers I chose not to ring back. There was a message from Chris. I called him immediately, and got through after only about twenty rings.

'I thought you'd want to know I've cleared up everything for Winston,' he said. 'In fact, he'll be back up here playing tomorrow, he says.'

'Tomorrow? The benefit match?' Throughout the year there'd be fund-raising events to give a senior player a nice bank balance for when he retired. On this occasion a Warwickshire XI would be playing an Oldbury Invitation XI.

'That's right. What I can't understand is how Winston – who plays for Middlesex – would be playing for Oldbury.'

Like Aggie, Chris found cricket something of a mystery.

'It's like this,' I said. 'Test cricket is the very pinnacle of cricket achievement, right? To be a test player you play for a county – Middlesex or Warwickshire, for instance. But you've got to learn your skills somewhere. Some men do it playing league cricket – like the Lancashire or Birmingham League. And even when they get signed up for a county – and only a small proportion do – they stay loyal to the club that nurtured them.'

'But how come you get from the *Birmingham* League to Middlesex?'

'How many West Bromwich Albion players were born in West Brom?' I parried. 'Anyway, this isn't the team Oldbury would normally field – it's made up of a mixture of regular players and ex-players – such as Winston.'

I could hear him suppressing a yawn.

'Well,' he said, with resignation rather than enthusiasm,

'I'm supposed to be *au fait* with everything in the community: I might come along for the last few overs.'

And I'd have to introduce them. Mike and Chris. Well, they'd survive, provided Chris didn't come all stiff-legged about a new man in my life.

'Of course, there's one man who won't be playing,' I said. 'Barkat Aslam. The man who wrapped himself round a traffic sign by St Hubert's Church.'

'Pissed, I suppose,' Chris said.

'I've only ever seen him drink orange juice,' I said. 'But I suppose someone'll be checking anyway.'

'You never change, do you, Sophie?'

'I solemnly promise that as long as I have a nose it will be stuck in somewhere,' I said.

'And the trouble is,' he sighed, 'it's usually stuck in the right place.'

'He had a big row with someone on Saturday night,' I said, my voice as neutral as I could make it. 'At a party out in Warley. But then, that was Saturday, and the crash was on Monday morning. He did miss the match yesterday, though. Funny, actually' – I hesitated: this wasn't the moment to introduce Mike as a factor – 'funny, other people thought he might have been sleeping off a hangover.'

Another huge sigh. 'I won't even mention the word coincidence. Look, I'm tied up all day. A Home Office woman for lunch; then a meeting with some people from the Crown Prosecution Service. And we're having a big briefing about this drugs business. We've got another kid in intensive care – the heroin's too pure. And a hooker's just died of an overdose – I'm wondering if there could be a connection. But I promise I'll have a word with one of the coroner's officers some time today – see if they've picked up anything interesting from Traffic.'

'I couldn't ask for anything more.'

And I couldn't do anything more. I dead-headed a rose or two, and watered a couple of shrubs that looked thirsty, and that was it. So I slipped quietly and anonymously out of the little cul-de-sac, pushing my bike until I reached the main road. No problems. I shoved off, heading for Edgbaston. Not the cricket ground, this time. Birmingham University Library. Time to get to grips with some reading.

'They've decided to go ahead with the match tomorrow,' Mike said as we prepared the evening meal. 'But the profits will go to Barkat's family instead.'

'Sounds a good idea,' I said, peppering the steak.

'Poor kid. Even if I never had much time for him.'

'Any special reason? Apart from him being a stroppy little bastard?'

He blinked.

'That's how you described him the other night. *In vino veritas*, perhaps?'

'OK. Though in general, I go for the *nil nisi bonum* bit when it comes to speaking of the dead.'

'Fair enough. But if there isn't a lot of *bonum* to speak?'

'There may have been lots of *bonum* in him. I mean, I hardly knew him.'

'You were in the same team, Mike. You must have had some idea.' It didn't take me long to get back into teacher mode, did it? Perhaps I should say that aloud. I did.

He laughed. 'How long did it take you to get into teacher mode in the first place?'

'About fifteen years, God help me!'

'In that case, I shall clearly have to forgive you. Here – would your stomach mind some wine while we talk? And we could sit in the garden.'

'It'll soon tell me if it does. And I love the smells out there.'

70

Honeysuckle, lavender, marjoram, thyme, coriander; then a stronger note of pinks and carnations. You could wrap yourself in the scents, bathe in them. The wine – a radiant Chilean red – had a bouquet that would have had my policeman friend wine-buff Ian Dale in paroxysms of delight. We should have been rolling round on an airbed, not sitting solemnly down to pick over the faults of a young man newly dead.

Mike swirled the wine in his glass, breathing deeply. 'That was the second smash he'd had in as many weeks, by the way. Third, if the rumours are true about the courtesy car. He'd virtually written off his team Peugeot—'

'Ah! I remember now. There was a bit in the paper. And – I hate to say this – but Guy was on to it, wasn't he? Something he said in the bar on Saturday.'

'When I was wondering how to get you out of that maelstrom of admirers. And wondering if Winston had had a change of heart, and maybe I shouldn't—'

'And I was wondering why of all the players in the bar you were the only one who didn't come over.'

And so on and so on.

Eventually we got back to Barkat.

'He was very arrogant, for one thing. You should ask the coaches about that! OK, he was naturally brilliant – I mean, brilliant – but without discipline and technique you've got nothing to fall back on on those days when you've got a cold or had a row with your mum. He had a bad attitude to net practice and training, too. All part of the same thing. But he wasn't just heedless – there was something calculated, as if he was trying to work out how far he could push people. Flashed his money around, too. I don't know. Just a callow youth, I suppose, in some respects. But he used to bring his mates along sometimes to parties like Saturday's – and I tell you, I wouldn't have wanted them in my back yard.'

'Anything specific?'

'So sharp they could have cut themselves. Harassed some of the wives. Wide boys, you know the sort of thing.'

'What was it – too much booze?'

'Other things. When I said "pissed" I might have said "smashed". Took a lot of risks, that kid. Your friends in the police'll find out soon enough.'

I ignored that. 'All in all he wasn't your favourite person.'

'No. But I wouldn't wish him – or anyone else – dead.'

'Not even Guy?' I risked.

'Now? Not even Guy. I'd like to wring his neck, but not kill him. Think of the consequences of doing someone in. I wouldn't like them. So although the world would be a better place without him, Guy can sleep at night without worrying about me.' He looked me straight in the eye. 'And so can you.'

Had my anxiety, my lack of trust shown that much? On one level I was quite right to be anxious: we'd only known each other four days, for heaven's sake. On another, what can you base a relationship on except absolute trust?

'I believe you,' I said. And meant it.

Chapter Nine

I spent an uncomfortable hour at the dentist's, this time under the care of a hygienist whose sadistic water jets found more sensitive spots than the most penetrating ice-cream. Mike had dropped me off and collected me later so we could go straight to the Oldbury ground together. There was no point, as he said, having two cars in such an insalubrious spot. When I asked him how he'd kill the time, he was unusually vague.

Oldbury Broadwell Cricket Club was tucked into a corner of Langley. This little town had once been a suburb of Oldbury, but was now, thanks to local government reorganisation, a fellow suburb of Sandwell.

To one side was the village street – the Black Country may be one amorphous mass to the outsider, but it's really a conglomeration of very different towns and villages, all with their own identity and their own accent. To the other side was the Titford cut. If you'd followed it along its winding way you'd once have been able to end up at the wharf where we should have boarded my leaving-party boat. It was still an industrial canal, with huge buildings, ancient and modern, on its banks. What had once been a coal wharf was now a haulage contractor's base, and no one now remembered how Uncle Ben's Bridge had got its name. But a brewery and a cement works lived along here, and the smell was still authentically Black Country. The M5 roared in the background.

A hundred years ago, someone had managed to squeeze a park and cricket ground into a gentle bend. Looked at from one angle, the pavilion was as picturesque as one on any village green. From another it was dwarfed by the great red walls of Victorian maltings. They were still in use, too.

Despite its clean paint, bright in the warm sun, Mike looked at the ground with some distaste. 'Not such a nice setting as Smethwick,' he said.

I clapped a hand over his mouth. 'You don't mention Smethwick round here! It's a foreign country!'

'It's just down the road.'

'Since when did being neighbours make you the same race? Once upon a time I went out with a Smethwick man.' I infused the direst gloom into my voice.

'What happened?' He looked as alarmed as I'd intended.

I shrugged fatalistically. 'What could happen? He came from Smethwick!'

'Of course. If-you-want-a-nigger-for-a-neighbour-vote-Labour Smethwick. The election they threw out Patrick Gordon Walker.'

I was impressed. 'You know your local history, Mike. You'll know that Oswald Mosley was once MP for Smethwick.'

'And I know an old, old man who remembers him bringing his wife here to canvass. And when she stood on a railway wall – not far from the Blue Gates – to make a speech, the wind took her skirt and blew it round her ears.'

'And emptied every pub for miles around, no doubt. I wonder if it won him any votes.' We got out of the car. 'Now, do you know Oldbury's claim to fame? Listen – I'll give you a clue.' I hummed.

He looked at me sideways. '"A Long Way to Tipperary"?'

'Spot on. Written by an Oldbury man – one Jack Judge, commemorated variously but possibly inadequately in the town centre. Go on, look impressed.'

'I am trying, very hard!'

I gave up. 'Look, there's Sal waving to you! That's some car she drives.' It was a huge Merc to match her huge house and huge garden.

Mike waved back. 'She's in charge of running the barbie at the end of play.'

'And there's Winston!' My turn to wave vigorously.

'He's got guts, that lad. There'll be quite a press presence here to watch him play. Or rather, not to watch him play. I wonder who that gorgeous young woman with him is.'

I'd guess every man on the ground would be wondering precisely that. And coming to the same conclusion as me. 'Trust Winston to come up with someone who looks like an African princess. Hey! That's Guy Timpson, isn't it? What the hell's he doing here?'

'One of Oldbury's Invitation XI – he must have been nurtured here too. And I doubt if he'd want to miss a chance of seeing how much shit he's managed to stir up. Time I was checking in, love. Sorry: it's just one of my things. I have to be early.'

'Same as Winston always touches the stumps before he starts his bowling spell?'

Mike nodded. 'Or Barkat had to put his right boot on first, never the left. Not that it did him much good, poor sod. OK. Here I go. Over the top!' He disappeared into the pavilion, waving ironically to the first photographer on the scene.

Winston sauntered over, dropping his bag to give me another of his public hugs.

'The bastards can make what they like of that,' he said. 'And I'd like you to meet Joanna,' he said, suddenly as formal as if he were presenting her to his mother.

We shook hands with equal formality. And then grinned at each other and hugged. Let the press make of that what they would.

*   *   *

The Warwickshire XI won the toss and chose to bat. Mike, in whites rather than Technicolor, sauntered out to join Joanna and me. 'If I were Guy I'd be glad Winston's in the same team,' he said. 'Winston's pace on this pitch, spiced up with a bit of righteous indignation . . .' He shook his head. 'I just hope he remembers we like each other.'

'It does look a bit green,' I said. 'They'll be flying round there all right. Thank God you all wear helmets these days.'

'Amen.'

I hoped Joanna would join in the conversation, but she stood there simply smiling and looking wonderful.

'Not much of a crowd,' I said eventually, regarding the thirty or so scattered round the boundary, 'considering the talent on show.' I smiled at Joanna to show I included Winston in my compliment.

She just smiled back.

'You'll find they come in little bursts,' Mike said, as if sensing my desperation. 'End of school; end of work; after the evening meal. Ah, here we go.' Mike led the applause as Oldbury took the field. The captain, an old county player, tossed the ball straight to Winston. Timpson made for the far end, slapping the big outer gloves against his thigh as he went.

The Warwickshire opener took guard; Timpson pulled on his gloves; Winston touched the stumps and paced out his run.

I started to focus my binoculars.

There was a terrible scream from the far end. Timpson was trying to pull off his gloves.

Winston kept on running. But he'd let slip the ball and was heading straight for Timpson. He dropped down beside him and was pulling the gloves too.

He stood. 'Ambulance – fast! And get a first-aider!'

Mike was on his feet. We all were. I was sprinting on to the square before I knew it. 'I'm trained,' I gasped to Winston. 'What can I do?'

'It's anaphylactic shock,' he said. 'He needs adrenalin now. Go and see if there's any sort of kit in his bag – or something that looks like a pen. And move!'

I bolted back to the pavilion. I could remember Sal's voice talking about wasps – *he has to be careful*.

Mike was already in the changing room when I got there. 'It's not bloody here!' He tipped the bag upside down. Towels, shades, that bruise ointment, all over the floor. 'It's not bloody here! He always carries this pen, and it's not here!'

I went through it too. Nothing like a kit, certainly no pen. And no ambulance yet. All I could think of was the anti-histamine tablets I carry for hay-fever and my asthma spray. I grabbed them and ran back to the middle.

Winston was still trying to give mouth-to-mouth when I reached him. He moved over for me, and started to beat Timpson's chest.

'There's no airway!' I gasped.

'I know there's no bloody airway. There's no pulse, either.' He looked despairingly at my little haul. 'Crush one of them and put it under his tongue. You can try the spray, but if he can't breathe he can't inhale.'

So unless the ambulance came now, he'd die. His face was enormously bloated, and huge white blebs were spreading all over him. I didn't want to look at the hand which had been stung. It was far worse than Halima's, grotesque, hardly recognisable as human.

At last we could hear the ambulance, but its klaxon took an age to get close. An age Guy didn't have.

What I'd never have expected was a fight within yards of us. But the unnatural silence was broken by sharp voices.

'What the hell d'you think you're up to, sunshine?'

'You leave the poor bugger be: we don't want your sort shoving their noses in.'

I glanced up long enough to see some of the burlier Oldbury lads shouldering a couple of photographers out of the way. Then, as I concentrated on my task again, the ground shook with the impact of running feet. They were seeing them off the ground. Briskly.

At last the paramedics were here.

They did their best, shoving in a massive dose of adrenalin, giving the first tracheotomy I'd ever seen, and applying oxygen. At last, still not giving up but obviously distressed themselves, they took him off to hospital. We all knew it was in vain. And even if he did survive, he'd be brain-damaged beyond repair, Winston said.

We stood round the stumps, a shocked little bunch. Half the men still hadn't registered quite what had happened.

'Just a bee-sting, you reckon? A little thing like that kill a strapping lad like him?'

I nodded.

'But this bee . . . He was wearing bleeding big gloves,' the same ginger-haired man persisted.

'Must have been in his glove, I suppose,' I said. And grabbing the gloves by the opening end, ran back to the pavilion. 'Find me a polythene bag for these!' I yelled.

They could only muster a black bin liner from the kitchen, but that would do. I sealed them in. The gloves and their still angry cargo of bees.

Chapter Ten

The two police kids who'd presumably turned up because of the 999 call looked as shocked as the rest of us. I wasn't surprised. Death by bee-sting was even more frightening than death by peanut: if Halima had looked despairing, sheer terror had distorted Guy Timpson's features, as if he'd known— No, I was being fanciful.

The young officers were clearly overawed by the company. I ran a quick finger count of the men gathered around. Three current England test players, eight ex. Maybe I'd have been overawed.

And we were all trampling on the square. The groundsman wrung his hands. I caught his eye and grinned sadly. No one else seemed to have noticed, so I touched Ron, the Oldbury captain, on the arm.

'What's up, me wench?'

'Haven't you people got a match on Saturday?' I pointed at the turf.

'Ah. You mean, better shift this little lot.' Gently, apologetically, he herded us towards the pavilion. 'And I reckon as how we could use a cuppa, eh?'

I could, for one. The urn was already steaming. A kindly woman poured, pressing extra sugar on us all. For shock, she said.

No one wanted to break the silence. Outside, a knot of spectators waited for an announcement.

'Best tell 'em it's off,' Ron said. 'Here – you two. Standing round like spare dinners. You go and tell them.'

The officers did as they were bid, and returned looking embarrassed. I felt embarrassed. There was something I ought to say but didn't want to. I wanted it to be someone else who said it.

'I just can't make it out,' Ron muttered into his cup. 'A fine bloke like that. And all it takes is a bee sting.'

'A lot of people are allergic to things,' said the younger officer. 'My big sister – she gets hay-fever every time she drinks milk.'

'Ah, but she doesn't die! One sting! And what I want to know is where the little bleeder came from!' Ron pursued.

'I'd guess it was more than one sting,' I said. 'And I reckon the bees were in his gloves. That's why they're in that black sack, there.'

'They could have' – the constable's voice was losing confidence – 'like, crawled in, like . . . I suppose . . .'

'But he always carried an Epipen,' Mike cut in. 'Always. It was even in his shirt pocket at that barbecue on Saturday. The Rutland physio always has a back-up. We all know about it. We used to joke about who'd want to stick pins into his backside.'

'And it wasn't in his bag. I can vouch for that.' I looked straight at the older constable.

He swallowed, his Adam's apple bobbing convulsively. 'Seems a bit of a coincidence, like.'

His mate nodded. 'Look, ladies and gents: I reckon as how I'd better have a word with my superiors. Will you excuse me?' He turned and spoke into his radio.

We made the smallest of talk just to spare him.

'Look,' he said, speaking to us again. 'There'll have to be an inquest, seeing as how the bloke died sudden. We'll need some witnesses. What we'd like to do is take your names and addresses, just so as we know who's who, like. And a contact number, please. You will understand, gentlemen, we'll need to seal the dressing room.'

'Seal it? So we can't change?' Ron demanded. 'What about these lads – professional players? They'll be needing their bags, mate.'

The Bears' captain nodded.

'OK. Point taken. Tell you what, I'll just talk to me boss again.'

Once into gear, they'd been efficiency personified, and we were soon free to go, albeit with the men still in their whites. Officers had checked each bag, though, inside out, before handing it to its owner. Not an Epipen in sight. They also sent for further reinforcements to clear away the press, who had regrouped strategically by the car park exit. I couldn't understand why they were holding back, until Ron muttered in my ear, 'Learned their lesson, I see.'

'Lesson?'

'Them two trying to take your picture when you were on your knees by – by— Winston, too. Doing that resuscitation. So a couple of the lads told them where to get off, and slung their cameras into the cut. Just so as they wouldn't forget and try again. Know what I mean?'

I grinned. 'I wouldn't fancy diving in there to retrieve them.'

He shook his head. 'Bloody hell, no. Listen here, me wench, there's this bloke I know has this narrow boat. And he's trying to free the propeller – there's all sorts of crap tangling it up. And he leans this bit too far and in he goes, arse over tip. Any road up, they fish him out all right, but then he finds himself in Casualty. They only pump his stomach out. And fill him so full of injections he can't sit down for a week. No, if them lads try fishing for their gear, they may catch a damn sight more than they bargained for.'

Winston and Mike were deep in conversation beside Mike's car. Joanna welcomed me with a smile as I approached.

'They're talking transport and how to avoid being followed,' she said. 'I think we should drop Mike's car as soon as possible and go on in Winston's.'

It was good to hear her speak, and such common sense, too. Winston hadn't yet acquired a vividly sponsored car, though I was sure Middlesex would soon be repairing the omission. 'So we drop that at my place and Winston takes us on?'

'Right,' Mike said. 'To Winston's mum's. We need to talk, you see. Because if anyone wanted Timpson dead, he and I must be amongst the prime suspects.'

'Me too,' I added hollowly.

The changeover was effected cleanly. Mike managed to squeeze his car into my new garage, which, since it was summer, was relatively empty. I hadn't even got round to erecting staging for over-wintering my plants. The lawn-mower would have to put up with a sojourn outside. I grabbed more clothes. I'd have to get rapidly acquainted with the workings of Mike's washing machine at this rate. Mike had gathered up my mail, and we swept out, locking up carefully. Winston's car doors were already ajar. No, no one tailing us. Unless it was a youth on a tatty motorbike. Winston drove like he bowled, however, and soon there was no one in sight.

Philomena must have regretted the moment I walked into her son's life, but she didn't show it. Instead, she pushed away the book she was studying and embraced me as warmly as if she were my own mother. She was a mite more formal with Joanna, but there was no doubt about her approval.

'You're the one who's on the dentistry course, right?'

Dentistry! At least she wouldn't be one of those dentists who filled your mouth with unmentionable instruments of torture and then inflicted on you a stream of controversial conversation.

'You're running up debts as fast as my Winston, no doubt,' Philly continued. 'And are you planning to go into practice straight away? Or go and play with a bat and ball – you sure need a medical degree for that!' She eyed Winston ironically.

'Soon as I can find a practice to take me, Mrs Rhodes.'

'Come on, girl, I Philomena to all de worl'!' she said, assuming the patois she occasionally favoured, usually to embarrass others when they discovered she was considerably more than a hospital cleaner with a rolling, bottom-heavy walk. In fact, her walk was as feigned as her accent; and although she was no longer slender, she certainly didn't fit anyone's stereotype. At the moment she was a senior theatre sister, with a string of qualifications as long as Winston's arm.

Before Winston could say anything, she walked to the open window and stuck her hand out. She brought it in. Perfectly dry. 'OK. It's lovely to see you all, but what on earth you doing here now? I don't see any rain.'

Winston gave a succinct account of the afternoon's play.

'Jesus Christ! The poor young man. And no adrenalin? Why no adrenalin?'

'Only a benefit match – they don't have the medical back-up they have at county grounds. No physio, even, today. And the St John's people still hadn't turned up when we left.'

'I wonder why not,' Mike said slowly.

I stayed steadfastly silent.

Joanna shrugged. 'Because they didn't know about the match?'

Winston shook his head. 'There's always some sort of cover. And every match I've been to, they've been pretty punctual.'

'Right,' Mike agreed.

'So why weren't they punctual today?' Philomena asked. 'And where was that young man's adrenalin kit?'

Four solemn heads shook.

'You want to know what I think?' she pursued. 'I think this is a matter for the police. And I tell you something else: if you're not where you said you were going to be, young Mike, I think the police may want to know why.'

Winston butted in. 'Told you why, Ma. The press are on to them.'

'Paparazzi or no paparazzi. OK. Call them boys in blue. Tell them you're here. Stay as long as you want. Plenty to eat – you know that, Winston. But just remember this: sooner or later, you have to go back – don't you?'

'Come on, Sophie. You know you've got to do it. You've got to call him.'

Even outside another cup of tea and a slice of rather heavy banana cake, I still felt unequal to the task of phoning Chris. For a start, even murder – if that was what it turned out to be – was beneath his immediate notice, despite the fact that whoever had killed Guy had had the bad taste to do it slap in the middle of Chris's patch. For another thing, however platonic our relationship had been of late, we had never officially ended it, and the news that I was going out with another man was hardly going to make his day. Particularly as that man had a fairly good motive for wanting Guy Timpson dead. I had a terrible feeling that Chris wouldn't share my strong impulse to believe him innocent.

Whatever Chris's feelings – and at this stage we'd no idea what they were – his colleagues were certainly interested in our whereabouts, as a quick paging of our answerphones demonstrated. We were both invited to contact them at Piddock

Road as soon as possible. That wasn't the only invitation, however. Sal's voice – gravelly over the phone – begged Mike to go to supper, 'bringing that nice little girl if you like'. I wasn't at all sure I liked the nomenclature, and was fairly sure I'd rather have spent the evening in a variety of other ways, but Mike seemed happy to go.

'She's a game old dear.'

'Old dear?'

'My mum knew her. She reckons she's nearer seventy than sixty. Well, you only have to look at the flesh at the top of her arms. At least she's abandoned low-cut T-shirts. She gave up fags last year, but makes up for it with gin. Mind you, I've never known her so much as squiffed. And Art's a good enough sort, I suppose. So long as you stick to me like glue, that is.'

'A man for etchings, is he?'

'Galleries full of them, I should imagine. Right: Piddock Road in person, d'you think? Or phone them and bring them out to Harborne or Bournville?'

While we weighed up the odds, Philomena's phone rang. For Winston. They wanted to talk to him, too. He nipped out to change into jeans and T-shirt. His mother sent him back to change into dark trousers and formal shirt. He didn't argue.

Joanna came along, presumably for the ride.

Chapter Eleven

For those of us used to the clean, modern lines of Rose Road Police Station, Piddock Road was another world. It was still in stately Victorian premises, complete with ornamental porch. The doors were heavy with their desire to impress. Inside, however, the reception area was pure bathos. Anyone who had fears about police overspending on home comforts would find nothing to grumble about here. Quite the reverse. Although the counter was chest-high wood, presumably a relic of days when intimidating Joe Public was a Good Thing, the rest of the original area had been sliced up cheaply, with no regard to once spacious, heat-eating architecture. The brown rexine chairs to which we were consigned looked saggy, but we were brought up short: someone had had to shove pieces of block-board underneath the cushions to stop the sitter descending to the floor. Or rather, to enable him or her to struggle out again. In any case, there were only three – was this a testimony to police efficiency? Or an assumption that some people would just have to stand? Winston was the one left chairless, but he didn't stand. He prowled. In the tight confines he was like a tiger in a bad zoo. Not that we had to wait long. The sixties door soon opened, to reveal a youngish, slightly built Asian, who announced himself as DS Harvinder Mann. He ushered us together into a badly converted and thus badly proportioned office which was probably freezing in winter, it was so cool now.

He shook hands with us courteously: 'Ladies and gentlemen – please sit down. No, not that chair, sir. It's a health hazard. All I want to do now is hear an account of precisely what happened before my colleagues arrived. If there's anything else I should know, I hope you'll feel free to tell me.'

They all looked at me. I looked at Winston.

'Would it be easier if you gave me separate accounts? In the form of statements?'

'More paperwork for you!' I said. 'How about a sort of chorus. Mike and I arrived at the ground at one-thirty-seven, approximately . . .'

The tea they brought us made me wish I'd asked for coffee, until I saw Winston's expression, that is.

Mann drank water.

'As I see it, you're convinced that he was all right until he put on the big wicket-keeper's gloves. And then all your attempts to save his life failed.'

'He needed a big dose of adrenalin immediately,' Winston said. 'He might have needed more than one dose, the reaction was so severe.'

'Are we talking some strain of killer bee here?' Mann prompted. 'There was a programme on TV just the other night.'

'Killer bees?' Winston echoed.

'American. Very dangerous, according to this programme.'

Winston mimed a cool dude swaggering along the street. 'You mean, with, like, shooters, man? Or maybe machetes?'

Mann pursed his lips. 'Killer bees,' he repeated. 'Venom in their stings, Mr Rhodes.'

Winston remembered he was practically a doctor and shook

his head with dignified emphasis. 'I'd have thought not. Ordinary bees stinging a man with an extraordinary sensitivity. But Sophie had the presence of mind to keep the gloves shut and then bagged them. Whatever sort of bee it was would have been trapped.'

Mann had a point to score. 'You're a medical student, Mr Rhodes. Did you feel qualified to administer this adrenalin?'

'A child could have used Timpson's gizmo,' Mike said. 'He'd shown us. There was some spring mechanism that released a needle to the appropriate depth. But it wasn't there. As soon as I guessed what might be happening, I went to the changing room and went through his bag. Sophie came and helped – I gather Winston sent her. Nothing.' He spread his hands in an eloquent gesture.

'Was there anyone else in the dressing room?'

He shook his head. 'The Bears had all changed and were sitting out front. The Oldbury lads were on the field.'

Mann turned to me. 'Ms Rivers – how did you know what you were looking for? Was it just guesswork?'

'One of my students died after a peanut touched her tongue last week. I saw her pen. And I looked up the condition in Birmingham University Library yesterday morning.'

I'd said the wrong thing, hadn't I? There was no doubt he'd stiffened.

'Looked it up?'

'I'd had a bad allergic reaction myself to something on Friday. I wanted to know the score.'

'The rash was still there on Saturday morning,' Winston said.

'You didn't go to a doctor?'

'I've been too busy dodging the press,' I said. And wished I hadn't. But there was no pulling back now, and the man would soon have found out about Guy's proclivities. 'Thanks to the late Mr Timpson,' I added, for good measure. 'Superintendent

Groom knows about it: I spoke to him on the phone yesterday morning too. In fact, he'd thought of putting in an appearance at the post-match barbecue this evening.' The words *penny* and *pound* swam together in my brain. What I did hope was that I'd mentioned my conversation with Chris to Mike – but I had a feeling we'd been doing other things and it might have slipped my mind. Nothing like a public confession, I suppose. I didn't have to move far to stretch my hand to Mike's. Did I dare?

'Tell me about the press and Mr Timpson,' Mann said.

'He took photographs wherever he went,' Mike said. 'Anyone, anywhere. We were all at a party on Saturday evening – all of us except Joanna, that is.' He smiled at her. 'One of the photos he took – one of Sophie and Winston hugging like the old friends they are – found its way into the gutter press on Monday.'

Winston told the story of our acquaintance. All of it. Mann looked impressed. 'We've hardly seen each other since then, though. I've been down in London at Queen Mary and playing for Middlesex whenever they asked me.'

Mann glanced at Joanna with some embarrassment and then looked Winston straight in the eye. 'You don't have a relationship with Ms Rivers?'

'I have a very good relationship with Ms Rivers. But not a sexual one.'

I nearly gasped. The old Winston would never have played with words like that.

'It's I who's in a relationship with Sophie,' Mike declared, gripping my hand. I awarded him an A for remembering that the verb 'to be' doesn't take an object, an F for forgetting it should be 'who am' and another couple of A's for the declaration and the manner of it.

'Of long standing?'

'I beg your pardon?'

'Mr Timpson's revelations didn't shock you? Upset you?'

'DS Mann, when you've been through what I've been through at the hands of Mr Timpson, you wouldn't ask that question. I'm happy to give a complete account, but perhaps in private. And maybe I ought to talk to a solicitor first. Just to sort out what's relevant, you understand.'

The solicitor I usually dealt with was on holiday, and his partner – in the solicitor's sense – was in court. So I rang Afzal, who promised to turn out as soon as he'd finished with his current appointment.

'You do realise, Mr Lowden, that you're not under arrest, not being charged with anything?' DS Mann said.

'Of course. Look, I loathed that man – had every reason to – but I wouldn't – Jesus—' He broke off, shuddering at the memory. 'How these two managed to do what they did – touch him when he was . . .' Another shudder. 'Whoever is responsible should be punished: it's as clear as that. And the sooner you people can – how do you put it? – eliminate me from your inquiries, the sooner you can nail the bastard who did it. OK?'

I admired his courage, but doubted his wisdom. None the less, I smiled bravely and tucked my hand into his.

At this moment the door opened and the uniformed figure of Chris Groom strode into the room. He'd always been good at taking in situations at a glance, and I was sure he wouldn't have missed anything. Especially not my flush of embarrassment. Nor the fact that I didn't remove the hand until I needed it to perform introductions, as if this were some social gathering.

He shook hands with the completely silent Joanna and clapped Winston on the shoulder with comradely affection.

'Thanks for sorting out that crap the other day, man,' Winston said.

Why was he back into streetwise mode? He'd never really liked Chris, but he certainly owed him this time.

Chris nodded. 'No problem. Everything OK now, is it? Excellent!' He turned to me, touching me lightly on the nose. 'Been sticking it in again, Sophie? Hello.' He shook hands with Mike.

'No more success than I had with Halima, I'm afraid.'

'Nothing would have saved him except proper medication,' Winston put in. 'An enormous dose of anti-histamine might have held things off. We crushed one of Sophie's hay-fever tablets and put it under his tongue; we tried with her asthma spray, too. We tried all we could, man,' he concluded, so abruptly that I glanced at him. His eyes brimmed with tears. The doctor losing a patient. A young man seeing death close to.

'You've all had a bad time. Look, I gather your solicitor's on the way, Mike, but I can't for the life of me see why.'

Mike looked him straight in the eye. 'If you'd publicly threatened to kill him as often as I have, you'd want a solicitor.'

Chris nodded, the personification of calm. 'OK. Point taken. But we shan't be leaping around making immediate arrests, you know. There's got to be a post-mortem, however obvious the cause of death might be, and then an inquest. DCI Peter Kirby will be in charge of the investigation. We've got all your details. You're free to go whenever you want.' He spoke into an internal phone. 'One of the lads'll lead you out of this maze.'

Winston looked at his watch. 'We'll push off then, right, Joanna?'

She nodded.

'See you, Mike. Sophie. You watch yourself, man.'

No hugs or handshakes this time. But I slipped out of the door after him. A constable almost as tall and black as Winston was waiting.

'Winston,' I began awkwardly. 'All this "relationship" business – and the press and everything . . . Would it be better if I kept out of your hair for a bit? Yours and Joanna's?'

He studied my face, then looked at Joanna, beautiful and impassive. 'Yeah . . . You may be right, man. But if you need me, you know where to find me.'

I nodded. 'Thanks.'

This time we did hug.

And Joanna smiled agreeably as they waved goodbye.

The four of us waited. The two tall men: Mike, still in his whites; Chris, shirt-sleeved but with his insignia heavy with authority on his shoulder. The smaller Harvinder in ordinary shirtsleeves; five foot one of me in a pretty top and summer-weight skirt. The tension started to gather. It was broken by the arrival of a breathless Afzal, in the wake of a middle-aged constable glossy with the sweat of overweight. Afzal greeted Chris and me with every appearance of pleasure, even giving me his usual chaste kiss. He nodded at Harvinder, and shook hands very formally with Mike.

'He hasn't been charged, Chris?'

'Nor will he be, I hope. But since you're here—' Chris's shrug gave the go-ahead to any sort of conversation they might want. 'Find one of the interview rooms that's been decorated, will you, Harvinder? Sophie, are you waiting for Mike? Fancy a tour of my new kingdom?' He held the door compellingly.

I followed him through thirties-tiled corridors guarded by heavy doors. Then we went into the outside world, the warmth of the air almost a shock after Mann's cool office. I hadn't noticed the smell before, but it was there: pure Smethwick. Heavy industry, still surviving and still, presumably, polluting. But still providing work. Best to suspend judgement, perhaps.

We didn't speak while we crossed the tarmac yard. Then he opened the door of the block that housed him.

'This used to be the magistrates' court building,' he said.

Whether it was its civilian origins or simply because it had had to be rejuvenated, it was certainly better cared for than the main body of the station. I followed him down carpeted corridors to his room. He ushered me in, and closed the door.

I wasn't looking forward to the next few minutes. It had been understood that we were now friends, neither more nor less. And that either of us was free to find someone else. But I wish I'd told him, face to face, before he found out. I owed him that. Just as I owed him honesty now.

'I've been going out with Mike less than a week,' I said baldly. 'But I think it's important, Chris. It didn't seem appropriate to mention it on the phone.'

He nodded. 'Tea? I make better stuff than they do over there. At least, Helena does,' he added, with an interesting smile.

'Please.'

He spoke into his intercom. Then he came back my side of his desk. 'Have a seat. Such as it is.'

I followed his eyes round the room, which was big and pleasantly airy. But it was clear that Chris's furniture budget had been as limited as everyone else's. No two items matched. I sat on a low chair at a lower table.

'This is supposed to be our conference room, would you believe?'

'Looks as if you've got everyone else's leavings,' I said. And wished I hadn't.

'I have. A guy from West Brom sent me the desk; Ian had a mate who found the filing cabinets. But if there's any money left over in this year's budget I shall spend it on a decent-height table and chairs. You can't expect adults to squat round that.'

'What about a new desk and chair for yourself? With your back you can't afford to economise.'

'My back? There's nothing wrong with my back.'

'Yet! How many Alexander Technique lessons did you have? Two?'

He squirmed. 'Well, I was very busy.'

'And always will be busy. But if you go on as you are, you'll find yourself taking time off: really hunched, you're getting.'

'Maybe I need some new glasses.'

'Maybe that too. OK, Chris. I'll stop nagging now. But that doesn't mean I shan't start again tomorrow.'

Helena knocked and brought in tea. I'd bought him a set of china cups and saucers as a nick-warming present. I hadn't expected to see them in use in quite these circumstances.

'Nagging Chris?' she asked, her voice mock-shocked.

'About his back. And the need for a new chair.'

'That's one Noah threw out of the Ark when he sailed up the cut,' she agreed. 'I'll get on to a friend of mine at Oxfam – the furniture depot. Would that be hair-shirt enough for you, Chris?' She bent to lay the tray in front of me. 'You take your life in your hands with this table,' she said. 'One of these days I won't be able to get up again.'

She grinned at Chris: this was obviously a familiar theme. And there was something about her smile that reassured me, too. She wasn't going to worship him. She couldn't be more than a couple of years older than he, and if I were as attractive as her in five years' time I'd consider myself very lucky. I wondered if I might indulge in a little matchmaking – or would it smack too much of wanting him to have a consolation prize if he couldn't have me? I gave myself a thorough shaking. If he and she couldn't organise it, I wouldn't have the temerity.

'I was suggesting to Chris that he ought to get you to prioritise his incoming mail. Stop him going under altogether.'

She raised an eyebrow. 'Well, I do have to read everything. And I could use different-coloured markers – urgent, today, can wait. That sort of thing. No problem.'

Chris looked cornered. Then he did the sensible thing and smiled. 'Are you sure it wouldn't be too much trouble?'

'I'll give it a try, shall I?' she said. 'See you, Sophie.' And she let herself out.

There was a little silence.

At last Chris made the effort to break it. 'He seems a decent enough sort, your Mike. Good player, according to the papers.'

I nodded. 'Be terrible if he were guilty, wouldn't it? Warwickshire couldn't afford to lose two major players. Any news of Barkat?'

He burrowed amongst the files on his overloaded desk. At last he shook his head and gave up. 'As I recall, it was multiple injuries consistent with wrapping your car round a solid object when you're doing eighty,' he said. 'It'll be here somewhere.'

'Any idea why he was doing eighty?'

'He was a young man, Sophie.'

'A young man with a lot to live for. OK. It'll turn up. Maybe it'll make interesting reading; maybe not. Maybe the speed cameras'll show something up.'

He looked at me hard. 'What are you getting at?'

'I've absolutely no idea. I know Timpson needled him with something he said about cars on Saturday evening. And that he was having a shouting match with someone at a barbecue later. And that he didn't turn up for Sunday's match. And that, like Timpson, he wasn't universally loved and admired. But I also know, Chris, that you're trying to run a very big ship. You can't shove *your* nose into every little case.'

'True. But I need to know enough to ask the right questions when I see my teams every day.' He stopped pushing the files on his desk back into piles and walked over. 'I may need to ask the right questions about this Guy Timpson business.' He looked me straight in the eyes.

I didn't flinch. 'You think I don't know that?'

'They may be awkward questions. And the people I may be asking about are your – people you care about.'

I waited.

'This business about Mike and his solicitor: I don't like it, Sophie. I really don't. It smacks of – of guilt.'

I wanted to shout at him: there was no way Mike would have done this. Then I pulled myself together. 'I suppose it does. But I bet your Peter Kirby's investigations will throw up a lot of people with grudges against Timpson. Well, me and Winston for a start. Probably his Rutland team-mates. Maybe the physio who keeps the spare Epipen. People at the party, perhaps. A lot of people knew about that bee allergy.'

'But did they all have the knowledge and opportunity to take advantage of it?'

And that was the question I didn't care to answer.

Chapter Twelve

'You really don't want to go out tonight, do you?' Mike said, stroking my hair back from my face.

We were at his house, now. Through the open bedroom window the birds sounded subdued. Perhaps late afternoon wasn't their favourite time.

'No. I don't. And neither do you. But you've got "Call of Duty" stamped all over your forehead.'

'Like your friend Chris.'

The stroking had stopped.

'Not as bad as that!' I laughed. 'What did you make of him, anyway, what little you saw?'

'He seemed decent enough. And Afzal did . . . except something was troubling him. A couple of times he nearly said something. Then he stopped.' He sat up, looking puzzled. 'Twice. Quite definitely. But he seemed very conscientious, very trustworthy.'

I rolled on to my side. 'Last autumn Afzal and I were . . . for a couple of days . . . interested . . . in each other. Nothing more. He's too strict a Muslim. He's getting married soon,' I added, not quite irrelevantly.

'Anyone else I should know about?'

No wonder we were still lying here, nothing having happened.

'Do you want me to catalogue them in an aria or merely list

99

them?' I sat up. 'Come on, Mike – I'm even older than you. I've been neither celibate nor promiscuous. But if you want a list you shall have it. So long as I get yours.' What I wanted to do was howl.

For answer he pulled me back down and buried his face in my chest. 'I'm sorry. I'm so sorry. One day we'll have confession time for all. Once and for all. But not today. Not after today. He really put me through it, that guy Kirby. I was glad of Afzal. He was very tactful, but very assertive when Kirby started to re-interpret things I'd said. Trouble is, Sophie, for all Chris was saying there wasn't even a case yet, in their minds there is. And I'm number one suspect.'

'Winston and I are equal second, then. But there must be a number of others in the frame. Unlike my clothes. I can't help thinking your Sal comes with an extensive, expensive wardrobe. All my decent stuff's still tucked up at home, under the tender gaze of the nation's press, no doubt. I only grabbed everyday things. I forgot about this evening.' The friendly WPC who'd run us back to Harborne to collect my car had deflected the press long enough to allow us to escape by dint of pulling broadside across Balden Road. 'Hey! Where are you going?'

He swung out of bed and strode over to the Victorian chest of drawers he used as a dressing table. He seized something. 'Come on, let's go burn this up.' He was waving a credit card at me.

I swung and strode too. To my bag. 'Snap!' I waved mine at him.

He started to laugh. 'It's no good, you can't manage high dudgeon dressed in nothing but your suntan!'

'Any more than you can manage dignity wearing only those bruises.'

*   *   *

By the time we'd discussed the matter to our mutual satisfaction, it was far too late to go hunting for clothes. A quick iron helped the skirt, and by chance I'd brought one silk top with me. But I'd have to organise something conspiratorial with Aggie pretty soon. She'd love it, toddling off ostensibly to Safeway but in fact to bundle into a taxi with a case of my clothes. If her bad hip were up to it, of course. Which it probably wasn't. No, it'd have to be something much more complicated, involving my college friend Shahida, perhaps, and the key Aggie guarded with her life.

I was about to let us into the car when Mike clapped a hand to his forehead. 'What am I thinking of? Best get a taxi.'

'I know mine's only little compared with yours,' I said, 'but it'll get us there.'

'It's safer tucked up in my garage, isn't it? And Sal doesn't know the meaning of the words "Not for me, I'm driving."'

'In that case let's call another friend of mine. Shahida's brother, Arun. He's saving up for university: runs a mini-cab. And before you ask, I never had a relationship with him!'

Although we'd been late setting out, Arun's sublime disregard for lane-markings and speed limits meant we arrived almost on time.

Sal greeted us with a glass of gin in one hand, an unlit cigarette in the other. She waved both about our ears while she kissed us. It was clear this wasn't her first gin.

'How did you suppose her voice got like that?' Mike whispered as she toddled off to get us unspecified drinks too.

'Come along, children. Through to the conservatory. We're all in here or in the garden!' she sang out in a voice like Louis Armstrong's.

All! My grimace to Mike took in my top, my skirt and the sandals I'd forgotten to clean. It might also have encompassed the hair which was overdue for a cut, and showed it, badly, and my rather sketchy make-up: we'd had to check to see if my lipstick was kiss-proof. It wasn't.

'Now, here's your drinkies! What, none of your usual nonsense about driving, Mike? He's such a pain, Sophie, you've no idea.'

I grinned. If this was not Sal's first glass of the evening, neither was it, to judge by the array of bottles on a trolley, likely to be her last.

'Such a dreadful thing! Poor Guy. Not that he couldn't be a pain, too, him and that blasted little camera of his. Anyway, here I was, all on my ownio – Art's swanning around France again, lucky old bugger! And I'd organised all that food for the barbie, and I simply couldn't bear the thought of all that waste – my mother's fault, telling me to eat everything on my plate. First it was rationing and we were so hungry we were glad to. Then it was the starving children. And now I can't throw a scrap away.'

Either she had a very brisk metabolism or she never put much on her plate in the first place. Certainly our tour of the garden on Saturday hadn't revealed an extensive compost bin for nice green recycling.

I murmured something noncommittal and drank from the glass she'd pressed into my hand. Champagne! Ah, but, as I discovered after a couple of sips, a champagne cocktail. God knew how much brandy she'd sloshed in.

What, I wondered, had she meant by the word *all*? There was no one here except – the drink demanded I say it – *us chickens*. I told it I was going to say nothing of the sort, not even in my head. Though maybe to Mike later.

Then I heard voices from the garden.

Mike gripped my wrist hard. 'You know who that is? That's Kirby. CID from Piddock Road. This could be a fun evening!'

What the hell was he doing here? I tried to work out

what the ethics might be, an investigating officer socialising with possible suspects. Even through the alcohol, however, I registered that it was more his problem than ours.

'Oh, just give him a funny handshake and you'll be all right!' I said.

'Funny handshake? If I knew what it was, I'd give it. But one club's enough for me. And any bricklaying's been strictly the practical sort.'

'And your little kitchen pinny's not the right colour, either!'

Clearly, the champagne cocktail contained a very great deal of brandy. I would turn my attention to the fruit cup when it was time for a top-up.

'Don't even think of it,' Mike muttered. 'She spikes that too. With absolute alcohol, according to rumour.'

Alcohol having its usual effect on my kidneys and bladder, I was soon using that downstairs loo again. Yes, the mirror and blade were still there. I tucked the blade still further underneath and pondered. Or would have done, had there been anything to ponder.

There was when I emerged. A young woman apparently trying to apply herself like body spray to Mike. He pushed her off, with what looked like controlled anger, and headed purposefully towards the barbecue.

Hmm. I'd wait to see what he said. Meanwhile, that food was a good idea. This time I'd make a point of eating. Another whiff of alcohol on a stomach that had welcomed nothing more than a light early lunch salad and that heavy cake, and I'd be lying on the grass waggling my legs in the air like an upturned ladybird. In any case, with steak smelling like that – and a little girlish chat revealed Sal and I shared the same organic, BSE-free butcher – there was no point in resisting. But steak this quality? Had she really bought it all for a public barbecue? Did it make sense?

'They have a lot of money,' Mike said, with quiet emphasis. 'They'd buy and sell you and me and not notice the small change.'

'How did they get it?'

He shrugged. 'The words wheeling and dealing might have been invented for Art – he has all these crazy schemes. But they usually seem to work. There's a haulage side somewhere, and I know he's got interests in furniture – brings it in by the container-load from southern Europe. Posh-ethnic. Goes well in big conservatories,' he added, neutrality oozing from his voice. 'They've got property all over – I heard him say once he could live in a different country every month and still be in his own home.'

'So why choose Warley? With all due respect to my ancestors, this isn't the most fashionable part of the world. If they must stick to the Midlands, why not Little Aston or Dorridge or somewhere?'

Mike shrugged. 'Why *not* Warley? Only spitting distance from the motorway. All his old friends here. They haven't got an ounce of snobbery in their bodies. They dig extraordinarily deep in their pockets for benefits.'

I nodded. 'D'you suppose we ought to be mixing?' Despite the afternoon's events, there were one or two Bears people. No doubt Sal had coerced them, too. 'It seems a bit ungracious to be sitting here on our own quietly stuffing.'

'When you're ready. It's easier to mill round tucking into strawberries and cream than dealing with steak – even steak this good. But we won't stay long. Don't forget I've got to be up early – well, we all have. Grace Road calls.'

'Seems funny starting a match on a Thursday and finishing it on a Sunday,' I grumbled. 'What if it's all over on the Saturday? Must hammer the gate receipts.'

'But what if there's an exciting finish? Sophie – are you sure you want to come with me? Four days of cricket isn't every woman's cup of tea. And if it rains, Leicester isn't exactly your tourist paradise.'

I raised an eyebrow. 'Since when was I every woman?'

To my amazement, Peter Kirby made a very determined effort to get into conversation with us, virtually dragging over his partner, who looked resentful until she discovered I was a fellow further education lecturer.

'D'you know what the boss at my place has done?' she demanded, gesturing with her strawberry spoon.

Since I didn't even know her name, let alone her college, that was scarcely likely.

'Only set up a camera so he can see who uses the union notice board! And he's sent round this memo telling us we all have to wear suits to raise standards – suits, when there isn't a chair or desk that doesn't shred tights as soon as look at them.'

I felt almost guilty to tell her about my sabbatical. I was right. She missed the word *unpaid* and, pushing her fingers through her hair, embarked on a wild dithyramb about her training woes. I could do no more than nod, but even that seemed to fan the flames. Meanwhile, however, Mike was deep in conversation with Peter, whose quiet, almost monotonous delivery was at odds with his partner's theatricality – and made it, moreover, impossible to eavesdrop with a view to getting involved.

When at last she paused for rhetorical effect – I suspect she must have been breathing through her ears – I jumped in, recommending her to talk to my NATFHE saviour, Seb. But this wasn't the advice she wanted.

Eventually, quite ruthless and actually rather rude, I interrupted. 'I hope you don't mind,' I said across her to Peter, 'but do you know if Chris Groom is coming here tonight? I know he meant to come to the original barbecue.'

He looked taken aback, but as much, I fancied, by the question as by the manner of it. 'I wouldn't have seen him as the partying sort.'

I wouldn't have seen Kirby in that light either, but didn't mention it. I merely raised an eyebrow, hoping he'd continue.

'Know him, do you?'

'There was a case where I work, William Murdock College,' I said, economising with the truth for everyone's sake.

'That fire business?' He nodded glumly.

'Is that your new boss?' the woman put in. 'That tight-arsed bugger? God knows why they've inflicted him on Smethwick.'

Kirby looked embarrassed. 'He'll be all right eventually – when he's got the hang of things. But he can't get his head round the fact that he's supposed to be running a whole unit, not just CID. Has these little friendly chats.'

The woman nodded. 'Can't bear a boss who shoves his nose in, myself.'

'Not like the old place, that's for sure,' he sighed. 'Knew where you were, there.' I tried to place his accent, getting no further than somewhere south of the Thames.

Mike said, 'It was lucky both of you managing to get jobs up here.'

'Oh, Sheil's been up a couple of years. I just got my transfer, didn't I? Don't know if it's worth it,' he added.

I would not enquire whether it was the job or the relationship that was disappointing.

Sheil set off to talk to someone else. Kirby hung back. 'You don't want to get the wrong idea,' he said. 'Early days for us all, isn't it?'

'I think you'll find he's as straight as they come,' I said. 'And very hard-working.'

He nodded. 'And this case. We don't often get the wrong man. Not these days.'

I suppose he meant to comfort us.

Seeing Sal propelling the drinks trolley in our general direction, Mike and I headed gently, and, we hoped, unobtrusively, in the direction of the pool. A young woman started towards us, but seemed to think better of it, and dawdled over to a young man, whom she greeted with every appearance of delight. Affection, indeed. Except to my mind there was very little affection there; just a great deal of physicality.

And then my memory gave me a surprise. I placed her as one of the waitresses from Saturday.

I shook my head. A family friend, maybe a student, earning some pocket money. Nothing to do with me. Something else was, though. 'So what's Kirby doing here?'

'It may be what you said earlier. The funny handshake brigade. I know Art asked if I wanted to be proposed, though I always thought it was more to do with the set of golf clubs he was trying to persuade me to buy.'

'Golf!'

'It's not that bad! OK, I don't enjoy it, but you'll be surprised how many of the lads do. And are very good at it. No, what I like' – and he dropped his voice dramatically, looking round in hunch-shouldered suspicion – 'is the odd game of bowls. And there's a very nice little club not that far from where you live. In the Moorpool Estate. I'll take you one day.'

I eyed him. Me? Bowls? 'I know I'm heading for forty but I'm not drawing my pension yet.'

'Fun. Promise.'

Mike didn't seem inclined to mix with the rest of the guests, team-mates or not. He couldn't avoid a quick word with the skipper, assuring him that unless the police nailed him overnight, he'd be playing tomorrow.

I was quite happy to drift along with him as a silent, smiling appendage. If I closed my eyes I saw swirls of new faces, heard a barrage of new names – and then everything merged into the faces and voices of two young men who would never party again.

'Cold?' Mike asked.

'Someone walking over my grave.'

'Oh, don't say that. Not you, Sophie!'

Poor love, they'd been his colleagues, if not his friends. No wonder he sounded so distressed. And there was another reason, of course, for his anxiety. Kirby, speaking into a mobile phone, was looking straight at him.

Chapter Thirteen

I wasn't called upon to explore Leicester when a couple of
vicious showers delayed the start of play. I wasn't in Leicester
at all. I was sitting in an interview room in Piddock Road
Police Station in the company of DS Mann and DCI Kirby.
I just hoped that the police invitation to me to converse with
them wouldn't disturb Mike's concentration. It had certainly
affected mine. My driving, though I was in my own Renault,
terrified me.

The conversation was curious. There was certainly more
than one agenda. Mine was to tell the truth: I certainly had
nothing to hide, for myself or for anyone else. DS Mann's was
probably simply to elicit the truth. As for Kirby, I wasn't at
all sure what his was. But it was subtly different from Mann's
or mine. The room, for a start: clearly not one of the newly
decorated ones. Whatever my dealings with the police in the
past, I'd never been shut firmly in a room smelling strongly
of unwashed men with a distinct undertone, however hard the
disinfectant tried to disguise it, of urine.

'You're fucking this bloke, right, Soph?' Kirby was saying,
his face uncomfortably close to mine.

It would have been nice to ask what business it was of his.
But of course, it was his business. Anything relevant to the key
players was relevant to any case he might be building up.

'You know perfectly well that Mike Lowden and I have

a relationship,' I agreed. Oh, the blandness of the phrase! Except what other term could I employ? 'We told you about it yesterday, and you saw us together last night, didn't you?'

He ignored me, though Mann certainly registered what I'd said.

'Timpson makes a pass at you and you tell him where to get off. He takes a photo you don't like. You decide to fix him.'

'Mr Timpson made no pass at me that I'm aware of. He was one of a group of people in the Tom Dollery Bar. His team captain gave him a lift to the barbecue many of us went to. I next saw him taking photographs in our hosts' house. I left almost immediately afterwards with Mike, and spent the rest of the weekend in his company. Except, of course, when Mr Lowden was playing cricket at Edgbaston. He got a hundred.' A hundred – for me! The truth, yes. But the whole truth? Did I need to tell him about that blow to Mike's chest? Or Mike's part in Timpson's dismissal? On the whole, I thought not.

'Sunday night?'

'We spent it together, at my house.' And Aggie had seen the car. Forgetting myself, I added, 'Hey, do you reckon there's a connection between the two deaths? His and Barkat's? There's got to be, hasn't there?'

Mann leant forward as if to enter some sort of discussion.

Kirby merely stiffened. 'I'm asking the questions, Soph.'

My turn to stiffen. 'If you wish to use my first name, it's Sophie.' How sensible Mike had been yesterday to summon Afzal. It would have been so comforting to have someone interrupting, referring to me with courteous restraint as 'my client' or 'Ms Rivers'.

'You want to get something into your head, sweetheart. There's a bloke you didn't like lying dead.'

'There's a bloke lying dead I did my best to resuscitate!'

'So maybe you didn't want to kill him, just humiliate him. And you overshot.'

I took a deep breath. 'I had no desire to kill him. I had no means of killing him. I had no opportunity to kill him.'

'But Ms Rivers, I think you did. When you ran back to the pavilion, to find that – that—'

'Timpson's Epipen. It wasn't there,' I said stupidly. 'I searched for it. It wasn't there.'

'It wasn't there because you and Lowden had slung it through the open dressing room window into the canal,' Kirby declared.

I could have vomited there and then. There was, wasn't there, just the remotest chance that Mike could have done that? This time the deep breath was mental. Mike had sworn he wouldn't hurt Timpson. But – and however hard I searched my memory I couldn't persuade myself he had – he'd never since sworn that he hadn't succumbed to some immense pressure I couldn't begin to understand. I must look normal – but the blood was draining from my face. Along with Timpson, Mike had been one of the first players in the pavilion – one of his rituals, he'd said. He could have seized a moment when Timpson's bag was open to grab the Epipen and sling it through a window – cricketers are used to throwing long and accurately. Motive. Opportunity. Means? Sure, there were bees in his garden, but to get them from his garden to Timpson's glove without my knowing . . .

'All I know,' I said, my voice thanking all those years' teaching for its firmness and conviction, 'is that Mike and I made a frantic check of Timpson's bag and failed to find anything. I couldn't tell you whether the window was open or not.' Though even as I spoke, my mind's eye showed it inexplicably closed, despite the heat. 'All I can tell you is that we did everything we humanly could to save that man.'

It was meant as an exit line, but I should have known Kirby wouldn't let me have the last word. He started asking about Mike's team-mates, and Timpson's. My head reeled with names. Mann looked uncomfortable: most of what Kirby was after was hearsay, after all. At last, at long, long last, Kirby announced he'd no doubt be seeing me again, and stomped off.

Mann hung back. 'I'm sure you realise that we have to pursue every line,' he said apologetically.

'Every legitimate line,' I shot back. And then felt churlish.

It took me all the effort of which I was capable not to demand to speak to Chris. Instead I nodded with a courtesy that matched Mann's as he showed me out into the midday sun. Somewhere out there a heavy industrial press was pounding metal. Other factories worked with chemicals. The smell took me straight back to school and the chemistry lab fume cupboard. Once it had been so thick you could have broken it into chunks. Now there was just an ominous residue.

My car shimmered.

'Sophie! What on earth—?'

It took me long moments to register. 'Helena!' I nearly fell as I turned towards her.

'You poor thing – what on earth's the matter?' She swung a plastic carrier bag to her other hand and took my arm.

Shopping? Did that mean it was lunch-time already?

I shook my head. 'Just questions about Guy Timpson's death.'

'But you didn't have anything to do with that!'

'I could have done. It's all to do with the questions—'

'What you need is a nice cup of tea,' she said firmly.

'But – look, I'm a suspect!'

'You're a friend of Chris's,' she said firmly.

'Which is why I can't run to him now.'

'You're not running anywhere, are you? Come on, can you honestly say you're well enough to drive?'

It was easier to follow her back into the building, under the surprised eyes of the receptionist and the more surprised eyes of the officers behind the big old counter. We trailed together through the corridors, out again into the now blinding sun, and into Chris's territory.

'Here – sit down. I think you've got one of Chris's heads. You poor dear.'

I sat. Within seconds there was a glass of water in one hand, a small pill in the other.

'One of Chris's. I keep a few spare in my desk in case he runs out. What have those men been doing to you?'

'They did absolutely nothing they shouldn't have done,' I said firmly. 'OK, I don't like Kirby's manner, but . . . You see, Chris and I always talked things through. But we would – we're old friends. I can't expect that sort of treatment from someone else, not till I've earned it, shall we say. Hey, I can see again.'

'Good. Now, how about that cup of tea?'

'Better not. I don't want to put you into a compromising position if Kirby really does see me as the prime suspect. Where's Chris, by the way?'

'On one of these courses. Financial management, I think. He gets in at seven, poor thing, goes off to Birmingham and comes back at seven. Just to keep on top of things.'

'Good job you're here to look after him. And me! Hey, let me write down the name of those tablets . . .'

The most direct route to Harborne from Smethwick is certainly not via posh residential parts of Warley and thence along the A4123. But I wanted to think my way round the place. I even took in an extra diversion, diving down into Langley, for a quick look at the scene of yesterday's events. A great deal of police tape was in evidence, and several uniformed officers. I parked near the Barlowe Playhouse, taking a circuitous route back to the club car park. Without drawing too much attention to myself, I now knew what my aim was – to see if that window at the back of the pavilion was open. I couldn't see, of course. Not unless I could scale a seven-foot fence. A man was getting into an elderly Lada. The groundsman!

From the anonymity of the road, I flapped a hand. He flapped one back. He pulled out from the car park, and, as if by chance, drew up twenty yards along the road.

'You all right, me wench? After all them goings-on?' He leaned out of his window.

'OK. OK-ish,' I amended. 'What about your square?'

'After all them coppers had been dancing on it with their bloody hobnailed boots? Do you expect it to be OK?'

I tutted in sympathy.

'Tell you what, it's a shame young Winston won't be bowling on it. He'd be mecking use of every little lump and bump, I'll tell you.' I should have been able to locate his birthplace to within a quarter of a mile, the way he pronounced *bowl* as if it were part of the human intestine. But I'd emigrated, hadn't I, to foreign parts. Birmingham. But I'd still bet he wasn't born far from Old Hill.

'I'm sure he would. Pity we couldn't have seen him in action yesterday. Hey, I could manage some lunch. Fancy a quick half with me?' Not that I'd be drinking, not after Chris's tablet.

We fetched up at the Finings and Firkin, a rather prettified pub still clinging on to some roots – it brewed its own beer, and that for other Firkin pubs too, in the brewhouse round the back.

He regarded me over the top of his mild. 'I should be paying for this, me wench. The way you was working yesterday.'

I nodded in self-deprecation. 'Team effort. And then it didn't work.'

'There'll be them as is glad it didn't,' he said. 'Couldn't half fancy some of them pork scratchings.'

I thought I'd prefer a bap, and then got him one as well as

his scratchings. He gestured his thanks with his glass. It was almost empty. I got in another. Mineral water for me.

'Who might be glad to see the back of Guy?' I asked bluntly.

'A lot of lads with wenches they fancy. Got his hands into a lot of knickers,' he said. He shot me an appraising look.

Laughing, I shook my head. 'Not mine! I've got a bloke.'

'So I saw,' he said drily.

If I'd hoped for a compliment about Mike I wasn't going to get one.

'Don't know what they saw in Guy,' I prompted.

He rubbed his fingers together. 'Lots of money to throw around. Not like some lads – not a lot of work round here. Not men's work. All right for you wenches – you can go and work at Merry Hill or some such. Shops! Now I remember when it was Round Oak making some of the best steel in the country.'

I was sure he did. What I wanted him to remember was something else. But it might take a moment to get back to there. 'There's a lot of nice shops there,' I said, keeping my voice in neutral. 'But I bet some of the local shops have suffered.'

'You'm right there. Have you seen Dudley centre? Dead! Gutted! And Oldbury – all them little old houses gone, all them shops. My gran was born down there – bloody bus garage now.'

'We're lucky someone hasn't tried to buy up the cricket ground and develop it – put some supermarket there,' I hazarded.

'Never heard of it if they have,' he said. 'Mind you, we could do with a bit of money spending on the club. Rising damp in the pavilion for starters.'

'Sounds expensive. Tell me, d'you get much trouble from vandals? Being next to the park and that.'

He considered. 'Had a bit of thieving. And there was a bit of trouble with folk trying to sleep here.'

'Sleep here!'

'Them beggars. Dossers. Used to come here and leave God knows what behind them.'

'Syringes, you mean?'

'Ah. Them too.' From his embarrassment, I deduced he meant condoms.

'What did you do about it?'

'I got a metal box and painted it up to look like a burglar alarm. Took no notice, did they? So then I nailed up all the windows and put some wire grating up. Round the back, anyway. Place stinks of sweat, of course.'

Funny, I hadn't even noticed.

'And you should see them showers. The grouting's gone green. Half the lads go home dirty, I reckon. Can't say as I blame them.'

Time to wind things up. Over another half I asked him about Oldbury's prospects for the rest of the season.

'We'll end up somewhere in the middle, I reckon. So long as we beat bloody Smerrick, that's all I care.'

Chapter Fourteen

I'd just picked up the A4123 when the car radio told me there'd been a gas explosion at a house in Edgbaston. Speculating that the reporters who'd been haunting my house might have been detailed to pick over the human misery up the road, I risked driving down Balden Road instead of the parallel Wolverhampton Road South. No cars. I parked. In the gutter were a couple of piles of fag ends and a mixed assortment of fast-food packaging: they'd evidently taken the opportunity to valet their cars. Checking in first with Aggie – I didn't want her alarmed by noises next door – I gathered up a pile of mail and an assortment of clothes and shoes. It occurred to me as I locked up that I loved my little house and wanted to come back to it soon. There was also the matter of Mike's car lurking in my garage. He'd had to cadge a lift over to Leicester. At least there was something I could do about that. If I loaded my cycle into the back of my car, and got both to Bournville, I could then trundle back by bike and stow it in his for the return journey. Five oily minutes later, the first part was achieved, at least.

The route to Bournville took me, of course, past Brown's, the butcher I shared with Sal. Roger was the sort of man people talked to. I wondered if he might supply me with a little gossip as well as some more meat. Not that I'd want him to betray any confidences, of course.

'Great couple,' he said promptly, weighing out diced chicken. 'Wonderful parties, I hear. They always invite me, but I don't fancy driving all the way back home and then coming back in again.'

'So you've never been out there?'

Perhaps my disappointment showed.

'Well,' he said, leaning closer, ostensibly to reach some pork fillet, 'I did once. Just the once. But it wasn't my scene. And my wife—' Roger pulled a face.

I waited.

'Come on, Sophie: you must have noticed . . . some of those girls . . .'

I must have looked like a hen with the gapes.

'Working girls, in my book.'

'But—' That would explain the way Mike had shaken one off.

Roger nodded. 'And then there were the – let's call them substances – that people were offering. The food was great, though.'

'It would be if you supplied it!'

'Of course. How did you get involved, Sophie?'

'Through my new boyfriend. Not, before you ask, the guy I was kissing in the papers. He was an ex-student.'

'Any vacancies in your classes?'

'Not for another fifteen months, I'm afraid. I'm on sabbatical till then, remember.' I followed his glance. Another customer. I used a more public voice. 'And half a dozen free-range eggs, please.'

'Is there any other sort?'

The new customer was safely checking the pickles and chutneys on display at the far end of the shop.

While he totted up my bill, I scribbled on a scrap from my diary. 'If you have any more ideas, you can catch me on either of these numbers.'

He looked at me hard. 'This sounds important.'

I nodded. 'Guy Timpson's death. I could be a suspect,' I mouthed.

The new customer was at my elbow. 'How much are these pickled shallots . . .'

Over a cup of tea, and to the comforting chug of Mike's washing machine, I wrestled with my conscience. I wouldn't care to count the times I'd stuck my nose into other people's affairs to uncover material some might have preferred to keep buried. It seemed right when I was trying to achieve justice for other people. And if it had been just Mike involved, I wouldn't have hesitated. But to try to save my own skin . . .

The last spin told me I was being ridiculous. I worked out where his washing line lurked when not in use, promising myself a similarly neat spring-loaded affair when my line gave up the ghost, and pegged out a cosy mixture of his shirts and mine. Right. I could do it now. But I didn't, of course. I re-assembled my bike, regretting the need for a helmet in the increasingly sticky heat, and went back to Harborne, to reverse the operation and shove the bike in Mike's boot. He'd got the car into the garage. But then he was tall enough to be able to see how far it extended. I'm five foot one, and needed a periscope. Parking by ear was not an accomplishment I wanted to acquire. Despite the power-assisted steering, it must have taken at least eight attempts to wriggle out, but at last, as hot as his clutch no doubt, I triumphed. It was only as I washed the oil from my hands for the last time that I wondered why I should have gone to the trouble to take both cars and one cycle to Bournville. Somewhere my common sense had abandoned me.

It was at this point that I realised Mike's answerphone was flashing. Did I dare take the messages? It was such a long time since I'd swept into a new relationship – come to think of it, had I ever dashed so headlong into such

119

intimacy? – that I couldn't remember the niceties of that sort of thing.

Hell, if I could peg out a man's underpants, I could take his phone calls. I poked the button. A frightfully correct woman's computerised voice confirmed that I had three messages. Message one was from Mike, hoping all was OK and asking me to phone him back on a mate's mobile phone. The second was a double-glazing firm. The third was Mike, asking why I hadn't phoned.

The friend's mobile was only accepting messages, so I left one, assuring Mike I wasn't in the Tower of London.

Not yet, I added under my breath. And with that in mind, I flicked through the hand-written list Mike kept by his phone. Yes, there they were. Art and Sal Appleby.

Fixing a smile on my face, I dialled. This was, after all, a bread-and-butter call. I'd had two lovely evenings at Sal's and not thanked her.

Her voice suggested she didn't wait to imbibe till the sun dropped beneath the yard-arm. But she croaked with delight when she heard who it was. 'Such a sweetie. Lovely to hear another human voice. Art's still swanning round France, bless him. Why don't you drop round for a drink?'

'Love to. But I'm tied up this evening,' I lied. I glanced at my watch. Yes, it was evening already. If not quite my drinking time.

'You naughty girl!'

It took me a few seconds to work that one out. And I wasn't sure if it was the right interpretation then.

'How about a coffee tomorrow, then? Or' – she yelled, her voice cracking – 'will you still be tied up?'

'Not as far as I know,' I said. 'Let me take you out. I certainly owe you.'

'I wouldn't hear of it, lovie. No, you come here. If it's still as hot as this, bring your cozzie. Have a little dip. Ten-thirty-ish?'

*   *   *

120

I was sunk into domesticity ironing shirts when the phone rang. This would be Mike, wouldn't it? I was already smiling foolishly when I took the call.

Chris!

'Look – can you pop round this evening? Something's turned up that might interest you. Nine-ish?'

He hung up when I'd done no more than agree.

The phone rang again immediately.

'There you are at last! Is everything OK?' Mike asked.

'As far as I know. But Chris wants to talk to me tonight. Informally.'

'OK.' From the chilling of his voice, it wasn't.

'I had a bit of a grilling from Kirby, you see. And went down with a migraine. Ended up taking one of Chris's magic pills.'

'You're all right now?'

'Fine. Fine enough to want to talk to Chris. Kirby's going to try and pin something on one of us, I can feel it in my bones. And Chris can point him in the way of justice, not just quick results. I think it would be a very good idea.'

'Hmm. I see.'

'Come too.'

'Hell, I can't. There's a bit of team-building shit going on tonight. Good job you're not over here, really. You'd have got ever so bored.'

'I'm not bored now. Just missing you . . .'

Chris was grinding coffee when I arrived. I reached out cups and milk, more at home in this kitchen than in Mike's.

'Your migraine cleared now? Helena left a note,' he added.

'Fine. Not even a hangover.'

'Funny, it takes me all this time to get medication that suits me and now I don't seem to need it.'

'You're getting on top of the job, then?'

He grimaced. 'That idea of yours about Helena and the post was a little cracker. She says she likes doing something useful, too.'

'She was certainly useful this morning. I'm not complaining about Kirby, Chris. He's got a job to do.'

Chris nodded. 'I've got to let him get on with it for a bit: this bloody course. Invaluable, of course – sorry! – but I should be out there doing the job.'

'You'll do it all the better for learning how. So long as you keep in touch with the teams.' Maybe it was a good way for him to learn a less interventionist form of management, too.

He nodded again, picking up the coffee tray. 'Let's sit in the garden. I know it's getting late but I need some fresh air.'

Perhaps it was just the effect of the dusk, but I thought the garden was looking rather dejected; perhaps it was because I no longer spent so much time out there tinkering while Chris took his endless phone calls.

A couple of late wasps buzzed us, then went on their way. The dusk settled.

'Something as small as that,' Chris observed, sinking back heavily on the bench. 'It was the bees. The PM results were quite clear. And the pathologist wanted you to know that without adrenalin there was nothing you or Winston could have done to save him. Just to put your mind at rest, there were no other recent puncture marks – there can be no accusations of foul play while you were trying to treat him.'

'Did I notice a slight stress on the word *recent*?'

Chris grinned. 'Off the record I'd say he was using stuff the MCC wouldn't approve of.'

'Using? You mean he was taking it or just carrying it around in his cricket bag?'

Chris stared. 'I meant using himself.' There was a note of doubt. No one had checked the cricket bag yet, had they? I'd bet my new filling that someone would in the morning.

'That's risking a long ban.'

'That's one thing he won't be worrying about now, isn't it? And there's evidence of other drug use. His nasal tissues were damaged.'

'I wonder if it was his blade and mirror I came across at a party the other night.' I gave him the details.

'I'll get Kirby to check it out.'

'I could check it out myself: I've invited myself to Sal's for coffee tomorrow.'

His face hardened. 'I don't know that that's advisable in the present circumstances.'

'I've been there twice in the last week. I'm sure another visit won't hurt.'

'Don't attempt to touch that mirror. OK?'

I nodded. 'All I intend to do is have a coffee and a swim. And keep my eyes and ears open. Promise. And,' I added not feeling specially proud of myself, 'if it's not advisable for me to go to Sal's, what do you feel about Peter Kirby and his wife spending the evening there? Oh, a bob-howler!' If there's one thing I'm not happy about it's big moths blundering round, and one had taken a fancy to the lighted kitchen window behind us.

'What did you call it? We can go in now if you want.'

'A bob-howler,' I said, over my shoulder as I beat my retreat. 'Not too much aitch, either, down Oldbury.'

'Funny,' he said, as we settled in his living room, 'how your accent has suddenly returned. I've never thought of you as a Brummie.'

'Neither should you,' I exploded. 'Hell, Chris, if you want to survive in Piddock Road, the very first lesson is that the Black Country is not Birmingham. They're – they're *new*comers. *We* are the salt of the earth. The fact that we go for cock-fighting and dog-fighting—'

'And racism and sexism!'

'—is an irrelevance. And what we have is a set of dialects, not some nasty composite accent.'

'Hmm.' His face was very alert. 'Isn't that what Brummagem meant in the old days – something glistening but definitely not gold? And didn't that character in *Emma* say—'

'—you could expect nothing good to come from Birmingham. That was only Mrs Elton, though. Scarcely Jane Austen's mouthpiece. But I don't know that either would have approved of the Black Country. All those tough women.'

'Like you! I didn't know bee-keeping was a Black Country hobby, though,' he added more soberly.

'Neither did I. Not a lot of nectar, I should have thought, despite that Urban Forest development. Where did they come from, Chris? And how did they get into Timpson's glove?'

'They must have been put there, mustn't they? At the same time as his Epipen was nicked. Incidentally, we're having the Titford canal – OK, the *cut* – dragged tomorrow. I authorised the expenditure just now.'

I couldn't hold back a chuckle. 'Poor buggers! Have you any idea what the average cut conceals?'

'A pretty good one. If necessary – if it's the only way of searching it – we'll drain it.'

'It's a hell of a stretch to have to drain. And I'll bet you my year off you won't find anything. Well, actually you'll find a hell of a lot, but not an Epipen.'

'Kirby still reckons someone threw it out of a dressing room window.'

'He can reckon all he likes,' I said. 'Tell me, have you checked on those windows for yourself?'

If the press had decamped from Harborne, there was no reason why I shouldn't go and sleep in my own bed, for all Mike's was a deluxe orthopaedic job, with lots of pocketed springs. In fact, it was so comfortable I might just sally forth into the city centre tomorrow and see what the sales offered. My mind on this and other domestic details, it took me some time to realise that a motorbike had been behind me for several junctions now. Just to test out my theory, I took a particularly circuitous route round the back of Harborne, only to find the motorcycle behind me after each turn. The last thing I wanted was an encounter with the press at this time of night. Or anyone else, come to think of it.

What I could do was simply turn tail and lead him straight back to Chris. Or any police station. Rose Road was near enough. As I hesitated, whoever it was pulled alongside me. I braced myself but he roared off, leaving me nothing but scared. As fast as I knew how, not even having the sense to take his number, I flung the car round and headed for Mike's. That was the only haven the biker hadn't yet found. And, come to think of it, it would be nice to sleep between sheets that smelt of him.

The house was in darkness when I let myself in, except for an upstairs light I'd left on. But the burglar alarm, which I'd switched on, was off. I froze. Someone moving upstairs stopped moving. I didn't even know where to look for a weapon. What I would do was flood the house with light.

And spotlit Mike, standing, braced for attack, at the top of the stairs.

Chapter Fifteen

'I just – I wanted to know you were all right,' he said. 'So I came back—'

'And I wasn't here. I'm sorry.' Perhaps I'd suppress the bit about wanting my own bed. 'I had this idea someone might be tailing me – thought I'd have to shake him off. But probably he wasn't.' I could see the alarm rising in his eyes, so I added casually, 'I was just deciding which police station to lead him to when he overtook me and shot off into the night. But I'm here and you're here and it's so good to see you.'

Mike had begged a lift back with one of his colleagues whose wife had just gone into labour. At least my various vehicular manoeuvres would make life simpler for him the following morning. Then he asked, very carefully, 'Did Chris have anything useful to say?'

'No,' I said, carefully ignoring the subtext. 'But I did. The theory is that one or both of us lobbed the Epipen into the cut. They're going to drag it, on the off-chance. But what I found out yesterday was that the windows have been sealed to stop vagrants getting in. So that cock won't fight.'

'I know one that will,' he said, smugly.

Mike, due to bat sometime that day, was clearly disappointed that I wasn't going with him to Leicester, and was reluctant to accept that sniffing round might prove a life-saver in the future.

'I just want to make sure the police have all the evidence available, not just the bits Kirby chooses to select.'

'Look, Sophie, we're not in a fascist state, you know.'

'I know. And I know forensic science is so far advanced it can make something out of virtually nothing. But I also know that the police have limited resources and if someone like Kirby doesn't want to spend money chasing something, someone like Chris is going to be happy keeping the purse-strings tight.'

'That doesn't make it your job.'

I nodded. He was right, of course. 'Why don't I whizz over to Leicester as soon as I've had coffee? I'd really rather be watching you, you know. And my car's here, and the motorway system's at my disposal.'

'If you come,' he said, 'I'll get a ton for you.'

'That's an offer no woman could refuse.'

Having neatly forgotten my costume, but equipped with all the paraphernalia I'd need for an afternoon's cricket-watching, I set off to Sal's as early as I decently could.

Sal, somewhat bemused by my presence on her doorstep, waved vaguely inwards.

'Go on, you have your dip while I get the coffee started.'

I clapped my hand to my forehead in well-feigned exasperation. 'I forgot my things.'

'You'll find plenty of cozzies – and towels – hanging behind the door in the conservatory. Help yourself.'

Should I? It was certainly tempting. But I pottered along behind her, thinking a spare pair of hands in the kitchen might help her as much as me.

She patted vaguely at the crockery in the dishwasher. 'Must be some cups somewhere.'

I grabbed a couple from under the morning paper, the one

in which I'd been featured, as it happened, and swilled them. I also had a systematic sniff at the milk cartons she produced from the fridge, discarding one or two. But she knew her coffee, grinding it to just the right density for her espresso machine, the sort I'd drooled over in the kind of kitchen shop you visit to look, not buy.

We drank it black. My turn to flounder now. What on earth should we be talking about? I should have prepared a set of questions. Two of her guests had just died unpleasant deaths. That was what I should be focusing on.

'I love your garden,' I said, nodding through the open conservatory door.

She sank on to a wicker *chaise-longue*, staring at her bare legs and scarlet toenails. 'Nice, isn't it? I do it all, you know. There were a couple of old houses over there.' She waved in the rough direction of the swimming pool. 'Cottages, really. When they came on the market Art bought them for me and knocked them down. Imagine having flats there. That's what they'd have put up, you know. Overlooking my garden.'

I tried to nod in commiseration. Imagine being able to buy perfectly good houses simply to knock them down. I could imagine preferring a view to the profits from flats, but never in a million light years being able to satisfy such a whim. I was clearly out of my league.

'There's another little corner round there. Behind that bit of fence. All the essentials in there. Mower: would you believe,' she said, throwing back her head and laughing, 'I've got one you can sit on? And a couple of nice compost heaps. And a wormery.'

'Wormery? I've never actually seen one. They're supposed to be quicker at breaking stuff down than a compost heap, aren't they?'

'I'm not convinced. Come and look, anyway.' Gathering her housecoat, she swung her legs over in an easy, indeed graceful, movement. She led me off to the far side of a fence staggering under the weight of clematis and honeysuckle. She'd certainly disguised it well.

'There,' she said, pointing to her expensive mower. 'That's Derek.'

'Derek?' I said blankly.

'After Derek Mountfield, see. The Aston Villa player. Years ago, now. But the name stuck. And what else could you call it, seeing that it's a Mountfield?'

I considered. 'Eric. Because it's red,' I added. 'Isn't he supposed to have discovered America?'

Her turn to be non-plussed. 'You could have had a try,' she said at last. 'Only with this dry spell . . .' She looked at the cropped lawn.

I shook my head. 'Don't want to shave it. Mine's really suffered. At least staying at Mike's means I can't nip out to have another little cut, even if I wanted to.'

She nodded. 'Nothing quite like mowing a lawn, is there? Clears the head wonderfully. I told Mike he was making a big mistake having that fancy paving instead.'

Had she seen it? Had she been round to his house? Or had they merely talked about it at one of her parties? 'It looks good,' I said, insisting to myself that I could assume the latter. 'And of course, it only needs a quick sweep – that must be a bonus if you're away from home as much as he is.'

'Like my Art. I hardly see him these days. I don't know what I should do if it wasn't for all you young people coming and cheering me up.' She peered at one of the compost heaps, sounding as if she were well into her dotage.

'Do you have children?'

'Children? Oh yes.' Her voice saddened. 'Abroad, though. Both of them. Lovely lads. So handsome! Well, with Art's genes, they would be.'

'And yours.'

'Well, I wasn't bad when I was young. Trouble is, I like the sun too much. All this covering up, I can't be doing with it. Not like these young men with their floppy sun-hats and sunglasses and sun-block. More like war-paint, if you ask me.'

'Have you known Mike long?' He had a past, after all. Just as I did, I told myself firmly. Oh dear, soon we'd be meeting all each other's old friends, judging and being judged.

'Knew his parents . . . Then he joined the Bears. He was ever so shy, come to think of it. Got himself a girlfriend. Then another. Then he got married to that nurse, Sandra. Oh, she was so pretty. Had a bit of a reputation, mind. But then – well, there was that Guy business. I felt so bad about it, since they'd met here.'

'They'd have met somewhere else,' I said.

She nodded, her face taking on a wistful turn. 'The trouble with young men like Guy is they don't know when to stop. I could tell you five or six who didn't want him to, mind you. I suppose you and he hadn't—?'

I shook my head emphatically. 'I'm with Mike.'

'Oh, you girls are so prudish. Where's the harm in a good bonk, for God's sake? What'll you do if Mike goes on an overseas tour? Buy a hot-water bottle? You don't suppose he'll wear a chastity belt, do you?'

'The situation hasn't arisen yet,' I said, my face stiff.

'The way he's playing these days it will. You take your pleasures where you can – we only come this way once, remember. Now, these are my worms.' She headed for a small green wheelie-bin.

'Do you – enjoy yourself? When Art's away?' Not with Mike, please, please not with Mike. To hell with being illogical! I didn't want to admit to myself that he'd done the wonderful things he did to my body to other bodies. Especially not Sal's.

My question had been too direct. She lifted the bin-lid and fished out a circular fibre mat, rather dog-eared.

131

'Poor things – they've been reduced to eating their moisture mat. Hasn't old Sal given you enough lettuce, then?' she cooed at a departing red tail. 'They don't like the sun. Not like me. Oh yes, I do have ways of keeping warm when the sun goes down.' She smiled, looking a flirtatious sixteen. 'Not involving electric blankets. Ah, is there any pleasure like a firm young body in your arms? Unless it's a firm young prick in your pussy.'

I liked the sentiment, blushed at the language. I've never been able to use that sort of word. My laugh sounded embarrassed even to my ears. 'He'd got a nice figure, Guy,' I said, feeling that something was called for.

'Very nice. Now I'd love to get young Winston with his kit off. Wouldn't you? But I gather he's a bit of a puritan, especially now he's got this girlfriend. Pretty girl, I hear.'

'Very beautiful,' I said.

'But I also hear she's boring.'

'She's certainly quiet,' I said, not admitting to her that I was disappointed that Winston should have picked such a dull partner.

Sal replaced the moisture mat and the bin-lid, clipping it firmly in place.

Mike had organised both a ticket and a parking permit for me at Grace Road. Arriving in the lunch interval, I got one of the stewards to take a note round to the dressing room saying I was waiting for that hundred, and settled in the now hazy sun to await developments. The scorecard told me he'd been promoted up the batting order; the scoreboard told me he'd be in at the next fall of wicket. I tried not to ill-wish anyone. Not Teddy, who'd reached forty-seven. Teddy, who was yet another person with a motive for wanting Guy out of the way. I shook my head. Teddy wouldn't do that sort of thing, surely. I could imagine him being driven to lash out in inarticulate rage, but not hatching such a devious plot. His name had never once come up in my conversations, amicable and otherwise, with the police. How long I sat with my head in my hands I've no idea; but I know it took a long time to discuss with myself the ethics of mentioning him should things ever get tough for Mike. It took the pavilion bell warning the players they had ten minutes before returning to the field to remind me I hadn't brought any food with me, and I made a quick sortie for a sandwich.

Whatever Warwickshire's number three had had for lunch, it plainly didn't agree with him. With forty-one behind him, you'd have thought he would be seeing the ball as big as a football, but he scraped and pushed ineffectually, eventually edging an easy catch into the gully.

I'll swear that as Mike walked out to the square, the clouds parted and the sun shone down on him. OK. Pathetic fallacy again. But it did. And maybe the slight change in the atmosphere meant the ball didn't swing so much in the air, and the bowling was consequently less dangerous. Mike started to accumulate runs, slowly at first, then with increasing confidence. A very old codger near me muttered comparisons with Denis Compton. Another spoke of David Gower. Yes, Mike made it all look so easy.

No one would ever have thought he was a suspect in a murder inquiry.

Nor would they for the rest of his innings. He just took charge, batting faultlessly till the close of play. 127 not out. His century – for me!

While I was waiting to join him, my mobile phone tweeted.

It was something I used so rarely, on all sorts of admirable grounds, ranging from my dislike of having my brain micro-waved to the inconvenience to the rest of the human race, that it took me a minute to realise where the noise was coming from. And then another minute to dig the wretched thing from the bottom of my bag.

Chris!

'I thought you might want to know I've found that file. Barkat's crash,' he said.

'And?'

'It makes interesting reading. Your nose is a sensitive organ, Sophie.'

'Tell!'

'Later. I'm sorting through other things at the moment. I'll stand you and Mike a drink. Nine-ish?'

'OK for me. I suspect Mike might have to stay over with the team. He's just got a lovely century, by the way! OK, see you nine-ish, Chris!'

At this point I remembered I should have been doing voice warm-up exercises. The second choir rehearsal I'd missed in as many weeks! I phoned in my apologies.

The whole team were pleased with themselves: 397 for eight – they had reason to be. They'd got maximum points for their first innings, and had put themselves into a strong position for the following day. This could well be a match that didn't run into Sunday. The idea of a whole day with Mike was very appealing. I might even hope for rain so we didn't feel honour-bound to jog or mow lawns – mine and, in general these days, Aggie's. We didn't stay long in the bar, however, Mike's eyes making it clear that he had in mind other ways of celebrating. These didn't include, of course, a drive to Birmingham to confer with Chris. In the car park I broke it to him quite gently that they had to.

'Why the hell—? You're quite sure you're over this guy? I mean, you seem to spend all your life having nice little chats with him.'

'That's why you're invited.' I could feel the name Sal dying to make itself heard.

'Wants to make a threesome, does he?'

I turned away. I mustn't throw Sal at him. Mustn't. I counted to ten. Turned back. 'Shouldn't have thought you'd have the energy,' I said. 'We don't have to set out till after eight, you know.' Sal's face receded.

I could see him making an effort too. He glanced at his watch. 'What are we waiting for? Follow my car!'

We left his sitting ostentatiously in the hotel car park, and drove back in mine. I'd phoned Chris to say we'd bring in a takeaway, and could blame the lengthy queue for the fact that it was nearer ten then nine when we arrived.

On the whole I was glad Chris kissed me – just a matey affair, on the cheek. He produced a bottle of Moët to help celebrate Mike's century, though the conversation first of all concerned my aversion to large buzzy moths. It was clear to me how much generous effort Chris was putting into establishing that, although he was still fond of me, he was prepared to see Mike and me as an item. I hoped that in a similar situation I'd do the same. That I hadn't welcomed his last girlfriend, a policewoman with a taste for whisky, as a bosom pal was, I liked to think, because she was an unpleasant woman. But I couldn't entirely convince myself.

Perhaps I could make amends if the Helena situation developed.

At last the conversation got round to Barkat's accident.

'Thanks to your nose, Sophie,' Chris said, 'I took a sniff at one or two things myself. Including the material recorded by the speed cameras, which, unlike those deployed by some forces, actually contain film at the present moment. And we have two cars belting along at an unnatural rate. Barkat's was – apparently – in pursuit of the other. Sorry – I know you hate policese. Anyway, at the traffic lights—'

'—where the incident occurred—' I supplied.

'—indeed – another vehicle appears to have crossed the

135

lights on red between the two cars.' Reaching for the light and dark soy sauce bottles and a fork, he illustrated his point. 'So the leading car sped away and the other came into intimate and irrevocable contact with the road-sign. Neither of the other vehicles has been traced. False numberplates. We're going to try some very clever and no doubt expensive computer enhancement to give us a fix on the drivers. I don't hold out much hope myself. Still, it's worth trying.'

'Interesting little scenario,' Mike said. 'So what was Barkat up to?'

'That, of course, is what I was hoping you might tell me. No, don't get me wrong! But anything you can think of in Barkat's behaviour that would at least give us some direction for our inquiries would be very gratefully received.'

'So you haven't got a CID and an expert or two in accident investigation on your staff,' I said.

'Nary a one,' he said blithely.

'Fair enough. For starters he seems to have an odd track record with cars,' I said. 'I first met him socially over a flat battery in a side road in Harborne. And the late and unlamented Guy – whoops, it must be that champagne! – teased him about it in front of a group of us in the bar last Saturday.'

'He'd got a team car, like the rest of us,' Mike said, 'and we gathered he must have crashed it. And we know he had a courtesy car, but that seems to have disappeared. Might be worth asking the Peugeot people what happened to it. I bet they didn't take it away just because they wanted to lend it to someone's mum. Guy wouldn't have mentioned it if they had.'

'The one I saw him with was a rather tatty specimen. Hang on.' I closed my eyes to rethink that jog. 'Metallic. Silverish. Metro, of course.'

Chris shrugged. 'The one he died in was a red Astra. No seatbelt, incidentally. I won't bore you with an account of his injuries. But there was one thing that struck the investigating officer as odd. A dent on the passenger door.'

'Wouldn't you have quite a lot of dents?' Mike asked mildly.

'My response exactly. But this officer was puzzled by one detail. Funny shape to the dent. And it had a puncture mark. She can't work out what made it and it's niggling her.'

Something was niggling me. Something at the back of my memory.

'Any road, as they've taught me to say at Piddock Road, I'd like to get a picture of the man. I know it's not my job, Sophie, so don't look like that. But you can't be a detective—'

'—and a good one—'

'—all these years without liking to shove bits into other people's jigsaws.'

'And very irritating it is too,' I said. 'When you've been saving that funny-shaped piece for your final space and some pest comes and puts it in for you.'

He grinned. 'OK. Let's assemble some of our pieces. We know he was married to a woman who, according to my officers, was so cowed they couldn't imagine her kicking her way out of a paper bag. In strictest confidence, Mike, do you know if he had a – shall we call it a less official? – relationship?'

'Funny taste some women have if he did. He wasn't my favourite person, Chris. And some of his friends were real yobs.'

'Some women do have odd taste in men,' I said slowly. 'The sort of woman who is battered by her husband and refuses either to leave or to shop him. The sort of woman who goes on the streets for her man. Funny, only the other day I saw a young woman jump out of a car, get chased and recaptured by a bloke – and try to kick his door in,' I finished in embarrassment. 'Smethwick. Waterloo Road. I thought it was what you lot would no doubt call a domestic. Kept my nose out, for once. I can't even remember the car – it was two or three ahead of me in a jam, and I only had a glance at it. No number or anything.'

'High-heeled shoe?'

I shook my head. 'No idea.'

'What did the woman look like?'

'Lot of hair, very short skirt.'

'A tom?'

'Eh?'

'A prostitute,' Mike interjected.

I shrugged. 'It was the day of Halima's funeral, Chris.'

'And your abortive party. I'm not surprised you can't remember things. Tell you what, I'll have a word with the investigating officer and see if she thinks a foot would have done that sort of damage.'

'What if it did?' Mike asked. 'How could a footprint be relevant to being killed in a car crash?'

Chris smiled. 'Sometimes the piece is such a funny shape you don't know if it's for this particular jigsaw. Or if it's a piece at all. But it's worth having a look at before you throw it away.'

Chapter Sixteen

It would have made more sense to sleep at either Mike's house or mine, but he'd left his contact lens case at the hotel. I resolved to buy him a spare and whatever solution he needed to keep at my house.

He drove back even more briskly than my Renault was used to, and we checked into his hotel room with still a reasonable amount of night to sleep through. In the same single bed. OK, it was silly, when he was a tall man and needed to stretch. But what greater pleasure than to lie so tightly that when one of us turned the other had to, and staying on the bed and hugging his back were the same thing? And to feel his arm wrapped round my ribs? That unfamiliar emotion was washing over me whenever I surfaced to turn: happiness.

I waited just inside the ground. In a re-run of last Saturday, when Winston had cadged a comp for me, Mike was off in the pavilion getting me a ticket. When he came back he was looking as sombre as the morning's sky. 'Someone's told Kirby that Guy had given Teddy a hard time.'

I was glad it hadn't been me.

'And now he's stuck in a closed room with him and Harvinder Mann until he's explained himself.'

'Why now? I thought the police had everyone's name on Wednesday? Why didn't they deal with it then?'

'They probably did. But Teddy's the sort of person to answer the questions they put to him without volunteering anything else. You must have noticed – you tried hard enough.'

'Like extracting teeth,' I agreed. 'Any idea if he knows his rights? A solicitor, for instance?'

'He's not under arrest so I suppose Kirby might not have reminded him.' He looked at me gloomily. 'Do you think we ought to contact Afzal again? Teddy's too easy to bully.'

'Yes, I'd say he's in for a really nasty time. Don't worry: I'll phone Afzal. But the police would still have to establish opportunity, and be sure he could have used the means. I don't see Teddy reading up on anaphylactic shock on the off-chance.'

'Who would? Not your everyday reading matter.'

'Not unless you're me with a dead student and a nasty rash. And no, I didn't do it, Mike.' I wasn't joking. I wanted to reassure him as much as I wanted him to reassure me.

'I know you didn't. And – yes?'

A small boy with autograph book was leading a pack of other small boys.

Mike signed, committing himself to ten minutes' good PR. As he took the second boy's book, however, he mouthed at me, 'And you know I didn't, don't you?'

I reached over the child's head and for a moment, in an awkward movement, we managed to clasp hands. Then he returned to his public duties. As soon as they were over, and we'd kissed goodbye, I phoned Afzal. All I got was answerphones.

The Bears' total was so good that the captain had declared their innings closed overnight. So it was the Leicestershire batsmen who would have to deal with today's conditions. The Bears supporters – and there were a good few faces I was beginning to recognise already scattered around the ground – were no doubt rubbing their hands with glee. The heavy atmosphere would make things more difficult for the batsmen as the ball would move off the seam in the air. The openers could be in for a testing hour or so. Certainly they were put under immediate pressure, with very hostile field placings. No, I wouldn't have liked to face sixteen stone of muscle propelling a hard ball at ninety miles an hour on a murky day like this, not with a ring of fielders behind me, waiting to snatch up any ball I might snick in their direction.

Teddy came sprinting on to the field several minutes after the start of play, and the twelfth man jogged off waving cheerily to him as they crossed. What a nice bunch they all were. And yet one of them might be a murderer. No. I couldn't believe it of any of them. Certainly not those I'd met the other day. The odd one might be the type to land an angry punch, but surely not the sort of cold-blooded killing of Wednesday. And what about Barkat's crash? Which of them might be hot-headed enough to lead a car chase at that speed?

Whatever the logic, I didn't want it to be any of them.

Play was too tense for me to concentrate on what I insisted to myself was someone else's problem. The ball was moving in the air so much, for the batsmen it was more a matter of staying in than of scoring. So the total inched along painfully slowly, although the Bears still hadn't taken any early wickets. No Barkat to call on to break the partnership.

There's a strange part of the brain that doesn't respond to instructions to think. On the contrary, it seems to prefer to wait until the rest of it is otherwise engaged – as mine was on the cricket – to fire up little ideas. I almost saw this one pop up, as if it were a piece of toast leaving the toaster. I'd have to use the wretched mobile phone. Wherever I used it I felt a poseur – or was it poseuse? I could imagine the barracking I'd get from some of my fellow spectators if I suddenly started to talk loudly – somehow mobile phones are synonymous with yelled intimacies. On the other hand, I didn't want to miss any play, so in the end I simply waited till the end of the over and sneaked back to where the stewards were checking tickets.

Chris was not at home. Fearing I knew where he'd be, I phoned Piddock Road.

'I thought this was supposed to be a weekend off,' I said, more in sorrow than in anger.

'You know I've got to try to keep my head above water!' he flared.

I tried a bad joke. 'You'd certainly better if you're anywhere near the cut. Come on, Chris! We only come this way once, remember. Any road up – which is the *authentic* Black Country expression, not just "any road" – I'm glad I've caught you. What did the overdosing prostitute look like? You know, the one you mentioned a while back that died.'

'There'll be a photo somewhere round here.'

I had a vision of all his files descending in a swift avalanche.

'Well, if you find she sported a short skirt and big hair you might get one of your team to check if there's any hair or whatever that matches hers in that car with the curious dent,' I said.

'Eh? Not one of your better sentences, Sophie, if I may say so.'

'You may. But Warwickshire have just taken their first wicket, so I'll apologise and ring off. Just one thing, Chris. Delegate. Don't try to do everything yourself.'

He chuckled. 'At least you're not suggesting I ask Helena to do it.'

'How about Peter Kirby?' I asked, as one incapable of any malice.

That could have been a bad mistake, I thought, as I headed back to my seat. Kirby already resented what he saw as Chris's interference, and the last thing I wanted to do was set them at loggerheads. And in revenge he might not prioritise the job. Claim there wasn't enough funding, or something. But I could scarcely phone Chris and tell him not to ask Kirby: there were some things best not stirred up with a long stick.

I worried about it all morning, however, as Leicestershire toiled to make runs and Warwickshire battled to take wickets. Progress on both sides was so slow as to appear tedious to those not in the know. But to watch the captain's tactics, the subtle changes in field placings, was like watching a game of chess. At last, the cloud cover started to lift, and the batsmen freed up. The Bears were faced with a long day in the field and an uphill struggle on the last day. So much for my plans for me and Mike.

It goes without saying that my field-glasses slipped to him from time to time. Apart from the obvious pleasure, it was good to watch a professional at work. He and Teddy had a natter between overs, and then he had a word with the captain. Hey presto! Teddy was bowling his first over of the innings. It was awful, all over the place. They took three fours and one six off his first four balls. The next was so rank bad the batsman just swiped at it and got caught on the boundary for his pains. The last ball was a real demon, and took another wicket. It would have been nice if he could have got a hat-trick by taking a wicket with the first ball of his next over, but his line and length were still all over the place.

None the less, lunch was a cheerful affair. A middle-aged couple next to me were plainly horrified by my meagre rations of sandwiches and water bought on the ground and pressed me to share their feast. It would have caused offence to turn down home-made chicken and ham pie, and have been a positive insult to refuse a second slice of the best treacle tart I've ever tasted. I did decline the stewed Thermos tea, however, on the grounds of a mysterious bladder complaint which had the woman – Dot – nodding sympathetically.

'I can't help asking, er, Sophie, but didn't you – weren't you—'

I had to wait: was it my tabloid appearance or my failed first aid Harold was trying to allude to?

'—in the papers the other day? When the Rutland man . . .'

I nodded.

'That was a bad business. Was he a friend of yours?' asked Dot, producing a damp face-cloth in a polythene bag. She wiped her fingers first, then passed the cloth to me. It was scented with lavender.

'I just happened to be there. And I've got some first-aid training. On a big ground like this, they've got the St John's people and a doctor. So if anyone gets stung out there today, it's not my problem,' I said.

'No St John's? But they're always there. Even at our village league matches. Birmingham League, they're bound to be,' Harold objected, taking the face-cloth absent-mindedly.

I nodded again, biting my lip. They were right, of course. So where had my brain been? Why, even Philomena had spotted the omission, the day it had happened. But it was someone else's brain that mattered. Not my job. None the less I must ask Chris later. I twirled my ring round so I'd remember. If I looked down and saw the little Victorian diamonds facing my palm I'd know there was something to do.

'Village cricket?' I repeated.

'We live out Uppingham way. Always come in for matches when we can,' said Dot.

'I'm surprised you're not Rutland supporters.'

'Oh, no. Leicestershire, all our lives. Some of our friends, they've been with Rutland through and through. Cock-a-hoop now they've made it into the first-class game, bless them. And the fund-raising they had to do to get their ground something like.'

'We used to go to some of their events,' Harold added. 'Dances and such. Skittles.'

My ears pricked. Poking round Birmingham and the Black Country was something I could do; sniffing round the Rutland team was not. 'Did everyone muck in?' I asked. 'Players and all?'

'Oh, ah. Most of them; some still had day jobs, though. You didn't see them so often. But they came when they could – brought their wives. Tom Butler's wife, now—'

'No, Tom was still playing for Gloucestershire, wasn't he?' Dot said.

'That's right. But they'd got roots our way, and she moved back here with the kids to sort out their house. Took a lot of work, by all accounts. Got a lot of help, too, mind – pretty young woman, you'd expect the young men to dance round.'

'So long as they only wanted to paint ceilings,' Dot snorted.

'What about the one that died?' I asked. Maybe a vague question would get answers I didn't expect.

'Him? No, I don't see him painting any ceilings,' she said.

'Oh, he liked a bit of fun. No harm in him. And all those photos he took – he'd have little auctions of them. Raised a lot of money that way.'

'What sort of photos?'

Dot coughed. 'Couples, dancing and that. Like that man on the telly, if you ask me. Liked to catch people with their trousers down, if you see what I mean.'

Harold roared with laughter. 'Goodness me, yes! There was that one he'd taken in the showers during an England match! All those—'

'I never saw anything funny in that.'

'And another thing – you know all these young men have their nicknames? You'll never guess what they used to call him, on account—'

'That's enough, Harold. Really! Ah, that's the ten-minute bell. I'm off to wash my hands.'

'You've just washed your hands, woman!'

With extreme delicacy she mouthed, 'Ladies'.'

I followed her.

'Lets his sense of humour get the better of him, my Harold,' she said. 'But these men never grow up. Still think they have to snigger behind the bike shed, don't they?'

'I'm afraid so. But most of the players I've met seem very pleasant. And I've no complaints about my boyfriend, Mike Lowden,' I added.

'Now which one's he?'

'He was fielding in the gully most of this morning.'

'Oh, the lad that got the century yesterday. Now he won't have any reason to like Guy Timpson. Well, it was in all the papers, dear. Before your time together, though, I should think.'

'Yes. Did Timpson – was he—' I sought for expressions that wouldn't freeze her up again. 'Were there any other marriages he – he upset?'

By now we'd reached the queue for the lavatories. Dot nodded meaningfully at the backs in front of us and pursed her lips. We waited in silence till cubicles became vacant.

Once inside, I stared at the ring twisted inwards. Now what had I done that for? Ah, St John's Ambulance. Quickly, I jotted in my diary. And turned the ring the right way round.

At last, with clean hands, we set off back to the pavilion. How did I restart our conversation? Delicately? Crudely? Or, since a smatter of applause announced the start of afternoon play, not at all?

By the tea interval, Warwickshire had started to get a grip on the game, but it was, as any spectator would sapiently have remarked, not over yet. Cricket is, as they might have added, a funny game, not over till the last ball's bowled. I slipped off to bring back a fistful of ice-creams.

'Oh, you shouldn't have,' Dot said.

'Well, it was a lovely lunch,' I said. 'One good turn.'

We smiled. People around us were stretching their legs, rubbing stiff backs. There was no one to overhear.

'This is rather difficult,' I said quietly. 'I've only been with Mike for a short time. And sometimes I don't always like to ask about his past. So did his wife and Timpson – you know?'

'Went at it hammer and tongs, one do we were at. It went round they'd been found in-flag-whatever-it-is in one of the loos. Lucky bloke.'

'You be quiet, Harold Field. It was shameful, not a matter for giggling about. The trouble was, everyone except the poor girl knew it didn't mean a thing to him. And then it got into the papers. But it could have been serious – well, there was more than a rumour about that other young girl, and they certainly broke up very soon afterwards.'

So Guy played at home as well as away, did he? In which case there'd be any number of men back in Rutland wanting to fix him. And maybe some vengeful women. Well, the police would know all about that. Wouldn't they? Surely Mike would have made it clear that it wasn't just his wife who'd attracted Guy's attention. And the Oldbury players would have mentioned a black sheep amongst their former players? Wouldn't they? It wouldn't just be me who'd bought that groundsman a pint. Would it?

Chapter Seventeen

It was overcast again on Sunday, and this time it was the Bears who'd be struggling against the seam bowlers. Let the openers just stick it out until the shine was off the ball – I wanted to see Mike in full flow. I settled myself in the members' stand, armed with another comp. My puritan mind told me, of course, that I should be paying full price for all this pleasure. But there was no point in rocking the boat of custom and practice just to salve my conscience. I was looking round for my pleasant companions of the previous day when it dawned on me that my name was being called over the tannoy. Had they found me out at last? But then when they asked me to go to the players' quarters, another fear grabbed me: Mike! Was he ill? I moved along the row in the briskest sideways shuffle I could manage, reached the steps, and ran. But it wasn't just the brief exercise that left me panting and breathless.

Mike was there – yes, he was all right, and I felt the deep rush of air fill my lungs with relief – with the Bears' captain, whose friendly smile transformed an otherwise grim face.

'This is a real cheek,' he said, checking that no one could overhear us. 'But Mike says you get on well with Teddy. And currently he's locked in the bog crying his eyes out, by the sound of things. He says – well, you'll hear what he says soon enough.'

'What about the Leicester staff doctor? Wouldn't he be more

appropriate? I mean, it's not that I mind, and I suppose I've done the odd counselling course, but I'm hardly qualified.'

'I suggested the doc to him when I saw him first thing,' Mike said. 'But he went grey and bolted. Sophie – can you give it a try? The kid's due to bat first wicket down.'

'If he's as bad as you say, I can't see me fishing him out very quickly, let alone getting him in a state to go out there.'

'OK, Mike – you pad up, then. I hope you won't be needed just yet, but you never know. Off you go, man. I'll take Sophie through.'

We kissed briefly.

'Remember your promise!' I said.

He waved, and disappeared into the changing room.

'Promise?' the skipper asked.

'Another hundred,' I said.

'Be good if he could. One of the England selectors has just turned up. And God knows he's ripe for selection for Australia this winter. Here you are.' He dropped his voice. 'I'll get you something to sit on. And organise a keep-out sign. Anything else you need?'

I put a hand on his arm. The sound of sobbing was heart-breaking. 'We may just need that doctor,' I said quietly. 'And a better place to talk if I get him out.'

He nodded.

As counselling rooms went, this was certainly not the best I'd been in, though I had been known at William Murdock to discuss the most intimate problems in the ladies' loo. At least there, however, I didn't have the background of regularly flushing urinals – though I consoled myself with the thought that poor William Murdock's probably wouldn't have flushed at all. And the place was clean, not stinking as it could have been. The outer door opened, and a chair appeared.

I moved it to by the door of the locked cubicle. 'Teddy?'

He yelled something. I didn't know the language but the

meaning was as clear as if he'd used the classic four-letter word. He yelled again and again.

I was out of my depth, wasn't I?

I waited till I could make my voice calm and reassuring. 'Teddy: this is Sophie. Do you remember me? We talked last Saturday? At Edgbaston?'

No response. At least I hadn't provoked the same anger.

'We went to that party—' Wrong. This time I'd provoked him into agonised sobs. 'I'm Mike's friend, remember. We talked about . . .'

I don't know how long I kept up my monologue of meaningless chatter. This dreadful echoing room, the rush of water, his sobs and my drivel. At one point I heard the outer door open and close. If only there were someone I could turn to for help! Couldn't they drug some tea or something? But I didn't stop. I had to think of it as if I were soothing a fretful child to sleep.

At long last I said, 'Why don't you come out now, love? I'm sure we could find somewhere nicer to talk.'

No response. But at least he was quieter, and I could hear his breathing slowing, steadying. I carried on. Childhood memories. School. The place I worked. Cricket matches. Anything and everything.

Without any warning, the cubicle door opened. He staggered forward into my outstretched arms.

A roar from outside told me that Leicestershire had drawn first blood. Mike would be striding out, fastening his helmet and his gloves, swinging both arms in huge backwards circles as if to warn the bowlers he was after them. He'd be taking careful guard.

I was holding a frail, thin child, who should have been out there doing the same things, with the joy I'd seen only a week before. What had reduced him to this? I held him to me. He sobbed into my shoulder: I could feel his tears soaking my sweater. And he was wet too, with sweat I presume, shaking as if in a fever.

I scrabbled some tissues out of my pocket, pressing them into his hand. His face was swollen, eyes and nose streaming. I tore off wads of loo roll when the tissues ran out.

I sat him in the chair and squatted beside him, taking a hand. He shook me off, turning his face.

Another roar from the crowd.

His eyes rolled wildly – yes, he should be out there, shouldn't he? Poor kid. Eighteen or nineteen, and on his own. So lots of kids were on their own at that age. But all the Murdock ones I'd known were more streetwise than Teddy, even the most sheltered.

My weak knee was screaming it had squatted far too long. Shifting the weight didn't make things much better.

'Look,' I said, 'it's not very pleasant in here. Why don't we find somewhere nicer. Splash some water on your face – it'll cool it down.' I proffered more tissues. He dashed them to the floor.

By now regular bursts of applause punctuated the whooshes of urinal water. It took me all the patience of which I was capable not to leave him there and walk out. I'd done my best, for God's sake!

At last a particularly loud roar roused him. He looked from me to the door. 'I should be – it's our – oh, shit.' More tears.

More tissues. This time he took them.

'The sooner you're feeling better the sooner you'll be out there. Come on, wash your face and we'll have a cup of tea.'

He got as far as the wash-basin and froze, staring at his reflection. It wouldn't cheer him.

At last, desperate for a pee myself, I marched to the door and flung it open. 'We can't stay in here. Come on. Time to move.' Joyce Grenfell couldn't have done any better.

*   *   *

152

A silent young man who might have been the doctor, since his scrutiny was close, was waiting for us in the corridor. He caught my eye briefly, as if to establish that I didn't need immediate back-up, and simply pointed along a corridor. At the far end were some double doors. I steered us through, and found another door open. Someone had vacated his or her office – her, I rather thought, from the abundance of plants and family photos on the desk – and moved the chair to the front of the desk, so it sat beside another, less comfortable one which might have come in from a canteen. There was a box of tissues, and a kettle so I could make us tea or coffee. Which I promptly did. My throat needed lubrication, and his hands needed something to clutch. And maybe those chocolate biscuits might come in handy.

From the distance another roar. Another Warwickshire wicket down. Please don't let it be Mike's!

From now on it ought to be plain sailing. All I had to do was get him to talk while I listened. All! It wouldn't be easy to keep him talking without asking questions, and my memory of counselling courses was that direct questions were out. Funny how your brain dries up when such skills are needed.

'You're very upset,' I tried.

Silence. Well, it was such a stupid gambit.

'Do you want to talk about it?' I hated the vague 'it', but since I didn't know what it was, I couldn't be more helpful.

He leaned across me to cram two biscuits into his mouth. He looked at the rest as if they might disappear. I picked up the plate and put it in front of him. How did I juggle his needs and the demands of my bladder? Hell, how could I leave him? And how much longer could I survive?

The process was long and painfully slow, exacerbated by the way his South African accent had thickened almost to the point of impenetrability. And I was always a jump behind, making wrong assumptions. The first was when he used the word 'test'. I associated this immediately with international matches, but couldn't work out why he should be worrying about them yet. Next year, maybe.

'No. No. The tests, man. The tests. For drugs.'

Drugs? Surely Teddy didn't go in for that sort of thing? Had he been reading about Olympic athletes being tested positive when all they'd taken was cold remedies? But I wouldn't leap in with cosy reassurance just yet. I had to let him tell me in his own words, at his own pace.

When I'd been to the loo. It didn't say anything in the counselling courses about the counsellor suspending interviews to respond to calls of nature.

'Look,' I said. 'I've got to pop outside for a minute—'

'*No!*' He grabbed painfully at my arm.

'The loo, Teddy. I've got to go to the loo. I'll be back in just two minutes. I promise.'

He clutched more fiercely.

'It's no good. I've got to go. Two minutes. OK?'

I sprinted. Since I didn't know where the ladies' was, I returned to the gents'. The keep-out notice was still there, and I wasn't at all sure I'd have worried if it wasn't.

'It was drugs, man. I'm sure it was drugs. I was talking to these guys, and they said . . .' It was as if my exit and prompt return had reassured him. I wished they'd given me equal confidence.

'First it was like I had this fever: all hot and sweating and my heart really going, and I thought I'd pass out or throw up. But then it was so lovely. And I was sitting in the corner and everything was so clear, and people, they were really listening to me, man. It was all like scenes from a movie. Not moving, but like photos you hold. And then my arms and legs, they said, Teddy, you're staying right here. And I was dead scared. I seen those old guys down the shebeens. And I'm Baptist, Sophie. I been to Sunday school and church all my life, and now I sinned like this.' He started to weep again. I picked up the words, 'And now I going to be sent back home in disgrace.'

I had to start asking straight questions. 'Why should you be sent home?'

'Because if I get sent one of them tests I fail it for sure, man. Stays in the blood.'

Random drug testing. That must be it.

'What did you do to get those strange feelings, Teddy? Did you smoke something? Drink something?'

'There was smoke. Sweet, heavy smoke. But I go away, man. I don't like the smoke. And then someone give me this big burger – oh, it was great: so thick and meaty and all this sauce and these onions. That's when I started to – God, those lovely colours, man. And everything so clear, like it had been cut out. I ask one of the lads here' – he jerked his head – 'and he say, "It sound like one good trip, man. Tell me where you get this weed, OK?"'

'So you think you've taken cannabis and are afraid it'll show up if you have to provide a urine specimen. Tell me, have you been asked to give one yet?'

But he wasn't ready for hard facts. 'And they'll cancel my contract for sure, and maybe I get deported. And I want to stay here, Sophie.'

I wondered why: he didn't seem to be having a very enjoyable time. But I simply nodded.

He took two more biscuits, then put one quickly back. How many times had he been told not to be greedy, that he must share?

'Do you have any family back home?' I asked.

For the first time he smiled. 'Oh, yes. I got three brothers, four sisters. I got the pictures in my bag. And my ma.'

Poor kid. I wanted to hug him better. And did. At least, I

put my arm round him. All that power and energy from such a tiny frame.

'She must be so proud of you,' I said. A son to be proud of, that was something, wasn't it? She could take the paper round to the neighbours – *Look what my lad's been doing*, she could say. Whereas I – but that way lay, if not madness, tears. Why I should be so upset now, I didn't like to think. I'd lived with the secret for years enough, for goodness' sake. And this certainly wasn't the moment to be indulging in self-pity.

'Come on,' I said, risking a bit of brisk logic at last. 'The chances are that you won't be asked for a specimen until all that stuff's through your system. But there are things we can do to prevent you getting punished for something that isn't your fault.'

There was a huge round of applause from out on the ground. I itched to be out there. Crazy, all those years of denying myself the innocent pleasure of watching my favourite sport, and now I resented being kept from it. I helped myself to a biscuit as consolation. He took two more.

'Maybe you should talk to the police,' I said, more thinking aloud than offering it up as a concrete proposal.

'No!' He was on his feet, wild-eyed. Peter Kirby had clearly given an impressive demonstration of the English bobby's tact and sympathy. 'They think I kill that man. They say I hate him. But I didn't, Sophie. I just wonder why he hate me.'

'I don't think Mr Kirby actually believes you did it; he just has to find out who did, and if it means being hard, that's what he does. But there are other policemen. What about a lawyer? A lawyer would write down all you've told me and tell you what you should do.' And I knew just the man, didn't I? Even if he hadn't returned my call. Afzal was so quiet and gentle I was sure Teddy would take to him. 'I know a very kind man. He's a friend of mine. Shall I phone him so you can talk to him?'

His nod was almost imperceptible, but I pounced. There was no reply from Afzal's office number, so I tried his home, then his mobile.

There was a noisy background of children's laughter. I hoped he could hear as I outlined the situation. Then he said, 'Please assure your friend that he has the law absolutely on his side. I would have to check – and remember, Sophie, this is by no means my area of expertise – but as I recall it's covered by the Offences against the Person Act, eighteen sixty-one. And should your friend suffer any professional damage, it would, I believe – no! I'm talking, Jalal! – sorry, Sophie – be possible for him to take civil action against the perpetrator – shh!'

'You're with your fiancée's family, I take it,' I said, laughing.

'Indeed. They are lovely children but very boisterous.'

'They need a dad to sort them out. Anyway, Afzal, I'm very grateful. Now, might I trespass a little longer' – heavens, this was catching! – 'on your time, and ask you to explain to Teddy exactly what you've said to me . . .'

Teddy looked at the phone as if it might bite him. I'm afraid I stood with one hand on my hip, the other thrusting the handset at him, until he reached unwilling fingers and grasped it.

There was another roar.

'I should be out there, man!'

'Not until you've spoken to Afzal,' I said curtly.

A century before lunch, and I'd missed it! I was ready to weep with frustration. And I hadn't finished yet. The club doctor wanted to speak to me, it seemed. And a senior Warwickshire official. It was difficult to know what to say without letting slip anything that Teddy would see as a betrayal. And I wasn't at all sure where I stood legally, either. In the end I told them both that I thought Teddy's crisis was over, but promised we'd see him back safely to his lodgings. A hot, sweaty Mike appeared briefly, assuring them that he'd take Teddy to the Bears' doctor the following morning and to talk to Afzal.

We had a few moments on our own. Ready to cry with exasperation and disappointment, I confessed I'd seen nothing of his triumph.

'I'd go and get another – oh, I'm still there! – but we only need another sixty. Never mind, now I know how to do it, I can always do it again. How about on Tuesday? We've got a day-night match against Glamorgan at Edgbaston.'

'It won't be before lunch, though,' I whined like a little girl. The effect was meant to be comic, but the feeling was absolutely genuine.

'OK. Wednesday, then. County championship game?'

'How about both?' I asked. 'Hey, I shall smell as sweaty as you do.'

'All in a good cause, though,' he said, holding me even tighter.

Chapter Eighteen

We'd agreed to sleep at my house on Sunday evening, on the grounds that I hadn't seen the place for some time, and that, according to Aggie, the reporters hadn't returned. As I drew my bedroom curtains, I could have sworn I saw a motorcyclist rev away. I felt quite rattled, not least because I didn't want to burden Mike with my fears. I'd have had to promise, wouldn't I, to pass them on to the police? And suddenly that was what I wanted to do. Perhaps it was a result of the strains of the morning that I felt weary to the soles of my feet. I slumped on the bed, and wrote on the memo pad I always keep there: *Phone Ian Dale*. After a moment I wrote another line: *Phone Dr Burrows – contraception*. If this was going to be the long-term relationship I hoped it would be, then there would come a point where something other than condoms was called for. And I ought to mention the allergy that had seemed so important when it flared up. I added, *and rash*.

Mike padded in from the bathroom. It was a good job I'd drawn the curtains, given that he was mother-naked. 'Ian?' he asked, not quite idly.

'A policeman friend of mine,' I said. 'His retirement party's coming up soon. The invitation's in that pile of post in the kitchen. He wants me to take Aggie. And you, once I've told him about you.' I hoped to God Chris would take Helena or someone plausible – it would break Ian's heart if he thought

159

Chris was languishing after me. But I didn't want to suggest going without Mike, lest *he* feel snubbed.

Mike nodded. Then he pointed to the next item. 'You mean the pill or something?'

'Whatever's the safest—' I was disconcerted: I'd expected him to be over the moon at the prospect of abandoning condoms.

'I don't want you taking any risks,' he said.

I waited. There was something else.

'My sister was on the pill. She had a blood clot.'

I didn't need to ask what happened. Perhaps that was why what might have been a jolly, indeed lascivious, conversation had been so bleak. I took his hand and pulled him down beside me. It wasn't just sexual relationships he'd had in the past, it was all sorts of other painful experiences. And there was nothing in the world I could do to take away the pain. 'I thought about the mini-pill,' I said at last. 'When I was with the only live-in partner I've ever had, it seemed to suit me. There's always IUDs, I suppose.'

'But aren't they more suitable for women who've had pregnancies?'

I'd never told anyone else. But I had to tell him. I took a deep breath. 'As a matter of fact—' I began.

'So long as you don't expect to need contraception tonight,' he said, yawning hugely. 'I'd forgotten how knackering all this activity is. Am I getting old?'

'You? You're a mere stripling,' I said. I didn't feel very young.

He fell asleep almost as soon as he'd wrapped himself round me. It was a long time before I did. All the anxieties in my head scampered round like hamsters on wheels.

Mike was still in the shower the following morning when I phoned the St John's Ambulance Brigade office in Birmingham.

A kindly man pointed out to me that the apostrophe s was redundant, and they no longer referred to themselves as a brigade. I squirreled away these nuts of information for future use, preferably against a pedant like Chris. He also told me how to book their personnel for functions and what to do if I wanted to cancel. When I narrowed down my function to a cricket match in Oldbury, he pointed me in the direction of their Dudley HQ. The usual person to make such a request, he said, would be the club secretary.

I thanked him and hung up. To me that suggested official notepaper – well, no organisation would want to make spurious bookings. And what about cancellation? I wondered if they'd do that over the phone.

Putting on my best Oldbury accent, I phoned Dudley. I just wanted to confirm with the duty officer, I said, that the Oldbury ground would be staffed for their remaining fixtures.

'Of course,' said the voice with a Tipton accent, rather shocked. 'It's all booked up in our records. Any reason it shouldn't be?'

'No. I've just been taken on as a sort of assistant to the club secretary,' I said. 'And I'm still feeling my way.'

'It wasn't you that phoned the other day, was it?' he asked, his voice suddenly sharp. ''Cause you didn't half land me in it!'

'In what way?'

'Cancelling when we were supposed to be there. Here it is. Phone cancellation—' He reeled off the time and date.

'Not me,' I assured him. 'If you tell me who phoned, I could bollock them for you.'

'It says here, Mrs While, pp Mrs J. Baggeridge. Mrs Baggeridge, that's who I usually deal with.'

'While?' I repeated.

'Hard to tell, she spoke so quick. Well, you know how they do, down Blackheath.'

161

I couldn't argue. In Blackheath they forget that dictum about God making plenty of time. I thanked him with great courtesy, apologising for my colleague, whoever she might be. I'd trace her if it killed me, I added.

I thought of that motorcyclist and hoped it wouldn't.

'Ian,' I said, a very few minutes later, 'I'm scared.'

We were on our second cups of breakfast tea, and Mike was complaining that I'd left the *Guardian* he'd just nipped out for in a mess, when the doorbell rang.

'You move very quickly when roused, Ian,' I said mildly, kissing him on the cheek. While he and Mike sized each other up, I made fresh tea. My absentee housekeeping had let me down. The only lemon surviving was brownish and tough. There were some lemon slices in the freezer, come to think of it, and I pondered whether to microwave one or slosh the hot tea on to it on the basis that that would thaw it. By the time I'd worked everything out it was beginning to thaw anyway – it must be an even hotter day than I'd realised.

'Attracts trouble like a fly-paper, does our Sophie,' Ian observed. 'You haven't a spot more hot water, love? This tea's a bit strong for me.'

In anyone else's book it would have been dismissed as more like a urine specimen. And that got me back to poor Teddy. The kitchen clock insisted it was ten already: any moment now I'd have to remind Mike that he was supposed to be playing Good Samaritan. But the last thing I wanted to do was suggest that I wanted him out of the way while I talked to Ian.

At last Ian put down his cup and pulled out his notebook. 'So tell me about this motorbike business, love.'

Mike glanced at his watch. 'Hell! I didn't realise – look, I must dash. I'll see you here for lunch, shall I?' He bent and kissed me in his usual way, which would not escape Ian's notice.

Nor did it. Mike was hardly out of the house when Ian raised his eyebrows. 'New young man, then?'

'I've told Chris I think it's important,' I said. I wanted to get that clear.

He understood and nodded kindly. 'I thought you'd do the right thing by him, love. And he seems to be getting himself involved. His secretary, of all people. Know anything about her?'

'Only that she's bright and efficient and kind. A bit older than him, I'd say. But not enough to matter. I think you'll like her.'

'He's bringing her to my party,' he said.

'So it must be serious,' I agreed.

And then, the important matters out of the way, we turned to the matter of my motorcyclist.

'. . . the thing is, I don't want to keep bothering Chris,' I concluded. 'He's head of that big operation and he's got enough on his plate without me adding to it.'

'You've got to tell the officer in charge, then. No doubt about that. Who is it?'

'Some bright southerner called Kirby. Likes to think he's a hard case – and he may well be. I didn't take to him any more than he took to me. And he's really upset someone I like. The kid Mike's looking after this morning.'

'Kid? They'd get specialist officers—'

'Kid as in eighteen but awash behind the ears. And in the throes of an emotional crisis thanks to some pillock who spiked his beefburger with what I suspect was grass – never having tried it myself,' I added sententiously.

'Have you told Kirby this yet?'

'Not yet, but—'

'Withholding information isn't a way to make friends, now, is it? Come on, I know you and Chris always had this special trust, but most officers can't afford that. Remember how you

163

got off on the wrong foot with Diane Stephenson, when you could have been friends.'

'I still blame her boozing for that,' I said carefully. 'And if anyone took advantage of her relationship with Chris, it was her. How is she these days, by the way?'

'She never got her promotion confirmed. Not that I'd have expected that, to be fair. She's gone back into uniform in Cornwall. Let's hope there are fewer pubs down there.'

'Poor woman.' I meant it. I think.

I was standing at my sink, reflecting on the virtues of being green and hoping they compensated for a cos lettuce plucked warm from my garden with a full complement of hyperactive earwigs. The radishes came with interesting bite marks, not as attractive as Safeway's cheerful red globes by any means.

There was Mike's key in the door. I wiped my hands on the front of my shorts and prepared to greet him pretty thoroughly. But he was talking to someone. Teddy.

'Hello, love. I knew you'd want me to bring Teddy back – he's had a bit of a morning and I told him you were the world's greatest cook.'

I thought of the disreputable salad, and mentally reviewed the contents of the freezer. It was the wrong end of the holiday for it to be adequately stocked. But there should be a flan or two, and a couple of supermarket part-baked speciality loaves. There was certainly a tub of good ice-cream. Well, we'd have to make the best of it. Whatever Teddy wanted, it wasn't *haute cuisine*. I was sure Mike's instinct had been right: he wanted company.

It wasn't until we were sitting on my tiny patio, the *ad hoc* meal almost over, that I asked Teddy how he'd got on. He looked wildly at Mike.

'The doc wants to settle him down somehow, but no one

wants him to have any tranquillisers or anything, so there's a possibility of acupuncture.'

Pretty remote if Teddy's expression was anything to go by.

'What a good idea!' I said, sincerely. 'Someone I know had a bad back nothing could sort out, and after a few sessions he's talking of swimming again.' I did not care to reflect on the similarities or otherwise of the two conditions and thought I could rely on Mike to remain supportive. 'Did you like Afzal?'

'Very nice. Very nice.'

'Afzal's preparing a letter to the Cricket Board explaining what has happened, and he wants to accompany Teddy to the police to make a complaint against the people who drugged him. Assuming they did. He's arranging for a private blood and urine test.'

'Who did it, Teddy?' Amazing that in all that conversation yesterday I never got round to asking him. Less surprising that he hadn't volunteered the information, especially when I saw the effect the simple question had on him.

He was on his feet, the pretty bowl which had held gross amounts of chocolate chip ice-cream in pieces.

'Hey, it's OK!' Mike had him by the arms. 'Come on, Sophie was only asking what everyone else will ask. Didn't Afzal, come to think of it?'

'I told him I didn't know.' He subsided back into the chair under Mike's gentle pressure.

This wasn't making sense. How could you complain to the police if you didn't know? Or could you just make a complaint and ask them to investigate it? Another thing I'd have to talk to Chris about.

'Why don't you want to tell me, Teddy? What have I done that you can't tell me?' Would playing the guilt card work? 'You know I'm your friend. I'd never let anyone hurt you.'

'I promised.' He was barely audible. 'I had to promise.'

'If you didn't promise, they'd do something to you?'

'I have to do something they tell me. They make me—'

'Sophie? Sophie, you there?' It was Aggie, peering over the fence. ''Cause I don't know what's wrong with your bell but some bloke's been ringing and ringing.'

'Thanks, Aggie. Battery gone again, I suppose. I'll get some more this evening. Let me know if I can get anything for you, now, won't you.'

'You get to your door, while it's still in one piece,' she said.

Whoever it was was framed against the bright sun. It took me a moment to fill in the details of the silhouette.

'Mr Kirby! Come along in. How can I help you?'

'I'd like – what the hell—?'

There was a terrific commotion in the garden. I hurtled through, Kirby at my heels. There was no sign of Teddy, none of Mike either. Just two chairs tipped over backwards and another smashed dish.

'Sophie? Sophie?'

Aggie didn't sound her usual chirpy self.

'You got a burglar, me love? 'Cause he's just shot over the fence, through my house, and out the front.'

No time to reassure her.

'Thanks,' I yelled, turning tail and hurtling back in Kirby's wake. Again the glare of the sun held us up for a second or so. Then, as our eyes recovered, we spotted them, sprinting hell for leather down Balden Road. Trusting Aggie would stand guard on her front step, I set off, again a pace or two behind Kirby. He had to stop for a number 10 bus going along Croftdown Road, so we were neck and neck as we reached the low wall of St Faith and St Laurence Church. We both saw Mike bringing Teddy down in a rugby tackle just before he reached the church door. I grabbed Kirby before he could throw himself on top.

He shook himself clear.

'Wait, for God's sake.' I couldn't shout, lest that terrified the poor kid even more, but I certainly left him in no doubt that I meant it. 'Leave it to Mike. Can't you see he's hysterical?'

'I suppose you want me to call a bleeding ambulance.'

It was tempting to meet sarcasm with sarcasm, but I fought it. 'I hope it won't be necessary. Look, Mike's getting through to him, I think.'

He seemed calmer. Mike stood him upright, a friendly arm around his shoulders. And collapsed, winded by a vicious elbow jab to the stomach.

Teddy flung himself at the church door: 'I want sanctuary!'

Chapter Nineteen

When Kirby started yelling into his radio I thought he'd changed his mind and was calling for police assistance. But I heard the word 'ambulance'. Perhaps the man was more sensitive than I thought.

Mike had stopped choking and was on his knees beside Teddy, who'd slithered down the door. Mike's hands were firmly on his shoulders. He may have been offering comfort but he was certainly trying to make sure he didn't bolt again. What was my best move? I turned to Kirby.

'Peter,' I said, 'the kid's going through some sort of breakdown—'

'Don't worry, I'm not about to get heavy. Tell you what, I'll back off, shall I? See if you two can handle him until the medics arrive. And don't say you can manage without them, because I can recognise a sick lad when I see one. We don't all wear woad down south, you know.'

I grinned. 'And you took the bone out of your nose specially for this occasion. OK. Do you want to go and wait at my house? I fancy the front door's standing open for you. Guarded by Aggie. You'll have to show her your ID or she won't let you near.'

He flapped a hand and withdrew.

Time to join Mike and Teddy. By now a sizeable crowd had started to cluster on the pavement, including a teacher neighbour of mine who opined in a loud voice that Teddy was out of order asking for sanctuary since he still hadn't got into the church. A familiar voice favoured him in non-academic language with advice about how he should conduct himself – Kirby had made a return sortie. He also suggested that anyone in Teddy's position deserved a little privacy and shepherded everyone back. Gradually the message sank in to even the most obtuse ears.

Meanwhile, whatever Mike was saying was working. Teddy was making visible efforts to straighten his shoulders and raise his head.

I located Peter Kirby, who had stationed himself on the far side of the road. 'I wonder if we'd do better without the ambulance,' I said. 'He's so twitchy even the sound of the klaxon might push him over again if he thought it was your people. If we can get him to the doctor who's already treating him, I'm sure that would be better.'

He looked doubtful, but spoke into his radio.

So there was Teddy back in my kitchen, drinking hot sweet tea, despite the heat, and devouring the last of my chocolate biscuits as if he'd not got outside a plateful yesterday. Peter Kirby – who'd originally come to talk to me, he insisted – went to explain to Aggie and returned to wait in my living room, not altogether patiently. I could hear him prowling around, and then striking a few chords on my piano.

The effect on Teddy was electrifying. 'You got a piano?' He was on his feet.

'In there.' I opened the connecting door.

He almost ran across the room. Kirby stood aside. Teddy played a few arpeggios.

'God, have we got a re-run of *Shine*?' Mike whispered.

We all waited. Teddy adjusted the piano stool, shoved back his sleeves, and started. Within a few bars we were jigging away. The rhythm was infectious. Kirby, shaking his head in disbelief, let his foot tap. And then inched nearer to the piano. What was he looking at? I inched too. Slicing its way up the back of Teddy's lower arm was a long scar.

The doorbell announced the arrival of the club doctor. Mike drew her into the kitchen to give her an update. I returned to the living room. The music had stopped, but Teddy was still beaming, and moving slightly, as if in his head it played on.

'Tell me, kid,' Kirby asked in a quiet, matter-of-fact voice. 'How d'you get that?'

Teddy shrank.

'No, I'm just interested. Nasty scar.'

Teddy muttered something I couldn't pick up. A name?

'That a place or a person?'

'A town.' He repeated it.

It meant little to me, less, by the look of it, to Kirby.

'Don't you remember,' came Mike's voice, from the now open door to the kitchen. 'In the tradition of Sharpeville? A funeral. Some police action. People were attacked with sjamboks and then with bullets.' He crossed to Teddy, laying firm hands on his shoulders. 'Was it just you that got hurt, kid?'

I knew the answer before I heard it.

'My dad. The police killed my dad.'

Mike had followed Teddy and the doctor back to the family where Teddy was staying to brief them and make sure they were happy for him to continue there.

'It's a responsibility not everyone'd want,' Kirby mused.

'I've got a fair idea where he'll end up if they can't face it,' I said. All I wanted was to be alone with Mike. But then, if in the middle of all my happiness I couldn't offer shelter and support, I didn't rate myself highly.

'Bit of a burden.'

'I like kids,' I said carelessly. I didn't add that we all have private debts to pay: I didn't want to sound insufferably pious. 'Another cup of tea? Or something cold?'

'I could really use a cold beer,' he said. 'It's been a bit of an afternoon, hasn't it?'

I fished a couple of Beck's out of the fridge, and, finding bottle opener and glasses, motioned him into the garden.

He didn't move. 'Ian Dale called me this morning,' he said abruptly.

I went out anyway. Can you feel your age when you're less than forty? All I wanted to do was sink into a deckchair.

Perforce, Kirby followed. He scowled at the low chair, as if unsure that it would support his weight. 'I wish you'd spoken to me direct,' he said. 'I've had Groom chewing off one ear, and now his ex-sidekick's having a go at the other.'

'They're both old friends,' I said. 'It's natural for me to talk to them. I wouldn't expect you and me to be on such relaxed terms – after all, you're investigating a crime I could have committed. And when I have tried to offer you friendly information, you've been pretty underwhelming.' I couldn't actually remember trying to on more than one occasion, but let that pass. Let him reflect on his habitual aggressive manner.

'Point taken.' His voice was grudging but he was obviously trying. He produced Rizla papers and a tobacco tin, gesturing.

Since we were outside, I nodded. 'So let me tell you what I've told Chris and Ian. Chris doesn't know about my tail yet, by the way, and Ian's not involved with you people in Smethwick. I phoned him because my tail's only appeared in the Harborne area.' I waited while he made a note. 'I've spent a lot of time listening to cricket gossip, which will probably confirm what you and your colleagues have already found out. Guy Timpson was a thoroughly nasty piece of knitting: he had a sex life that would have embarrassed a tom-cat and took nasty photographs. He'd got a tube of Lasonil in his bag.

Was that just for bruises incurred on the field of play or was it to take away marks where he injected himself?'

'You know I can't answer that.'

'Was there a woman he'd recently taken up with? And dropped? Or got pregnant? According to gossip, there'll be a lot of women round Rutland and even out in Oldbury – he must have maintained very close ties with his old club – whose relationships will be safer without him. And the interesting thing, of course, is that it was a woman who cancelled the St John people for the Oldbury match. I don't know whether they'd have done any better than Winston but someone wanted to make sure there was no first-aid cover.'

'And how would you know that it was cancelled? And that a woman called?'

'Same way as you, I suppose. I phoned up their Dudley headquarters and asked. According to the man I spoke to, his caller had a Blackheath accent. What I couldn't get was a name. Something like While, but your guess is as good as mine. Did you have any better luck?' I leaned forward – that looked like ground elder coming under the far fence.

Kirby lit up again. 'Why are you doing all this? Poking around?'

'Because . . .' How could I explain all my fears and suspicions? I left it at that, and started again. 'OK, let's talk about Barkat's car. Have you found anything to link him with the woman I saw in Smethwick, kicking a car door in?'

He looked genuinely nonplussed.

I had a terrible feeling I'd put my foot right in it.

'I'll tell you what we did find in Barkat's car,' he said. 'A fancy mix of illegal substances.'

'I wouldn't be surprised if it was he who—' I stopped, abruptly. Without Afzal's or Teddy's agreement, that was one thing I couldn't reveal.

Kirby was no fool, however. 'Who what?' he prompted.

'When Teddy's well enough, I'm sure he'll talk to you,' I compromised.

He flung his hands in the air. 'For God's sake, woman!'

'I'll do my best to get him to talk,' I said.

He sighed.

There was something I should have picked up earlier. 'Is Chris still on your back?'

He looked at me sharply.

'You mentioned it the other night.'

'Hmm. Well, it's more peaceful with him on this course. To do him justice, he tries to keep in touch, though. Leaves me updates on e-mail. I do the same. I don't mind that. I'll fill him in on everything this afternoon, don't you worry.'

'Thanks.'

After that, we'd done little more than fence with each other again. He left soon after, leaving me baffled. Why on earth had he bothered to come all the way over here, just to ask me to talk to him? Neither of us was much further forward, except that I now knew about Barkat's drugs, and he knew I knew something that was official police knowledge that he didn't. And that wasn't going to do much for his health and temper. I'd have to have a word with Chris.

One person I very much wanted to talk to was Afzal, to thank him for seeing Teddy. Amongst other things. He was still at his office.

'Any chance of him talking to the police about being fed whatever it was? To complain so they can sort it out?'

'I'm working on that – I'm seeing him again tomorrow.'

'Has he told you who it was?'

There was a long silence.

'I wish I could talk to you in confidence, Sophie. But you know that as the man's solicitor I can't, not without his permission. He has given me a description of the people involved, however, and I can assure you they do not include Guy Timpson.'

'What about Barkat?'

'Nor Barkat,' he admitted wearily. 'As I've told Chris Groom.'

So someone else had been talking to Chris instead of Kirby. I was tempted to feel sorry for the man.

My toaster of a brain chose that minute to spring into action. 'My God! I wonder if they've looked at the film in Guy's camera.' I explained about the candid shots. 'Wouldn't it be lovely if they were recorded for posterity?'

'Are you a betting woman, Sophie?' Afzal asked drily. He added, laughing, 'Come on, surely it can't have escaped you that the person who killed Timpson would have thought about that?'

Swallowing any pride I had left, I phoned Peter Kirby. The switchboard took the call eventually, but I heard his extension ring out, getting me nowhere and adding to the phone bill I was supposed to be keeping in check for the forthcoming unpaid year. Neither did the switchboard pick me up again.

I suppose I was hardly surprised when I heard Teddy's voice outside the front door. He made a beeline for the piano. Mike steered me into the kitchen.

'Just for tonight,' he pleaded.

'It's fine—'

'You see, a couple of the lads have bad stomachs and I may have to—'

'It's no problem—'

'—persuade him to play. Might even be therapy for him—'

'I was just going to make up the bed for him.'

When what I was saying eventually penetrated, his smile was reward in itself.

'He's a nice kid. He needs looking after.'

Mike laughed, hugging me. 'I can never get over the fact that some bloke didn't sweep you off your feet years before this—'

'Maybe I take a lot of sweeping.'

'—and marry you and share a lot of kids with you.'

I pulled away from his arms. In the living room, Teddy was now singing along.

'There's something I've got to tell you, Mike. Something I've never told anyone else. Not Chris. Not even my own mother.' This wasn't how I'd planned to do this – if my insomniac agonisings could count as planning. 'No. Just listen. When I was Teddy's age, not much more, someone I knew – raped me. The classic never-happens-first-time syndrome – I got pregnant. Somewhere out there' – I gestured wildly – 'I have a son. Now do you understand why I couldn't dream of turning Teddy away? I just hope some kind woman's looking after my boy.'

Chapter Twenty

I don't know what I expected. Of myself or of Mike. I'd gone to extraordinary lengths to conceal this secret for nearly twenty years, and now it came exploding out, with no control, no art, no nothing. There wasn't even a theatrical silence – Teddy was still bopping wildly away in the living room, singing occasional phrases. I turned, gripping the edge of the sink. I didn't want to see Mike's face while he considered his verdict. And I saw myself like a prisoner in the dock – how could anyone endure those long moments of ritual when all they wanted to know was what future they might have? If any. Oh, I exaggerated my own case. Of course I had a future. But I knew from every second the piano jangled away that the future might not include Mike. And I hadn't realised quite how much I wanted it to.

Teddy sang on.

There was movement behind me. No, he wouldn't leave without saying anything, certainly wouldn't leave Teddy here without any explanation. Perhaps, after all, I'd chosen that particular moment to ward off huge emotional scenes. I'd never been good at them, had I?

The piano needed tuning. I'd better see to that this holiday. Fine holiday it was turning out to be.

Hands gripped my shoulders, turned me. I was pressed to Mike's chest. Maybe it would be all right. 'It's OK, Sophie, my love, it's OK.'

The words didn't sound as good as the thudding of his heart under my ear. But they sounded good enough.

He moved away, but only to turn the chair and sit on it, pulling me on to his knee. My God, how many years was it since anyone had done that!

'Do you want to tell me all about it?'

I suppose I did. Not that he'd understand much from the disjointed sentences that rushed out at him. The man high on drugs and Christmas and discovering the consequences up there in Leeds on a bleak February day. Knowing I couldn't abort or keep the child.

'Why? Abortion wasn't impossible, surely? Twenty years ago?'

He didn't understand, did he?

'It was for me. Not because I couldn't have got one legally. Of course I could. But because of whose child it was. And I can't even tell *you* that, Mike.'

'But—' Perhaps he sounded confused rather than angry.

'My family would have guessed straight away if I'd even so much as hinted I was pregnant. So I fed them all sorts of lies about what I was doing during the vacations I should have been back in Oldbury. I was the first of the family to aspire to such things as uni, so it was easy to con them. There was a charity that gave me some money . . . Anyway, just in time for the next academic year, I had Nicholas and handed him over to his new parents. Nineteen years ago.'

Neither of us spoke after that. Until he pushed me far enough from him for him to lift up my face and say, 'Jesus, Sophie – you must be the bravest woman I know.'

What *did* he mean? I gaped, tears trickling into my open mouth. Funny, I hadn't realised till then that I was crying. But there was a wet patch on his T-shirt front.

'No support? Not with all that going on? And you still went on and got your degree?'

I shook my head. 'Funny: I managed my second year all right. I did quite well, actually. Then it all went pear-shaped and I had to take a year out. Breakdowns aren't looked on too kindly in Oldbury, either, so . . . Well, I stayed up there and muddled through.'

No need to burden him with all the details. I closed my eyes against the excruciating moments that burst from where I'd buried them so long. I may have put up my hands to fend them off.

The fridge clicked on, humming loudly.

'Anyway,' I said at last, 'I let the adoption people know my address when I moved here, and there's a letter on file. If he should ever want to contact me . . .' I shrugged myself back into teacher mode. 'My experience of kids that age makes me doubtful. He's more likely to be furious with me. Maybe when he's older – kids of his own, perhaps . . . Hey, what are you doing?'

He'd set me on my feet and was burrowing in my glory-hole. For a moment he disappeared altogether. Then he reappeared flourishing a bottle.

'Champagne?' My mouth hung open.

'Champagne! Something to celebrate. Your son. Your gift of life. And your gift to me of your life's secret.' By now he was in tears too.

Him clutching the bottle, me the glasses, we clung to each other.

Which was how Teddy found us.

He stared at us in obvious puzzlement. Why should two people with streaming, swollen eyes be ready to swill that happiest of drinks? And why did we shout at him when he took the bottle from Mike and started to shake it for us?

Gently Mike wrested it from his grasp, and found a replacement, which he clothed in the instant-chiller jacket.

Teddy touched the glasses. 'So what is the celebration?'

What indeed? My heart might be light now; indeed, I actually felt dizzy, disorientated, with relief. But when Mike started thinking, then that might be a different matter. Raw emotion was one thing, brooding on it another.

Surprised I could move, I reached for a third glass.

'Sophie's just told me something that makes me very happy,' said Mike. He reached for the tea-towel, swathed the bottle and prised the cork with the minimum of drama. 'There!'

'Oh, she's going to marry you! Please – let me tell you how happy I am.' He shook us robustly by the hand, and flung an arm round Mike's shoulders. 'When will it be? The wedding?'

'I'm not . . .' I began, helplessly. 'We're . . .' Was that where we were heading? Marriage? All that commitment? Him to me, me to him? Not yet, surely? Except, why not?

'The sooner the better,' said Mike. And looked me in the eye as if he meant it. 'So long as you play at the party afterwards, Teddy.'

At this point the doorbell rang. It was Chris, looking very natty in a white tuxedo. I could have screamed. There was Teddy, grinning as if he'd invented an early Christmas, ready to blurt everything out. I couldn't face the semi-comic, semi-tragic denials, amendments, whatever, not now.

'Some dinner I can't get out of,' he said, briefly, going straight through into the kitchen. 'Anyway, I was passing so I thought I'd check up on things.' He must have noticed the generally heightened emotion overheating the place, but didn't remark on it.

I introduced Teddy, and Chris went into social gear straight away, talking about Birmingham and places he must visit while he was here. If he associated him with the hunt for Guy or Barkat's killer he gave no hint. He certainly didn't ask any questions about the afternoon's alarums and excursions. But then, he and Peter Kirby wouldn't have had time to discuss them yet. Would they? In Kirby's place, I'd have phoned the boss, wouldn't I?

'They've dragged the cut!' he announced. 'Found a variety of shopping trolleys, several mattresses, assorted vehicular impedimenta – and sod all in the way of Epipens. But the mud's so thick the team says they'll have to drain it if we want a thorough check. Expensive and time-consuming. I wish – purely in the interests of my budget, you understand – one of you would confess.'

By now it was dawning on Teddy that he was in the company of another policeman.

Chris smiled kindly at the widening eyes. 'It's OK. I'm joking. I want to get justice done, and if that means draining the entire West Midlands canal system I'll do it.'

Teddy sat down heavily. At least if he was intimidated, he wouldn't blab, would he?

Chris continued, 'I reckon we're on to a loser, all the same.'

'You think the Epipen might have been removed from his bag at some other time?' I prompted.

'I was going to say the mud's so glutinous. Why, what do you think?'

I shook my head. 'Whoever removed it would have wanted to be absolutely sure, wouldn't they? And if they were trying to do it in the dressing room, there was always a chance someone would come in. Too risky all round. I'd have done it beforehand. I suppose the PM didn't indicate anything else?' I asked, almost at random.

'He'd eaten a large meal not long before. I asked the pathologist to check in case he'd eaten anything he was allergic to – like your Halima – but he found no obvious allergens. And the reaction would have taken place much more quickly, he thought, given its intensity.'

'Large meal?' Mike said slowly. 'Most of us eat pretty sparingly before a match.'

I nodded my confirmation, as did Teddy.

'I'll get Peter to pursue that in a bit more depth,' Chris said. 'Naturally we're trying to build up a picture of his last hours. It might have needed two people to do it, of course. One person to keep him occupied while the other one did his bag over.'

Did we have witnesses? The days had been so hectic I could no longer remember where we'd slept, where we'd eaten. Of course. We'd slept at Mike's. I'd been over it enough times with Kirby. I'd been to the dentist's – that was it. And Mike had picked me up. An hour later.

'Sophie – are you sure you're all right?' Chris asked at last, looking at me intently.

'Just panicking about alibis,' I said.

'Yours is OK, of course. And we're just waiting for your neighbour, Mike, to get back from Skyros to confirm that conversation you say you had about cats,' Chris said drily, accepting almost absent-mindedly the glass of champagne Mike thrust at him. 'Thanks. If she does, you're both in the clear *if*, that is, the theft took place then. As is this young man. But it's a big if. We need to pin down the last time anyone saw that bloody Epipen. And we've got the East Midland people working flat out on it, too.'

'Can we go back to the cut for a minute?' I asked. 'Apart from no Epipen and a lot of truly stinking mud, did you find anything of interest?'

'A couple of cameras, for instance?' Mike cut in. ''Cause if they belong to the people I think they do you could put them back. The gentlemen of the press,' he explained, his voice dripping with irony.

'I'd like three cameras,' I said. 'The press ones, and the neat little job Guy used to take all his jolly candid-camera shots. I suppose it hasn't turned up, Chris? I don't remember seeing it in his bag. Though since I was going through it like a dose of salts that isn't surprising. Or was it in his car somewhere? Locked out of sight of the Black Country's light-fingered best?'

Chris sipped slowly at the champagne. I sensed he was creating a nice dramatic pause, so the impact was wasted on me. Not on Mike and Teddy, however, to judge by their faces.

'Funny thing is,' he said at long last, 'try as we may we can't discover how he arrived at the ground. His own car was safe in the car park of his local railway station. See, we can manage some things without your help, Sophie. So we presume he travelled by rail. But no one saw him on any of the trains he could have taken – no one we've run to earth, at least. Though there's still time. Sometimes people take an incredibly long time to come forward. So what I'd love to know is not just how he came to eat a huge lunch, but everything else about his activities that day.'

'His favourite hobby was bedding other people's wives,' Mike said. 'But I can't see it going down all that well on *Crimewatch*. "Were you bonking this man on the morning of . . . ?"'

Teddy looked shocked, and took himself sharply off. The piano danced into action again.

Chris raised his eyebrows.

'He's staying here tonight.'

'Oh, Sophie – don't you ever give up collecting waifs and strays?'

'He's a nice kid. Missing his family,' I said. I stole a glance at Mike, whose smile was such it should have been framed. 'Tell me, how are things going between you and Peter?'

Perhaps I'd started talking Chinese.

Chris looked at me as if I was. 'Fine.' Then he added, more graciously, 'Trouble is, he doesn't like my poking my nose in, and I'm trying to see what a bit of hands-off management will do. Being on this bloody course helps. First and last thing every day I leave him notes and e-mails, and I had the idea he was supposed to be reciprocating.'

I said nothing.

'How much longer's your course?' Mike asked.

'Finishes on Wednesday, thank God. I'm too old for all this learning – every time they introduce a new concept I can feel my brain withering a little more. And then it's business as usual.'

'If you've got to work with this bloke, whom I must admit I didn't take to either,' Mike said, 'can't you find some sort of compromise? Talk to each other in the pub over lunch or something?'

He was rewarded by two ironic laughs. 'In the public sector,' I began.

Chris continued, as if we'd rehearsed it, 'Lunch is for working. In my case I have all these lawyers and civil servants and community leaders all of whom want a good meal by way of compensation for venturing out into the sticks. Which means no nice, matey chats. Jesus, Mike, I used to work in this great team out in Harborne. Now I'm flying solo, without a compass, without a map, and with all these people imagining I can pilot and navigate the fucking thing.'

'You need to exercise some of that stress away,' Mike said quietly. 'And I know what you're going to say. That you don't have time. But I'll tell you this for nothing: everyone gets a grave and a headstone if they want one. Not a lot have "I wish I'd spent more time in the office" carved on it. What time d'you get up?'

Chris looked startled. 'Six-thirty. Why?'

'I'll be there at six-thirty-five for a jog. OK? Tomorrow?'

'But – I mean, this meal—'

'You want to live, Chris? You be there.'

'I'd better be at that meal or I won't live. OK. Six-thirty-five. You coming too, Sophie?'

'Depends whether it's to be a run or a jog. And if young Teddy gets nightmares.'

He still didn't ask about him, did he? I wondered how long he'd remain in ignorance. And – just to prove I could – I said nothing.

The talking continued – on and off – all evening. I thought I'd hate him probing, but each detail he extracted seemed to clear the air a little more.

'There is one person who knows,' I said eventually, while he laid the supper table. 'We'd been to the same school and gone to the same uni. Different courses. But I swore him to silence – well, I suppose it was blackmail really. He was trying to bonk the entire female population of the north-east, with a determination that would have horrified his family. So we had a mutual protection society. In fact, we gave the general impression that we were going out with each other – very useful for alibi-ing. Funny thing is, we've stayed friends – see each other from time to time for a drink. Mind you, he's risen like yeast – he's very high up in arts administration.'

'He? Does he have a name?'

'Tony Rossiter.'

He shook his head: it didn't mean anything to him. 'Shall we need spoons for a sweet or shall we eat cheese and fruit?'

I motioned with my head to the living room. 'I'm fairly sure there's some home-made ice-cream somewhere right at the bottom of the freezer and I guess I know someone who might like it. It'll be as hard as the devil's head, of course. Still, if we leave it out for a bit . . .'

'Does the father know?' he asked while he was stacking the dishwasher.

'No. It's one of those little announcements I keep putting off.'

'Well, nineteen years isn't all that long, I suppose. What'll you do, give him the news with his pensioner's bus pass?'

'Probably. No, to be realistic, it must be soon. If Nicholas' – the name sounded odd on my lips – 'if Nicholas can legally find me, and if he wants to, and if he succeeds, given I left that letter saying I was happy to be found, then I suppose he might want to know. And – and the father should – if he wants.'

'Sophie, my love. I'm with you. No need to tie yourself in knots. You want to be able to tell the kid who his father is if he asks. Right? And you should warn the father first. It's OK. There must be a reason,' he added, tipping powder into the machine and starting it, 'why you never have. Or would you rather not talk about it?'

I turned. I could see both of us full face in the mirror. 'Because I was in love with him. For all those years I was in love with him.'

'But he raped you! For God's sake, how can you love a man who did that to you? And for all those years—' His voice slid from anger to exasperation and disbelief.

'Because – because love's like that, isn't it? Sometimes? There's something about it in *Persuasion*. About it being a woman's lot to love a man when all hope has gone.' I'd loved him during his first marriage, during all his relationships with other women, well into his second marriage, a year or so ago. And he loved me. As his mate, big sister, nurse-maid, whatever. But not as his woman. And if he'd ever known I was the mother of his child he'd have disappeared into the wide blue yonder and I'd never have seen him at all. Never again. And I couldn't have contemplated life without Andy.

'Do you – do you still? Love him?'

I couldn't bear that pain in his voice. I turned to face him. My hands found his. 'I love you, Mike. I can't pinpoint the moment when I stopped loving him, nor the moment I started

loving you. But the first did happen, just as much as this has.'
I smiled, and reached to kiss him.

He held back. 'I can't get my head round all this,' he said.
Then his face softened. 'But I believe you. I promise you I
do.' He gripped my hands. 'Come on, let's have a turn round
your estate. I'd rather smell honeysuckle than washing-powder
fumes.'

Later that night, the condom burst, but my period started the
following morning anyway. In the past I'd have spoken about
a lucky escape. Now I wasn't so sure.

Chapter Twenty-One

'A jog. That's all. Promise. Not a flat-out run. I wouldn't want Chris to have a heart attack on me, now would I? Just a little loosener. So get yourself up and get those trainers on.' He was stretching, provocatively, irritatingly.

I regarded him from the safe side of the bedclothes. 'Nothing else?'

'Not as far as I'm concerned,' he said, grinning to acknowledge his wilful misunderstanding. 'But you might shock Teddy. He's coming too.'

It always seems a bit of a cop-out to me, to drive to wherever you're proposing to take your exercise. But Chris's house was sufficiently far from mine to justify the three of us piling into my Renault. It sighed almost audibly as we returned: it preferred not to have to ferry sweaty bodies. But since Chris had whizzed off to work without offering us a shower, let alone breakfast, that was what it had to put up with. He'd put in some frantic moments at Piddock Road, shaving, showering, changing, before he hurtled off to his course.

Over breakfast, while we waited for our turns in the bathroom, Mike and I planned our day. I was due for a major Safeway shop – my cupboards and freezer were virtually empty. The latter ought, in any case, to be defrosted before it was much older. If only I were more domesticated, I might find such activities fulfilling. My excuse to myself was that

I was so short that mopping the melted ice from the floor of a chest freezer was one of those activities that nature had designed me not to do. Chris had been dragged in to help in the past. It could be the first bit of serious housekeeping Mike and I did together. Then there was the slight problem of the spring-cleaning. The cleaning chemicals I'd bought at the start of the holiday regarded me balefully every time I went into the glory-hole.

'You all right?' Mike asked, intent on scraping the last of the flesh from his grapefruit.

'*The end of pleasure is pain*,' I quoted from somewhere. 'All this lovely gadding around watching cricket, and when the summer stops I'll wake up and find I still haven't done my spring-cleaning.'

'Leave it,' he shrugged.

'The problem is, that's what I said last year. And the year before.'

'Team effort, then,' he said. 'Isn't Teddy ever going to get out of that shower?'

'Jesus!' I dropped the tumbler I was holding. 'You don't suppose – oh my God!'

I was up the stairs in threes. But it was all right. Even through the bathroom door I could hear him singing the songs he'd been playing yesterday. I trailed down the stairs far more slowly than I'd gone up. Youth must be a damn sight more resilient than thirty-something, that was all I could deduce.

As I dawdled along the hall, the phone rang. I stretched a languid hand. Peter Kirby.

'No, nothing new. I thought you might just like to know we're draining the canal.'

'Are you indeed? What are you expecting to find?'

'Timpson's Epipen, of course.'

Talk about *déjà vu*.

'Tell you what,' I said, 'just let me know how many cameras you find, will you?'

As an exit line, it was OK. But it left me with an unanswered question: why had he bothered to phone? If he'd asked after Teddy it might have made sense. Shaking my head, I went back to the kitchen.

Mike and Teddy toddled off to Afzal's and would then go on to Edgbaston for some light training, promising me a ticket for the match, despite my reservations that I was taking too much Warwickshire money.

'Think of it as payment in kind for what you've been doing,' Mike said. 'For Teddy,' he added. 'By the way, I think it might get a bit rowdy tonight – the supporters seem to think this sort of match is a cross between the Last Night of the Proms and a challenge to drink the bar dry.'

'How does it affect your concentration?'

'Hardly at all – if you happen to be winning. If you're up against it—' He shrugged, expressively.

The trouble with having a shower in an empty house is that your head keeps on coming up with things it ought to think about. Or in my case, one thing it didn't want to think about. My relationship with Mike.

No, there was nothing wrong with it, nothing at all. In fact, despite all the emotional ups and downs, I knew I was happier than I'd ever dreamed possible. And he seemed happy, too. But there was no getting away from the fact that prompted by Teddy he'd spoken about marriage – only to be interrupted by Chris – and I'd never made the effort to broach the subject again. And neither had he. Or perhaps that should have been the other way round. It was his suggestion, so if it was serious, it was up to him to raise it? Yes! No, that sounded like an excuse to me. For my inactivity. Surely I trusted him enough to say, *Look here, did you mean what you said about marriage, because if you did I'm free on Tuesday?*

What if he'd changed his mind?

I couldn't bear it if he'd changed his mind!

Hang on, Sophie, I told myself firmly, you've spent the last twenty years avoiding commitment. You can't suddenly have yearnings for security as exemplified by a bit of paper and a ring? No, you tell him thank you for the kind offer of marriage but say that one shouldn't fix what's working very well. That's what you should say.

He's probably thinking exactly the same thing, cursing his mouth for even mentioning the word. Not that he did. Not really. It was Teddy.

Except he looked at you as if he liked the idea.

Cleaner but no wiser, I came to the horrible realisation of what this shower must be doing to the country's limited water-resources and turned off quickly. Time to shop!

Having spent an enormous amount at Safeway I spent a proportionate amount of time lugging carrier bags from the car and unpacking them. There were a couple of bags for Aggie, too, bulky, heavy items, which I dropped off inside her kitchen – it was her day for the chiropodist.

As I stowed stuff, I realised I was feeding not one but three people, assuming Teddy would stay as close as he could to my piano for as long as he decently could. I looked back at my previous week's expenditure: if I went on at this rate there was no way I could survive for my year without pay.

I looked at the bill again, and at a bank statement which lay malevolently on the top of this morning's post. A scan of the building society statement I'd filed without daring to look at it confirmed the worst. An unpleasantly large chunk of my savings had gone to pay for the Masters course I was starting in September, and I still had to pay for a holiday, if

I was going to have one, that is. I could always tell myself that all this cricket-watching was my holiday, but somehow it didn't feel very restful. The conclusion was obvious. To be Lady Bountiful you need the right resources. OK, I'd have to cut the holiday. And I could always find a part-time job. I'd done that before, in much less agreeable circumstances.

Gloomy enough to kick a cat, had I had one, I decided the best way to cheer myself up might be to go and irritate someone else. Besides, I'd never seen anyone empty a cut.

They'd done it by the time I got there, of course. If I'd wanted powerful cascades through the locks the Oldbury end, I didn't get them. What I was in time for, however, was the smell. There was plenty of that, the sort of smell you encounter when you've not cleaned out the school aquarium for a couple of months and the water filtration system has collapsed with exhaustion. That smell, squared.

I wandered towards a knot of shirtsleeved officers pretending to be too macho to notice. No Kirby, not that I could see, but Harvinder Mann was there, his complexion more green than olive. He smiled when he saw me, and trotted over.

'You shouldn't be here, you know,' he said. 'Officially.'

'I know I shouldn't. But if a DCI goes to the trouble of letting me know what's going on – where is he, by the way?'

Mann smiled again. 'He claimed he had unavoidable business elsewhere. I think he might have suspected the consequences of stirring up all this mud.'

'Stirring things up always makes a bit of stink, doesn't it?'

He looked at me sideways, as if appraising me. 'Sometimes a bit of a stink is necessary. Provided you're stirring the right things. And you'll be amazed at what you can find, Ms Rivers.'

'Sophie.'

'You'll never guess what they found in the canal, for instance. Something rather unexpected.'

The Epipen! My God, they'd found the Epipen!

'Come and look.' Now I came to think about it, his smile was teasing rather than threatening. 'But if I were you I'd find some tissues or something to cover your nose.'

I groped in my bag and found three or four folded into a wad. I separated them and gave him half.

The tissues, despite the smell of Polo mints faintly lingering on them, were unequal to the task. Trying not to gag, desperate to breathe only through the wad, I none the less followed Mann through the police line and looked where he pointed, with an air of conscious drama. As well he might. Lying on the towpath, in a rapidly drying pool of water, was a huge snake. Huge. Upwards of twenty feet long. That huge.

Mann laughed, then thought better of it and covered his nose and mouth again. He motioned me away. I needed no second bidding. He followed, equally briskly.

'If only Timpson had had the good taste to be crushed or strangled to death, I think we might have found our villain. A python, Sophie. Non-venomous, but impressive for all that. What I can't understand is how it got here.'

I dredged in my memory for long-forgotten facts about snakes. 'Don't they like water?'

'Water, yes – but *canal* water? What self-respecting creature would swim round in *that*?'

'Well, it isn't swimming now. Perhaps it tried and the toxins in the cut killed it.'

Another laugh. 'I'd have thought you'd be more observant. They'd already sent for someone from Dudley Zoo, but some intelligent soul decided it was going to bite him and slammed it on the head with a shovel. Heavens, where do these people keep their brains?'

The more I saw of Mann, the more I liked him. Particularly as he set us in motion again, across the park. Little groups of locals eyed us, but since neither of us was in uniform we were presumably dismissed as unimportant.

'How's that poor young man this morning?' he asked.

I jumped. For some reason Teddy hadn't been in my thoughts.

'Peter tells me he had some sort of fit yesterday.'

'Hysteria. He seems better this morning. We took him for a jog and he's going to see his solicitor – I just hope and pray he can persuade Teddy to talk to you people. He's got lots to tell you. Did Peter also say how he comforted himself?'

Harvinder smiled. 'I hope your neighbours like music!'

'They don't usually get it that loud or that long. Fortunately the house is joined to my neighbour's by the hall, not the living room wall. She's a wonderful old woman. I'd hate to do anything to upset her.'

'I gather she handled the media with aplomb. You're being left alone now?'

'They've discovered some other nine-days' wonder.' I found a bench, and sat on it. What little wind there was blew towards the cut. 'They'll probably be back for this story, though.'

'We've already invited them round.' He smiled and stretched, lifting his face to the sun.

'Have you got a policy about such things?'

If I expected a response it certainly wasn't the one I got.

'Snakes alive!' He zapped into a wonderful Southern drawl.

'And, indeed, "Lawksamussy, Mis' Sophie",' I added.

'Well, actually we have. We like to tell the public as soon as we can. Chris Groom actively endorses the theory that it should be the man doing the job who talks to the press. And guess who got the short straw? Next job, as it happens.'

'What about internal communication?' I asked. 'You know, between different departments, different officers – that sort of thing.'

He straightened and looked at me. I met hard stare with hard stare.

'I take it there's some significance to that question?' He was no longer smiling.

'You take it right.'

He was the first to drop his eyes. But not by much. He regarded his fingernails for a moment then looked up again. 'It's a very interesting question, Sophie. It's one I've given some thought to myself. But unless I'm very much mistaken, that's the first of the radio vans. I'm about to become a media star.' He tossed imaginary locks of hair with a prima donna gesture, smoothing them theatrically with the back of his fingers.

'So you'll no doubt want to be alone,' I responded, my voice gravelly.

He stood up, face serious again. 'Have I got your phone number?'

I told him.

We walked back to the smell in silence. My car was waiting patiently but resentfully. I checked my shoes carefully before I got in: there was no point in annoying it further, was there?

I parked in the garage, for once, assuring the now shocked and disorientated Renault that there were times when it was entitled to a little privacy. In any case, the roads around the county ground were no place for it: they'd be solid with other cars. I would take a bus to Five Ways and another to the ground: Mike, who had a parking place guaranteed, could deal with the traffic at the end of play. Except it was very much my turn. If the Bears won, as I devoutly hoped they would, there would be some beer sunk tonight. Not, however, enough to give any of the players a hangover: they started another four-day match on Wednesday. Too much for legal driving, however. And I'd let no car defeat me yet.

Not even a BMW Seven Series, I recalled with a moment's wistfulness.

I had time to make a sandwich and change, provided I was terse when I returned the calls on the answerphone. For once I employed a little common sense and changed first. It wasn't until I'd splashed on some of last summer's duty-free perfume, to chase away the smell that insisted on lingering in my nostrils, that I could consider eating. I put together a sandwich bulging with non-organic but non-earwiggy salad and mature cheddar cheese. That should keep me going. Now for the phone calls, one eye always on my watch. Nothing was going to stop me seeing Mike try for another hundred.

Not even Chris, as it turned out. It was obvious that he was catching a snack too: we'd have to talk and munch alternately.

'I thought you'd like to know that we have a match between the dead tom's hair and some found in Barkat's car,' he said. 'They phoned through here. Made a nice change from columns of figures, I can tell you.'

'"Tom"! Can't you think of a less pejorative term?'

'You mean, like "whore"? Come on, Sophie: my term's got fewer syllables than "working girl" or whatever, and it's much less ambiguous. The important thing is the connection, though.'

'With the drugs, you mean? All the illegal substances they found in his car?'

'I don't know what you're talking about.' His voice was dangerously quiet.

'Well you bloody well ought. Kirby's cock-a-hoop about it. Now, put prostitute dying of an overdose together with a car that's been carrying illegal substances and what do you get?'

'I do not believe this. Are you telling me Kirby's told you something he hasn't bothered to tell me?'

'I wouldn't put it like that myself. You're on this course, right? And communicating with notes or e-mail, right?'

'I told you.'

'Do you have a "message received" facility?'

'Of course. But—'

'Do you check it?'

'Of course. But—'

'In that case, are you sure that it's Peter who gets and acknowledges your messages? That some other kind person doesn't do it for him and forget to mention it to him?' I'd practised being inexorable long enough: it was time to let him get a word in.

'What the hell are you implying?'

'Just take Mike's advice and take him out for a quiet drink that no one else knows about, no one at all, not Harvinder or Helena or anyone. Just you two. And get your heads together. I've got to go now.' I dropped the receiver and prepared to scamper. The phone rang within seconds. Let it. I had an innings to watch.

Chapter Twenty-Two

I was too old, wasn't I? Too old for all the chanting and Mexican waves and silly wigs and obscene language. OK, cricket's only a game, and a carnival atmosphere never comes amiss. But it all seemed so contrived: young men coming to drink and yell, not to watch the game. I sat among other Victor and Victoria Meldrews, some of them younger than I, to be fair, lamenting the incursions of the loud, vulgar, drunken yob element.

'This lot here who don't know leg-spin from a leg bye. Only applaud the big hits, not lovely subtle shots like that – well played, sir!' My elderly neighbour got to his feet to applaud the delicate cut that brought the Bears' opener his fifty. Then he sat again. 'The whole world's dumbing down. Nothing on TV these days worth watching; Radio Four going to the dogs.'

The Glamorgan total was a reachable 223. Warwickshire were making a steady start, which reduced the likelihood of Mike fulfilling his ambition of getting a century in this match too. In any case, to be realistic, individual high scores requiring a slow build-up and lots of concentration were less important than everyone making a good total briskly, even if it meant taking a few risks. Hundreds were a very rare occurrence in one-day cricket. Or rather, day-night cricket.

In fact, the way the Bears were going, Mike might not be

called on to bat at all. I'd probably be more disappointed than he – after all, playing was his job, no more, no less.

A couple more overs, and then one of the openers got run out, risking a single that wasn't really there. According to the scorecard, Teddy was due in. Whoever had made the difficult decision to let him play had been fully justified. His bowling had been tidy, if not inspired. His fielding had been spot-on and he'd run the Glamorgan wicket-keeper out with a stunning return from the covers. He'd also held on to a brilliant but disputed catch which had dismissed their captain one short of his fifty. But the PA system announced – and I was on my feet cheering with all those I'd condemned as yobs five minutes earlier – that Mike Lowden had been moved up the order. Yes, he was running on to the field now, whirling his arms in that familiar delightfully threatening way.

My mobile phone rang. I switched it off.

No, he didn't get a fairy-tale hundred. A not-out eighty wouldn't do his average any harm, and he had the honour of hitting the winning runs with a towering six which landed about three yards from my seat, but it wasn't the same as a ton. Mike didn't seem put out, though, joining me in the bar, where I was with the teddy bear lady.

'I told you they'd make a lovely couple, Reg,' she said smugly to her husband, as Mike wrapped his arm round my shoulders and kissed me.

'All your idea, was it, Kath?' Reg demanded, waiting to shake Mike's hand in congratulation. 'Lovely innings, Mike. We'll be seeing you picked for Oz if you ask me, young man.'

'That's just what I told you, Reg. With this sort of form you must be top of their list, Mike. And you'll be going too, no doubt, young Sophie?'

It was as if someone had squeezed my heart, it hurt so much.

That was what all his success meant, wasn't it? That we'd be separated.

I shook my head, and hoped my voice would find its normal pitch. 'I shall be on a course – West Midlands University. So he'll have to go without me.'

'Well, you'll be able to go over for Christmas. And some-times they make them "no women" tours anyway, don't they? To make the men concentrate more, they say. Does it, Mike? Or does it just mean you lads can get up to other things?' Kath demanded.

He rubbed his hair, still glistening from the shower. 'It's tricky, isn't it? The lads have to stick together as a team, but believe me, you can get heartily sick of someone by the end of three months. So there's an argument for letting women come. But often they'll get bored, and they have their own difficulties, which sometimes spill over on to their partners. And if only a few of the women are there, it can be tough for the blokes who have no partner or whose partners are back home. Not easy either way. I suppose the logical compromise is shorter tours. Less cricket altogether.'

'Come on, you're only young!'

'No. We've all seen what the pressures can do. Look at brilliant men like Mike Atherton. You're not just playing the opposition, you know. You're playing the media. Look, Teddy's stuck on his own again—' Mike grinned apologetically.

There was far more noise coming from outside the ground than you'd have expected at ten-thirty or whatever time it was we left the bar. The smoke and beer fumes were making my eyes sore and Teddy, even with one of us on either side of him, was clearly unhappy. He'd been not out, too, with thirty-four – no cause for disappointment. He stuck to us like a leech as we headed for the car park, joining in the conversation with the briefest monosyllables.

Mike flipped me the keys. Raising an eyebrow I flipped them back and produced from my bag the duplicate set he'd given me.

After a certain amount of exploration I located the lights, and we set off. There was a little tail-back by the car park exit. The noise had intensified, and we could see that there was more than one set of flashing blue lights. Cars leaving the ground have to negotiate a fast, busy dual carriageway, and accidents are not unknown, either there or further down the road where cars turn into and out of Cannon Hill Park. So we prepared to squeeze past mangled metal.

What I was totally unprepared for was a pair of naked buttocks pressing up against my side window. I dug in my jacket pocket for my house keys, wound down the window an inch or so, and shoved a key as hard as I could into a specially fleshy bit. Then I rewound the window, easing the big car forward so that the police who were trying to clear the road would have a nice clear view of the car and its obvious team colours. I'd welcome a bit of protection. A hefty policeman in riot armour grabbed my mooner, frog-marching him away with neither haste nor dignity. Every few paces he had to stop to allow him to retrieve his shorts, drooping in the region of his knees. The mooner still rubbed his bum from time to time.

In the ground the deep dusk had been cut by powerful floodlights. Now, despite the street lights, it was imposs- ible to make out precisely what had happened. A couple of coaches were halfway across the road, surrounded by a lot of glass. Scuffles had broken out in several places, though the police were still managing to stop them from coalescing into a riot.

I inched a little further. Ideally I wanted to turn right towards Edgbaston, Harborne and home, but I'd have no objection at all to turning left and taking a circuitous route, especially when an orange-wigged, rugby-shirted young man built like a tank started to urinate on the car in front. As he peed, he yelled obscenities in a pure public school accent.

Anything to get out of this. As I looked for the best escape route, one of the youths skirmishing over by one of the coaches pointed at us and yelled. He rushed forward. It was touch and go whether he'd get to us before a policewoman my size got him. He was clearly after Teddy and, even as he went down under the WPC, was yelling and making obscene gestures. Others took up where he left off. I zapped the central locking on.

The big car rocked violently, a youth at each corner. As the police flung them off, others were there to take their places.

'Teddy – what the fuck are you doing? Get that seatbelt back on!' Mike rapped.

'If I go they'll leave you alone,' he said.

'Course they bloody won't. They don't like me much, either.'

I spotted an opening and shot forward, only three yards, but enough for the police to grab a few more bodies. I was pointing right: OK – I'd swing left, and clog the accelerator again. The police cordon split, and I headed for the gap. It closed behind us. I didn't hesitate.

'Good car,' I said, patting it lightly on the bonnet. 'Well done.'

Teddy stared at me.

'I couldn't have done that in mine,' I said. 'Too light. And the power steering helped too. Still,' I added, as Mike removed their bags from the boot, 'there's a lot to be said for a little anonymity, isn't there?'

'I've never seen anything like that,' he said. 'Never. I mean, noise is one thing. But that was a nightmare. Makes me quite yearn for the Long Room at Lord's. I see young Winston got a good set of figures again, by the way . . .'

I made hot chocolate, and longed passionately for my bed. Mike went up to use the bathroom first.

Teddy sat down opposite me at the kitchen table. He looked straight at me. 'The police saved our lives tonight,' he declared.

I nodded. I didn't think we'd been in quite such grave danger, but it wouldn't hurt him to get a rosier view of authority figures.

'Afzal thinks I should tell the police about the men who spiked my burger.'

I nodded again, more enthusiastically. 'He's absolutely right.'

'He said they'd protect me from the men who threatened me.'

'Of course they will.'

He looked at me, as if he wanted to believe me.

'You must, Teddy. And you must see them tomorrow. Before you even go to the ground. Someone like Harvinder Mann could come here. You liked him when you met him on Saturday, didn't you?'

He stared at the table. His features moved, tightening and relaxing with his thoughts.

From upstairs Mike yelled that the bathroom was clear.

'I liked Harvinder. But Mr Kirby – I think he would be better.'

I tried to follow his thought processes, but as Mike yelled again I gave up.

'Off you go and clean your teeth,' I said, as if he were eight. 'Don't take too long. It's very late.'

Meanwhile I phoned Ian, who tended to keep later hours than me. He answered first ring. God, not the bedside phone!

'It's OK, love, no need to apologise. I was having a read while Val finishes her bath. Go on.'

'There was a spot of bother at Edgbaston tonight. I was

wondering if you'd let me know if the grapevine throws anything in your direction.'

'Big area, Edgbaston,' he said doubtfully.

'Sorry. I meant the cricket ground. Confusing, isn't it?'

'What sort of bother?'

'Drunken yobbery, I'd say. But it just could be more than that. It seemed to be directed at Teddy.'

'The South African kid? A bit of race, you mean? OK, love. Now, before you go, we've got another wine-tasting competition coming up. Get your diary . . .'

Mike was asleep by the time I got to bed. I slipped in very tentatively, not wanting to wake him. But he reached for me and pulled me into our sleeping position, and I was still smiling when I fell asleep.

Chapter Twenty-Three

Mike and I split the morning's tasks quickly and easily. I phoned Peter Kirby to suggest that he or Harvinder talk to Teddy in what he almost certainly saw as the safety of my home. I phoned Afzal too. He should probably be here. When their interview was over, I'd then drive Teddy, hell for leather, to the ground.

Meanwhile, Mike was sorting out breakfast and clearing up. He'd go on alone to Edgbaston, telling whoever ought to know that Teddy would be there by start of play, though it was almost inevitable he'd miss net practice. I joined him, enjoying working by his side, while Teddy attacked the piano again.

'Have you made an appointment with your GP yet? That allergy.'

I gestured. 'When have I had time?'

'It's your health.' He passed me the phone, kissed me, and left.

The surgery was engaged, of course.

While we waited, Teddy drove me almost to distraction. He'd pick things up and put them down, pithering with fragile china I was beginning to acquire after all my collection had been smashed some years ago. Then he'd go and jab a few bars more on the piano. If I slipped out of the room, afraid that I was going to yell, he'd follow me. He was worried that if we went into the garden we wouldn't hear the doorbell. When the post arrived the poor kid nearly wet himself. He followed me into the kitchen.

I was always very systematic about dealing with the post. On a good day at least. The idea was to put stuff in appropriate piles – used stamps for Oxfam, envelopes for the paper bank, their contents in some sort of order for action. I was reading through an airmail from an ex-student when I noticed that Teddy was busy with a pencil on the back of one of the envelopes. He was working on a face. Intrigued, I none the less returned to the letter. But I did no more than skim through it: I wanted to see what he'd done.

I didn't recognise the subject. But I was sure I would if ever I met her. And would like her, the way those eyes gleamed from the work-weary face.

'My mum,' he said shyly.

'That's very good.'

'Sometimes when it rains I do pictures for the team,' he ventured. 'I could do one of you if you like.'

'I'd love one of Mike. Hey, I must have some paper somewhere.' I trotted upstairs, returning with some printer paper and a set of heritage pencils I'd treated myself to at some stately home or other. As an afterthought I found a rubber and a clipboard.

'There you are,' I said, handing them over casually.

He took them as if they were gold. 'For me?'

God, what a heel I'd been. I'd never even thought of giving them to him. 'For you.'

His smile turned the knife.

At last – though only forty minutes from when I first called – Harvinder and Peter arrived. Teddy fled to the loo. Just as they were about to tear their hair, Afzal arrived, the calm authority of his voice soothing me, and encouraging Teddy to emerge.

So there we all were, sitting round the dining table in my still un-spring-cleaned living room, everyone looking at me as if I'd somehow become the chair. Familiar if unlovely territory.

If that's what I had to do, I'd better get on with it.

I looked at Teddy, who picked miserably at a table mat, slopping coffee.

Even to me, the two officers looked intimidating. They started talking about detailed descriptions, serious accusations – all making him withdraw further into himself. At last, unable to bear the misery on his face any longer, I cut across Peter's spiel.

'Teddy – you know that picture you did earlier? Why don't you have a go at drawing those men?'

As he ran off to get the paper – we could hear his footsteps up the stairs and into and out of the spare room – Kirby grimaced. 'We're going to need pretty solid ID.'

'Give this a chance,' I said.

Clutching the pitiful little gift as if it were true bounty, Teddy slipped back into his place.

There was an embarrassed silence.

Peter said something inaudible to Harvinder. Afzal smiled at me, and strolled over to the patio door, opening it and breathing deeply.

'It's looking good,' he said. 'All those pink and purple flowers.'

'Petunias and fuchsias.'

'We need some rain,' Peter said. 'We get all this cloud and nothing much happens.'

'So long as it comes overnight and dries up in time for the cricket,' I said. 'Ah, Teddy – that's great.'

He demurred. Predictably. But I suspected he knew that what he'd done was good. He passed the sketch over to Afzal: it was of a strikingly good-looking man, probably in his thirties. 'I did this, too.' He fished a crumpled envelope from his clipboard. 'I – it's not good, I'm sorry.' His shrug added even more apology. 'This is one of them, too.'

Afzal took that as well, smoothing it flat. It showed another handsome face, shaded in pencil to suggest a suntan. But the hair was white. I'd no idea who the man was. Or had I? He was very like the one Mike and I had seen arguing with Barkat in that quiet corner of Sal's garden. By the sandpit. When Mike had ridiculed my desire to interfere. If only we hadn't dashed away so early, I'd have met him.

No, come to think of it, I couldn't regret leaving early.

Afzal beamed encouragement, passing the sketches on. Peter reacted to the one on the envelope. Not by much. But I'd swear he recognised the face.

'You're sure this is accurate?' he asked.

Teddy flung up his hands. 'I – I—'

'Just get on with the others,' I said. 'What do you mean, Peter, accurate?'

'I mean, this is the basis for a pretty serious accusation.'

'It was a pretty serious crime,' Afzal observed. 'Let's assume for a moment it is accurate, we need something to go on, and I'd have thought a pencil portrait would be better than – than a pen portrait,' he concluded in embarrassment.

There was silence, interrupted only by the scratch of the pencil.

'It's much more lifelike than your average photofit,' Harvinder agreed. 'What are the others like, son?'

Teddy slid the sheets across the table. This time it was Afzal's turn to blink in recognition. I waited with interest for my turn. And yes, my eyes must have flickered, too. Not that I knew the face, but there was something familiar about the thick neck and heavy shoulders.

'This man – he didn't do anything. He didn't laugh or anything. He just stood.'

'You couldn't do a back view of him, could you?' I asked.

Teddy nodded and got to work.

'We'd need a formal statement to go with these,' Peter said.

Afzal nodded courteously, and produced a thin sheaf of papers. He even had a copy for me, which Kirby registered without comment. It repeated pretty much what Teddy had said on Sunday, rendered carefully coherent by Afzal. Then he passed over another photocopy, which turned out to be of a letter he'd sent on Teddy's behalf to the England and Wales Cricket Board, and then another, sent to the Warwickshire authorities.

Teddy pushed a sheet straight to me: those bulky shoulders. No. I couldn't place them. Not yet. I'd have to wait for the answer to pop up when it was ready.

Truculently, it seemed to me at least, Kirby cast his eyes over that too. 'The trouble is,' he said, jabbing the pile he'd taken from Harvinder, 'however good they look, we've really no idea how accurate they are. I mean, what would a top barrister make of them? It's not as if Teddy's a regular artist, is it? Tell you what, we'll take them anyway, and get someone to flick through a few files – see if we can match any mugs.' The distinct impression was that someone would be wasting his or her time. 'OK?' He smiled around the table, gathering agreement. 'That OK by you, Teddy?'

Teddy nodded absently. He'd crooked his arm round his paper like a child doing a test, but we could see his pencil moving swiftly from side to side as if shading something in. No one spoke. At last, chin jutting for the first time, he lifted his arm and pushed a sheet across the table. His eyes sought and held Peter Kirby's.

Kirby had the grace to blush. Then he tucked the sketch under his chin, adjusting his expression slightly so it matched the one on the sheet of paper. He smiled. 'OK, kid. I take it all back. Mr Mohammed—'

'Afzal,' he suggested gently.

'Afzal. OK, we shall need to talk to Teddy properly. Will you want to be there?'

I opened my mouth to say I thought they were already talking to him properly or what were they doing cluttering up my living room.

But Afzal spread his hands. 'What better time than now?'

I wouldn't improve things by getting irritated. I stood up. 'You've got till ten-twenty. The club will need him then.'

Brewing fresh coffee and replenishing the biscuit plate, I refused to let myself worry about those familiar shoulders. Tapping gently, I pushed the door open. For once Teddy didn't seem to be on the defensive. He knew he'd scored with that drawing. They nodded their thanks; I left them to it again.

This time I managed to get through to the surgery. Success! There was an appointment available a week on Friday. As I put the phone down, it rang.

'Just thought I'd tell you what I found out about last night,' Ian Dale said, with no preliminaries. Perhaps senior ears were listening.

'Fire away.'

'Some silly sod cycled into a coach. Tight as Andronicus.' Ian wouldn't use words like 'pissed' to a woman. 'And when his mates came to pick him up – no, just a bloody knee, that's all – they realised there were a load of lads on the chara.'

I grinned. I loved Ian's blithe use of words long out of fashion.

'So they decided to have some fun. I don't think, to be

honest, the Glamorgan kids were averse. And then it got a bit more personal, like, when some Warwicks supporters took exception to one or two Welsh remarks, and vice versa. Sort of thing you expect with football, not cricket, isn't it?'

I agreed, and reminded him about the wine-tasting. Everything was quickly sorted.

I was checking over the supplies I needed for my day's cricket when the kitchen door opened and Afzal emerged carrying the empty coffee things. He put the tray carefully on the table before shutting the door behind him.

'You recognised some of those guys, didn't you?' he said.

'Two. And only half-recognised. I saw one at a party, talking to Barkat.'

'You'd better tell Kirby.'

I nodded. 'Who knew him too, I'm pretty sure. He tried not to react but I'll swear he did. I suppose you didn't notice anything?'

He shook his head. 'You could be in for an amusing conversation. I can't make the man out. It's as if he can't decide whether he's the hard guy or the soft guy. It was the same when he spoke to Mike at the beginning of this business. Half the time he seemed reluctant to probe, half he was downright offensive.'

'Mike didn't do it, you know.'

He didn't meet my eyes. 'I'm sure this morning's work will go a long way to proving that. It was a brilliant idea getting Teddy to do those sketches.'

'Not mine. His. Almost,' I conceded as Afzal laughed. 'Oh! The other guy—'

I stopped. Someone was opening the door to the living room.

Harvinder. He smiled as if interrupting something intimate.

213

I jumped straight in. 'That white-haired man . . .' I explained what I'd seen at Sal's party.

'And look what happened to Barkat. Funny, Sophie, we've talked to scores of folk since this inquiry started, but I've never come across anyone remotely like that.'

I raised my eyebrows. '*He* has.'

Harvinder jerked his thumb and mouthed his boss's name. 'He recognised him?'

'I'd go on oath,' I said.

'You might have to. I don't like this business. When I was at college I had this woman teacher who reckoned she could pluck ideas from our heads we didn't know we had. She wrote the question in the middle of the board and drew all these lines radiating from it. Spider-charts, she called them. This case looks like one of her spiders.'

'I call them sunbursts, on account of I'm not an arachnid fan. Hell, Harvinder, why don't we try that. One for Barkat, one for Guy – see what they have in common?'

There were noises from the living room – chairs being pushed back.

'I think we may have to do them separately, but I'd like to see the result. Have you thought any more about the non-communication problem?'

'A lot. Don't ask me what to do about it, though. Maybe something'll come into my head while I do my sunburst.'

And maybe it wouldn't. Not publicly. It was up to Chris to move, not me. And I wasn't going to breathe a word to anyone, not even to someone I liked as much as Harvinder. Who could I – who, more to the point, could Chris – trust in all this? I watched the two officers thanking Teddy and shaking hands formally with Afzal, and stood on the front step seeing them off. Afzal dawdled, inspecting a nasty infestation of greenfly on one of my favourite roses – another job my love-life had put on hold. I sighed – there'd soon be plenty of away matches when I could garden and clean to my heart's content. Unless I became a camp-follower. Mike's theories about team wives seemed at odds with his practice, so I couldn't predict what he'd prefer. As for me – but Afzal, having waved Kirby and Mann off, sauntered back to me.

He looked straight at me. 'You've placed the other man, haven't you?'

'I saw him leaving your office, trying too ostentatiously *not* to be seen. And he was – he was at that party.' I laughed. Thank you, mental toaster. 'Pissing into a swimming pool. I suppose you can't tell me who he is?'

He shook his head. 'Not by name. But the funny thing is, Sophie, in a way he was in the same fix as our young friend. I'm certain they wanted to blackmail him: *unless you do what we tell you, we'll blazon your drugs escapade all over the tabloids.* My client – the other client, that is – is in the public eye, too.'

'Could he not be persuaded' – why did I always start mimicking his formal delivery? – 'to speak to the police?'

Afzal raised his hands, palms upwards. 'Do you think I haven't tried?'

Crying *Oy vay* in a tone that matched his incredibly Semitic gesture would scarcely be tactful. I pulled what I hoped he'd take as a sympathetic face. We both knew that if he couldn't persuade whoever it was to go to the police, I'd have to tell Chris or Kirby myself.

'How's Fozia? And when's the wedding? And when am I going to meet her?'

'Well, and soon to both the other questions. Since she's a widow she wants a very quiet wedding, just for our families. Immediate family, that is, otherwise we'd be in the hundreds, I think. And then a civil ceremony: it would be lovely if you could come to that.'

'Try and keep me away! And a wedding list?'

'We have all the contents of two family homes. We have no need of anything.'

'Well, you'll have to have something you don't need, won't you? Thanks for being so good with Teddy. It's a pleasure watching you.'

'You seem – very much on edge, shall I say? Is everything all right between you and Mike?'

'Fine. As fine as it can be. Apart from—' My wild gesture incorporated the crime that was enmeshing us.

He nodded. 'Chris'll soon sort it out. Teddy is a charming and talented young man, but the last thing anyone needs at the start of a relationship is someone like him to look after.'

So he wasn't finding his fiancée's children easy!

'Get him out of your hair. There's no reason, surely, why he should stay with you. He's got perfectly good lodgings.'

'Trouble is,' I said, 'it's me who's got the piano.'

I got Teddy to the ground with a few moments to spare, and, thanks to Mike's forethought, was even allowed to park in the players' car park. The Renault crept into a space between two Peugeots, no doubt feeling a touch intimidated.

Apart from the roar of traffic along Pershore Road and Edgbaston Road, the ground was very quiet: I suppose that was natural on a Wednesday morning. Even the teddy bear lady was missing. But there was enough of a hum to remind us that Warwickshire were heading purposefully up the league table, that several of their players were in exceedingly fine form and that a good day's play was in prospect. It would have been better if we'd won the toss, from my point of view at least. But I told my brain to come up with at least one useful idea during the morning's play, and settled down to watch.

As Glamorgan's opener took guard, a motorcycle roared

past the ground, heading over-fast for the city. There was another factor I could insert on some chart or other – my own, perhaps. When Chris had been talking to Mike and me about Barkat's fatal accident, he'd mentioned a third *vehicle*. At the time I'd assumed it was jargon for a car. What if it wasn't? What if my motorbike and Barkat's were the same? I shivered, and not with the cool of an English summer's day.

Chapter Twenty-Four

Four-day county championship matches aren't necessarily exciting for every moment – hence the constant striving of the cricket authorities to achieve a balance between the sort of serious cricket that prepares players for the prolonged intensity of the international Test scene and fast-moving limited-over games that will fill the grounds with paying spectators. Today's was the sort of game that would have had sneerers pointing accusing fingers: Glamorgan were scoring very slowly, but the Bears were unable to take any wickets. Mike was fielding out in the covers, Teddy at square leg. Neither had done anything spectacular so far. It would be interesting to see how Teddy bowled, though the overcast, cool conditions wouldn't favour him particularly. Barkat, now – he'd have been useful on a day like this.

Barkat. Apparently of its own accord my organiser with its pencil found its way on to my lap. I didn't have enough space for a sunburst – I was used to the wide expanses of college whiteboards, palimpsests though they were, no one apparently having the correct markers in the first place or the right chemicals to erase their mistakes.

Nothing daunted, I started to scribble, deliberately trying not to list ideas in any order but to slap them down as they occurred to me. Later, if play didn't perk up, I'd turn my attention to Guy Timpson.

BARKAT

Seen in Harborne, Smethwick and Sal's
\
        White haired man
        – WHO? And how
        does Kirby
        know him?

  talk to Peugeot (not my job – police)
/
CARS – why so many? – accident-prone or what!!!
|

*chase – any chance of computer enhancement? – Chris
or Peter!!!*
|

drugs – prostitute

At this point Glamorgan lost their first wicket. I didn't see
it, of course. And with an ordinary county match there's no
big screen to watch a replay from every angle. I even had
to look at the scoreboard to see how he'd gone: lbw to the
opening bowler, in what would probably have been his last
over, given the length of time he'd been toiling away. So
would he be kept on, or allowed a rest? Normally the more
vociferous spectators would have been free with their advice.
Today, possibly as a result of the previous evening's violence,
everyone seemed very subdued.

They kept the bowler on.

OK, what about—

TIMPSON

WHERE ARE – Epipen
          – camera

Drugs – personal use/distribution? – source of supplies?

Why did he spend so much time in Oldbury if he was based in Rutland? – Connection Sal – if any, apart from party. (She seemed to know him well!!! – sex?)

all those other women

revenge?

women men

Connection with press? Blackmail? Bank account? (Interesting!)

There was a smatter of applause for – oh, yes, for a boundary. I pushed the pencil back into its holder, but then fished it out again, if only to chew. *Blackmail* – there was Afzal's client, too. Not to mention poor Teddy, who was now, it seemed, about to bowl. Why hadn't Guy tried to blackmail me, rather than simply send the photos to the press? Well, he'd only have to look at me to see I didn't have much money – I'd been decidedly low couture, hadn't I? Or should it be *bas* couture? And he'd know that although Winston had potential, he'd have student debts to pay off. More money from the press, then. Or was he just acting out of malice?

My brain was getting tired – pretending it was a toaster was far more efficient. And meanwhile Teddy had bowled a maiden over. The piano therapy seemed to be working. What a talented kid he was: I can play from music, and not badly, actually, and I can sing well enough to be in that choir I'd been neglecting. But I couldn't improvise the way he could, with both hands and voice. And his skill with the pencil –

thank God for families probably almost as poor as his own clubbing together to get him his education. And thank God for the changes in South Africa as a whole: other talented Teddies would get an education as their right, not as charity.

An appeal for a catch! Not out. Not a murmur of protest from the crowd. If only Mike bowled. If only anyone could do anything. If only I could talk to Chris. Maybe him and Peter Kirby together.

What I really, really wanted to do was see Timpson's house. Inside. For myself. I was sure the police would have any number of photographs I might wheedle my way into seeing, but I wanted to get the feel of the place. Where did he keep all that was private? His addresses? His files on people like me and Winston? His contacts? His accounts? I'd met a sensual, selfish man – but there was a lot more to him than that. He wasn't just a womaniser, by all accounts: he was trying to outdo Don Giovanni, without the sort of music that might have tempted even me. In these days all that sexual activity was risky – how many women had Giovanni infected, come to think of it? Still, no doubt Leporello would have had some pots of ointment to offer. What was the male equivalent of nymphomania? I ought to know, though God knows it was rarely used. Perhaps because so few people could pronounce it. Satyriasis, that was it. So was it a problem with his self-image? Some hidden hurt that drove him? I wanted to find someone who liked him, to shed another light. The nearest so far was Sal, who'd laughed away what she saw as peccadilloes.

Sal! If only I'd had space to draw a spider-chart I could have put her at the middle. Couldn't I?

There was another appeal. This time it was successful. The Bears rushed together in hand- and back-slapping celebration, as if they'd toppled an international giant not an ordinary club player. Eighty for two. And nearly lunch. Not exciting.

One person I could ask about Sal, of course, was Mike. I had a terrible niggling ache of suspicion that he hadn't been as frank with me as he could have been about his dealings with her. Indeed, so far most of the honest revelations had been on my side, after, of course, what he'd told me of his wife. Gloom and disgruntlement were settling nicely when Teddy tossed up a lovely, airy ball and got the third wicket with the last ball before lunch.

After lunch the play started to go the Bears' way – a steady fall of inexpensive wickets. Teddy bowled tidily and took three of them. Mike fielded briskly but wasn't involved in any wicket-taking. Halfway through the tea interval, reading away through one of those books I needed for September, I was summoned by my mobile phone. Aggie!

'I'm sorry to bother you, me love, only I've been and done something really stupid.'

'How can I help?'

'Oh, there's nothing you can do. It's what I've done, isn't it? This man on a motorbike came to me door with a letter or something for someone whose name I didn't know.'

Motorbike? My heart started pounding uncomfortably.

'Kent or Kant or somesuch,' Aggie was saying. 'My address. So of course I said it wasn't for me. And he says maybe it's for next door. No, I say, no one that name living there. So, he says, who does live there? And I only went and told him, didn't I? Gave him your name and all. I'm ever so sorry, me love.'

So was I. But by not so much as a squeak of the voice would I let Aggie know. 'No problem,' I said briskly. 'You know getting into my house is like getting into Fort Knox. And to find me all he'd have to do is look me up in the phone book or electoral register. If that's what he wanted, of course. He might really have been after that Kant or Kent.'

'Hmm. I don't reckon . . . Nice kid, very polite, all the same. Perhaps one of your students playing a joke or summat.'

'What did he look like?'

'What can you tell under them great helmets? Oh, he tipped his visor back a bit, but not so I could see his whole face.'

What I wanted to do was ask about his ethnicity, but Aggie had no truck with my PC language. So I said, 'How did he speak? Any accent?'

'Nothing special. You know – like all these kids speak. I looked for any – what did Chris call them? Distinguishing marks? – but he was clean-shaven and he'd got nice straight teeth. Couldn't see his eyes, of course, 'cause of that visor, but I'd guess they'd be blue. Very fair, he was.'

Good for Aggie.

'Like Chris. I don't know why you two don't just do the sensible thing and settle down,' she continued. 'All this on-off stuff.'

'He's got a nice woman-friend,' I said. 'Helena. You'll be meeting her at Ian's party.'

'Hmm. I'd better meet this Mark of yours. All this jumping over me fence and running through me house like he owned it.'

'Mike. He'd have come round yesterday to explain except we got tied up with the police and a doctor for Teddy. That was the black lad who hopped your fence first.'

'You and your young men. Anyway, this call's costing me an arm and a leg, isn't it? Being as it's to a mobile. Oh, I've put what I owe you for me heavy stuff through your door, me love. You couldn't get me some bathroom cleaner next time, could you? Only me tiles are a disgrace.'

Oh God. I shoved the phone away and dropped my head into my hands. This was all I needed. Not that I blamed Aggie in any way. She was one of the most helpful souls on God's earth, kind too. And what I'd said was true: my address was public knowledge. I tried to convince myself the enquiry was genuine, from one of my students, perhaps. No, surely not. The vast majority of them were Asian or Afro-Caribbean in origin, and although many would have passed, had they ever wanted to, as Mediterranean, none could be described as fair. I cast mental eyes over this and last year's intakes, and found no one. It had to be the guy who had been tailing me.

I know I yelped – I might have screamed. Something was pressing against my hand, something soft.

I saw huge bees, killer wasps! And then, opening my eyes, flinging my hands wide, I knocked away – a small bear.

'Oh, I'm so sorry.' It was the teddy bear lady, of course. 'We've only just come and this little chap thought you needed cheering up a bit.'

I hoped my smile looked genuine enough. My hands shook a bit, though, as I stuck one out for the bear. 'I certainly do,' I said. 'Do you think he'd come and sit on my knee for a bit?'

The arrival of the players on the pitch spared me any explanations. With a little bit of help, the bear applauded vigorously.

Drizzle and bad light brought the day's play to an early halt, and no one seemed to want to spend long drinking. I set off home with Teddy; Mike would come on later as soon as he'd picked up clothes and other stuff from his house. What he'd make of the posse of police cars outside my place, I'd no idea. Teddy certainly didn't greet them with any enthusiasm, but I packed him off into the living room while I found out what was going on.

Aggie had been going on, of course. She'd phoned Ian, after an afternoon no doubt spent agonising, and now several young constables were scrabbling round looking under my shrubs and behind my tubs to see if any package lay concealed. 'For package, read explosive device,' one young woman said, peering into the depths of a trough of petunias.

'For explosive device, read bomb,' I amended.

But there was nothing, nor in the back garden. Ian emerged from Aggie's, kissing her soundly on the cheek. He sent the damp and miserable kids back to the station, and invited himself in, not for further tea, but for the bathroom, I suspected. Aggie's loo is surrounded by a tubular frame supporting a high seat, these days, and I suspected other people, like me, preferred a more conventional one.

'In one sense I'm glad someone else has seen him,' I said, putting on the kettle anyway and finding some biscuits. I wouldn't fill the plate, knowing Teddy's propensity for emptying it. 'So it's not a fig-leaf of my imagination. But I wish – I wish they'd just count me out of this one, Ian.'

'Not surprised you're rattled, love. At least you've got someone to keep an eye on you!' He stood up to greet Mike, who had, of course, missed the drama. 'No, not for me, thanks. No more.' He paused, drawing in breath deeply and catching my eye. Not for anything would he complain about Aggie's brew, but he'd had more than enough tannin and caffeine for one day. He was running his tongue over his teeth, as if to clean them. 'She must have been worrying about this business all afternoon, bless her – only called me half an hour ago. Just as I was leaving for home, matter of fact. But at least she can rest content that there's nothing untoward in your garden.'

'Tell you what, Ian, why don't you eat with us? Wednesday's Val's keep-fit night, isn't it? She won't be expecting you. Grilled chicken. Organic.'

He grinned. 'Seeing as you've talked me into it.'

One thing I'd forgotten to buy was a new bottle of Fino. Ian liked his sherry as dry as it came. Mike sized up the situation at a glance, and dragged Teddy off to get some. The chicken could marinate in honey, garlic and lemon juice while it waited for them. Ian fussed over my last bottle of Pouilly-Fumé, trying to get it to the right temperature. I laid the table and prepared the vegetables: a few courgettes from my garden which the slugs had already tasted, broccoli that was free from the horrible little caterpillars that infested mine when I'd last tried to grow it, but no doubt drenched in insecticide to achieve its perfection, and new potatoes.

'Here, try this,' Ian said, as proud as if he'd bottled the wine himself.

The bouquet was heady with fruit and flowers and that curious flintiness. I sipped. And bent double with the pain.

'For God's sake – what's the matter? Sophie? You all right?' Mike's hands were on my shoulders.

I put down the glass and tried to straighten. 'It's OK.'

'It's obviously not. Here—' He tried to sit me down.

I resisted: it was more comfortable to stand. Meanwhile Ian plodded over to a far cupboard and returned with my antacid medicine and a large spoon. He sucked his teeth. 'I know it's chicken and that's as fine a wine as you'll come across, but I think you should stick to red if your stomach's like that.' He turned to Mike. 'Teacher's tum, she calls it. Stress. That business this afternoon, I suppose.'

'Business? What's been going on?'

'Pour Ian some of that and I'll explain as I cook. No, nothing for me till I've eaten, thanks.'

'Why didn't you tell me?' Mike demanded as we settled down for the night.

'Because I didn't know. Not until I came home and found half the West Midlands Police Service hunting for slugs.

Anyway, you can see I'm being looked after – Ian and Aggie. What's the matter?'

He pulled a face. 'It's just that – I don't know – you're surrounded by all these people who've known and loved you since the year dot . . .'

'I'd rather be surrounded by you.' But I sat up. 'It's a problem we both have to face, coming comparatively late into each other's lives. I'm at sea with Sal and your friends, you with mine. It'll take time. And effort. We'll manage, won't we?'

He nodded. 'Provided you promise me one thing. That I can meet Aggie tomorrow.'

Chapter Twenty-Five

I declined a jog but had the satisfaction of seeing Teddy and Mike lope off, Mike with a small rucksack on his back so he could buy the cleaner Aggie wanted. Meanwhile it was perfunctory housework time, a dash round with the vac, if not the duster. The bathroom had its share of attention while I cleaned my teeth. It was just like being at work. Except I wasn't used to chopped-up bristle scumming my wash-basin. I would have to establish a few house rules about that, and about the hair in the bath.

Then I popped a few defrosted rashers of bacon under the grill: eggs? Mushrooms? It depended how much of a feast the men wanted. My credit-card bill arrived in the middle of all this activity, putting me off my food.

Breakfast over, I let Mike take the cleaning stuff to Aggie. Teddy needed a certain amount of dragooning into the world of tidying up, during which I initiated him into the rites of dishwasher-stacking and table-wiping. If he was to be my lodger, he'd have to do his share. And maybe that was an option for the winter: what about taking a lodger? If – and at this stage it was a big if – I were going to join Mike in Australia, I'd have to raise money somehow, and I wasn't sure my brain was up to part-time work and full-time study. Let the mental toaster come up with something in that field.

Meanwhile I prepared my picnic lunch. Lots of bland stuff.

My stomach had scared me last night. It's one thing to have gastritis because you're working so many hours there's no time to eat; another to get a twinge just because life ruffles you a bit. There was some chicken, some salad . . .

Hell! Even the ring of the phone was enough to raise a twinge. Teddy seized the chance to scuttle off to the piano. I had to shut the door on him to hear the caller. Chris.

'Are you all right?' I asked. 'I hardly recognised your voice.'

'Bit of hay-fever. Look, I need to talk to you. This morning OK?'

At this point Mike pushed open the front door.

'Hang on a moment.' I covered the phone. 'Are you batting at number three this morning?'

He nodded, beaming.

'And are you going to get that hundred for me?'

Another nod; another beam, and a hand on the nape of my neck.

I uncovered the phone. 'Sorry, Chris,' I said. 'It'll have to be later. This evening, perhaps?'

'It's important.'

Idly I wondered how many times I'd made him wait. I couldn't recall any. Despite the full-time job, which for some reason he'd never considered as taxing as his.

'OK. I'll clear this evening. Will you eat with us?'

'I'd rather speak to you on your own.'

Mike might have overheard. I flashed a look at him. Certainly the laugh had gone from those clear blue eyes.

'In that case, eat with us first and talk to me while Mike and Teddy wash up. Eight-ish?' And I put the phone down. I don't know what Mike felt about my response, but for once in my relationship with Chris, I felt grown-up.

Edgbaston was gleaming after the rain, the hanging baskets

a-glow. On the other hand, the pitch might be tricky for an hour or so, especially if it had sweated under the covers. I said nothing to Teddy about Chris's call: sufficient unto the hour . . . Mike had looked at me with great tenderness each time we stopped at lights, and reached for my hand when he could.

There was much more buzz around the ground this morning, and there was no doubt in my mind that Mike was the crowd-puller. But then, I was biased. I tried not to ill-wish either of the openers, and, when I saw the way the ball was skidding and lifting on the damp pitch, rather hoped they'd stay put as long as possible. The rain had left the outfield slow as well, if slippery under running feet. All in all I thought I'd settle for a good solid century rather than an ill-fated attempt to score quickly and get out foolishly.

Both the openers were soon out to nasty, whipping deliveries. Which brought Teddy and Mike together just – I swear – as the sun broke through. Steam rose from the rows of seats. I tried to remember the effect rapid drying would have on a pitch, but failed, as Mike was dropped by first slip off a well-nigh unplayable ball. He took fresh guard – a psychological error, I thought, as it gave impetus to an already hostile opening bowler. Yes, a vicious bouncer – which Mike calmly hooked for four, the proper response to a ball coming in at that pace and that height. That was the keynote of his innings. Teddy lacked his experience of drying wickets, but was apparently untroubled, though he seemed happy to play second fiddle to Mike. It was a totally absorbing contest, fine bowlers not giving any chances to even finer batsmen, who none the less slowly but inexorably took control. Maybe that hundred was possible after all.

I was standing applauding the third six of the over when I was aware of a shadow falling on me.

It took me a moment to register.

'Chris!' I turned and then, thinking better of it, sat down again.

He did not respond to my smile. 'What the hell are you doing, slamming down the phone on me like that and leaving your mobile switched off? This is police business, Sophie. You don't mess around with the law like this.'

For a moment I suspected him of self-parody and started to giggle. Mistake. Big mistake. Chris always took himself seriously, didn't he?

I gestured like a hostess for him to sit. I couldn't keep my eyes off the pitch. This, then one more over before lunch, and Mike was on eighty-seven. It was possible. Just.

'We have to talk,' Chris said.

'Fine. Look at that!'

An elegant leg-cut bringing in three. Ninety.

'I repeat, I'm here on police business. To talk to you.'

'I thought you were on that course . . . Oh, you can talk all you like – yes!' Teddy had stolen a single to give Mike the batting for the last over. 'At the end of this over.'

'Now.'

'For God's sake, Chris! Just sit down a moment and enjoy this!'

By now there were forcible suggestions from spectators whose view he was blocking. He sat. 'Do I have to arrest you? Because as God is my witness, I will.'

'For what? Asking you to wait three minutes for Mike to score ten more runs? I wouldn't have thought it of you.' I was ready to weep, mostly with anger but also with the unfairness of it. Last Sunday I'd missed everything, and now – but Mike had hit a majestic six. Four to go. But no more this over. Mine wasn't the only sigh.

The umpires walked briskly to their new places. The clock said there was half a minute to go. They could have brought the players in for lunch. But perhaps even umpires are human – especially this one, who in his day had been a fine batsman. He signalled another over. And earned an ovation all to himself.

Another stolen single from Teddy, scampering as if the hounds of hell were after him to give Mike the strike again.

By now even Chris was quiet. In spite of himself, he was watching the players. Two to mid-wicket. A chance of a single he had to ignore. And then – yes! – another boundary, even if it were the sort of stroke best forgotten, sneaking through the slips.

As one, we rose to applaud. The true aficionados were trying to work out how long it had been since a Warwickshire player had scored hundreds before lunch in successive first-class matches. I was in tears, much to my surprise, and found people coming to pat me on the back, as if they were touching Mike by proxy.

He played out the over and cantered off the pitch, the Glamorgan players generously applauding him all the way.

'All that,' said Chris, 'for a man who I have reason to believe has committed one of the nastiest murders I've come across.'

We walked in silence to Chris's car, which was baking after even such a short time. He turned the ignition and opened the windows. We were no more private now than if we'd been standing in the open, but no doubt it felt more like it to him.

'OK,' I said, 'tell me.' I wouldn't let a doubt creep into my mind, let alone my voice.

He drew in breath slowly, heavily, and let it out in a sigh. 'How can I?'

'That's what you came all the way here to do, isn't it?'

'As a matter of fact it isn't. I came to thank you for

bollocking me the other day. Peter and I had a most productive half-hour over a beer last night.'

'Never mind that now. Mike. You were accusing Mike of murder, as I recall.'

'We've just discovered that Michael Lowden had access to Timpson's house.'

'Access to Timpson's house. How come?'

'I should never have mentioned—'

'Well, you did.' Probably because he was jealous of Mike, come to think of it. If ever my face had glowed with naked love, it had glowed for Mike this morning. Poor Chris. He'd had ample time, no doubt, to reflect on our bad times in bed as well as the good, the tensions always controlling our relationship. I'd never looked at him like that. Nor anyone else, come to think of it.

He was staring at his hands, the knuckles white on the steering wheel. Not that he'd ever have driven like that. Too well trained. A good driver. I'd put my life in his hands without hesitation.

Or had I put it into the hands of a killer?

'If you really think Mike did it, shouldn't you be talking to him?' I said at last, my voice as sharp as if I were back in the classroom. Mike would be expecting to see me, wouldn't he? A sneaked kiss by the dressing room, blind eyes turned. All my body wanted to think about was his tenderness this morning, and half my brain wanted to join in. But the other half was beginning to work with unpleasant clarity.

Chris bit his lip.

'We've been mates too long for this,' I said. 'Do you really in your heart think Mike killed Timpson?'

He stretched out his fingers: 'He had motive, knowledge – you didn't tell me he was a biologist, did you? – opportunity.'

'He'd have had a greater motive to kill him before I came

on the scene – I take it you know all about Timpson's affair with his wife? Yes, he'll have told you himself. I'm sure he also told you about the degree in biology. But opportunity? Come on, Chris, you know as well as I do he couldn't have removed the Epipen and disposed of it that lunchtime – damn it, you told us that.'

'He could have taken it earlier. When the bag was still at Timpson's house.' He dropped his voice. 'He has a key, Sophie.'

I knew something didn't make sense, but he overrode my protest.

'We've been talking to Mike's ex-wife. Sandra. She says she left Timpson's keys in a box of stuff still in Mike's house. He could have got access,' he repeated, stubborn as a schoolkid with a dodgy excuse.

'Not that she isn't an ex-nurse herself,' I said, 'with what might be a bit of a grudge, come to think of it. Might resent both men – want to land Mike in it as well as bumping off Timpson. Two in one fell swoop.' I wondered why the angrier I got, the more frivolous my speech became.

He looked at me coldly. 'She has a cast-iron alibi. She was working in France all the relevant period.'

I looked at my watch. 'I have to go and speak to Mike,' I said. 'I missed his last hundred altogether with that Teddy business – I don't want him to think I didn't see this. I take it, by the way, that Sandra couldn't just have zapped back here, done the deed and skipped back again? I wonder if Art what's-his-name could have . . . Anyway, the offer still holds, Chris. Come and have supper with us all; if you want to talk to me alone, that can always be arranged.'

'You simply haven't grasped what I've been saying. How can I sit down to eat with a man I suspect of murder? OK, I haven't a warrant. But as sure as hell I want to check out his house. I'll walk round now with you, shall I, and tell him. Officially.'

He got out of the car without waiting for a reply, and had to get back in for the electric window-winders to work. At last he looked at me.

'OK. But I'll want to go round to Mike's with you both.'

'I shan't object. He might, of course.'

'Will anyone else be there?'

'Peter Kirby, possibly. Or Harvinder Mann.'

As we approached the dressing room, another thought struck me: 'He's halfway through an innings. If you drop this sort of thing on him it'll hardly improve his concentration. Not to mention the interest the media will take.'

Chris never had been any good at dissembling; I could see the battle between fairness and the law being played out on his face.

'Switch your phone on. OK. So you'll call me the minute he's out,' he said, turning on his heel without waiting for an answer.

One thing about teaching is that it develops one's acting skills impressively. Your heart can be bleeding but you still have to go in there and teach *Hamlet* or whatever. So I didn't think Mike would pick up too much of my anxiety. I hoped not. In the event, he was a mixture of elation and disbelief.

'What we are going to do,' he said into my hair, 'is have the celebration of a lifetime. Teddy'll have to put up with an evening on his own – or go back to his lodgings. You and I are going to have a night to remember.'

I hoped so. Indeed, I hoped so. Meanwhile I had to make the Judas kiss.

Mike was back at the wicket, and though he must have seen

the ball as big as if it were the moon, he was trying to take a back seat to Teddy, giving him as much of the bowling as he could. A little knot of fans had gathered close enough to talk to, if I'd wanted conversation. The sun continued to shine. The teddy bear lady had found a small pair of shades, and her bear was basking in the heat, despite the vicissitudes of a thick fur coat.

Dead on three, the phone tweeted. Sick, I slipped to the back again, and took the call.

'I been thinking, me love, about that young man of yours. Mark.'

'Mike.'

'Now, I know he brought me that cleaning stuff and I'm not saying I'm not very grateful, but I reckon he's too much of a charmer for you. No, you listen to me. He goes all over the country with this job of his, and all over the world, from what he was saying. Are you sure he hasn't got a girl in every port? A man like that, as would charm the ducks off the water, he'd be bound to have lots of women, wouldn't he? Stands to reason. And you don't want to get yourself a bad name, you know. It won't have done you any good to get in all them papers with young Watson. No, you want to know what I think? If it's really over between you and Chris, I think you should get back to young Azfal.'

'Afzal. He's getting married to someone else,' I said as baldly as I could. 'And you know I owe Winston my life. No, Aggie, I respect your judgement, but I love Mike and—'

'Love! You've only known him five minutes. Be talking about getting married next! You hold your horses, me love. Now, the reason I phoned is this. This woman was asking for you this afternoon. Nice-looking woman. Asked for you by name. Didn't let on anything, of course, not after yesterday. Well, she's left you a note. I'll give it you when I see you.'

When she could just as easily have got the woman to push it through my front door. Aggie! Blast her! I stumped back to my seat, worrying a hang-nail.

'Bad news?' asked the teddy bear lady.

I shook my head. But I might as well have nodded, for Mike chose that moment to scoop a ball he should have left alone straight down the bowler's throat.

Chapter Twenty-Six

If Mike was lying, he was as expert as I was.

'Keys to Timpson's place? What the hell are you on about?'

Chris, his face as grim as I'd ever seen it, stood his ground, a policeman from the tips of his shoes to the crown of his balding head. Peter Kirby stood shoulder to shoulder with him. Feeling I'd obscurely betrayed Mike, simply by phoning to announce his dismissal, I now moved as close to him as I could. His hair was still wet from the shower, and he smelt clean and sweet.

'Let's just go and take a little look,' Kirby said, reasonably. 'That'll soon put everything straight. Tell you what, we'll all go in one of our cars, shall we?' Without any visible gesture, he started to move us along – years of training, I reflected bitterly.

'Not a good idea,' I said. 'The place is swarming with the media. One sniff and they'll be baying after Mike. And you. Look, why doesn't Mike put it about that he's got problems with his contact lenses. Maybe that's why he dollied that catch.' I risked an affectionate grin. 'We'll meet you at his place.'

'And I suppose you'll drive him straight there, no thoughts of a quick nip-off down the motorway?' Peter's voice dripped with irony.

'I'd have thought his face was well enough known to make that a pretty remote chance. And Chris knows I keep my word.'

'Does Lowden keep his?' Peter asked.

'I'll pick you up at the traffic lights, shall I?'

Chris looked at the three of us in turn. Without prompting, he stuck out his hand and switched on a brilliant smile. 'Yes, a great knock, Mike. It was a privilege to have seen it.'

Perhaps he too had seen the reporter.

Publicly, Mike said, 'Thanks. I hope you didn't miss too much of that course to watch.' He dropped his voice. 'I'm still working, you know, during the hours of play. I'll have to get permission to leave the ground.'

'That shouldn't be a problem, not if you've got lens trouble,' Chris said.

Mike turned back into the building.

Kirby flapped a hand. 'I'll be by the lights, then.'

Chris grinned and waved him off. Did all this acting mean he had a residual doubt? Or was it just his natural loathing of publicity? Anyway, after a toothy grin to me, which failed signally to reach his eyes and activate his crow's-feet, he waved and headed off, presumably to the car park.

Mike seemed a long time gone. What must he be thinking of my part in all this? How could I explain or excuse myself if he thought I was on Chris's side?

He was still in his Bears tracksuit when he emerged, taking my hand and, despite the searing heat, setting off briskly for the car park.

'Your car or mine?' he asked.

'Keep dabbing your eye. Mine. Less obtrusive.'

Everyday voices, prosaic chat. If he was anxious, he didn't want to scare me. Two minutes of private conversation should clarify everything. But that was something Joe Public was determined to prevent. The handsome hero with the tissue-covered eye had to have his hand shaken by all and sundry, and even as I nosed gently towards the gate there were still thanks to be given.

Despite Peter's half-irate, half-chummy attempts at conversation, I didn't speak during the short journey to Bournville. I could have blamed the glitter of the half-melting tarmac, the heavy traffic, other drivers' carelessness. Instead I concentrated on getting there in one piece. Chris didn't help matters: he was waiting in Pershore Road, and when he picked me up he stuck to my rear bumper as if I were towing him.

'We have a witness prepared to testify on oath that you have keys to Timpson's house,' Chris said flatly.

'I don't know what you're talking about.' Mike gripped the kitchen table.

Like the rest of the house, the room was airless, baking. I struggled to open the window over the sink. Peter reached across to help me, five-ten to my five-one. Easy.

'OK, Mike. Put it this way. When you and your wife divorced, you failed to return some of her property. What Peter and I should be doing is asking our officers to turn over your house, piece by tiny piece. What I am doing is asking you to hand the property over to me. Including the keys. After that – well, we'll see.'

Mike leaned dangerously towards him, open-mouthed. 'Failed to return some of her property! The bitch! The fucking bitch! Sure I've got some of her property. It's in my bloody loft because she couldn't get it into her flat. She could have had it any time she wanted it. Shit!' He slammed his open hand on the table, then had to pick up the salt and pepper mills which he'd upset. 'She's your witness, is she? Very reliable, I'd say.'

Chris ignored the sarcasm, watching him calmly. 'All right: let's go and have a look at that loft.'

'You have to pull down the cover – there are steps which let down from the loft itself,' Mike said, leading the way upstairs. Chris followed, then Kirby, then me. 'Do you want to go up or shall I? I know where it is, after all.'

'There's room for two of us, surely?' Chris was in menacing mode again.

Nodding, Mike retrieved an aluminium rod with a plastic hook from a corner and opened the door. Heat poured from the aperture like water. The ladder descended section by noisy section.

'After you,' he gestured.

Chris nodded and set off.

I don't think I've ever seen him move so fast. He was down that loft ladder like a monkey down a stick. He flailed at the loft hatch. But it wouldn't close, of course, not until the ladder was back in the loft. He thrust the rod at Mike. 'Quick, for God's sake! Can't you hear them, man?'

We all could. Not so much the murmur of innumerable bees as an angry saw in action. First one, then two insects found the gap. Others would follow.

Slotting each section back into the next, Mike worked as if he didn't know the word panic. But the buzzing was getting louder. At last! But the half-dozen or so that were out hurtled furiously round the tiny landing till Mike could slam them into the bathroom and bedroom.

'I take it you want me to get the pest-control people in before you venture up there again,' Mike said, trying to be cool but beginning to shake. I thought it might be laughter but it could have been reaction.

Chris, on the other hand, was ice-cold. 'I think we may have found the immediate cause of Timpson's death,' he said. 'I have to warn you—'

'You don't have to do any such thing,' I said. 'No! No more. Remember' – I spoke from bitter experience – 'once you've arrested someone you can't just un-arrest them. Where's your insect spray, Mike?'

'The cupboard under the sink.'

I ran downstairs and came back flourishing it. If Chris had been swift in his descent, I was like lightning as I opened the doors, squirting insecticide. After a few minutes, I ventured into the bathroom and brought out a couple of my victims on a wad of toilet paper.

'Two bees or not two bees,' I said. 'Wasps. In fact, not even wasps. I'd say, Chris, you've managed to stir up a hornets' nest.'

'I shall have to have expert confirmation about how long the nest has been there,' Chris said. 'And I shall want SOCO people to establish that no one apart from the pest-control people have been in the loft. And then I shall want to see where Sandra's boxes are and what they contain. Until then, forget the official caution.' He smiled, ruefully. After a moment, he lifted one of the bottles of Beck's that Mike had produced from his fridge. 'Cheers.'

Mike nodded coolly. 'What were you expecting to find in Timpson's house, anyway?'

'Expecting to find? We've been over that house with the proverbial fine-tooth comb, don't think we haven't. We've found repeat prescriptions for Epipens, pens in his kitchen and pens in his bedroom – he was one for taking precautions, it seems.'

'But not quite enough,' Mike said drily.

'You know,' I said, 'I'd give my teeth to see inside his house.'

'What on earth for?' Mike asked, tipping his chair back to the vertical.

'You don't have to go that far,' Chris said. 'You could

come to the incident room – cast your beadies over the photos.'

'It's not the same as getting a feel for the place,' I said.

'You and your intuition,' Chris said dismissively.

'Observation,' I said. 'The bit of the brain that picks things up without the conscious part knowing.'

'I can't see what good that would do,' Peter objected. 'You've got to know these things, haven't you?'

'You're not just thinking about picking up vibes,' Mike said slowly.

I shook my head. 'Don't know what it is. Tell you what, Mike, why don't you don a suit of armour, nick the keys, zap me across to Rutland and let me prowl round his house, and then pop the keys back into Sandra's box or whatever so no one'd be any the wiser?' Except the SOCO team, of course.

'Love to,' he grinned, probably at the sight of the policemen's outraged faces. 'But I'm supposed to be back at the ground as soon as maybe. And you and I have a date this evening with some good food and something fizzy – *after*, that is, a little celebration in the bar. Tell you what, Chris, why don't you drop us back at the ground? Don't want to upset any of your colleagues in Traffic, do I? And believe me, any bags we blow into tonight are going to go grass-green!'

They would have done, too. The celebrations in the bar continued till the shadows were deep across the ground. Mike was summoned from time to time to talk to the press, the sea of fans and colleagues opening and closing round him. High on mineral water, the pair of us, we had to share his triumph with them all, didn't we? We were part of a team.

At last he pulled me gently to one side. 'There's talk of a nightclub. What do you think?'

I'd never wanted to give private explanations, receive private reassurance so much. I smiled. 'Your night. You choose.'

'In that case I choose you. Let's go eat. Any ideas?'

'Plenty.' But very few of them to do with food or drink.

Someone had flicked the switch to morning horribly early! Or rather, so late that Mike had flung himself straight into the shower. I'd volunteered – foolishly, as it transpired – to get some breakfast together. But all the essentials seemed to be hiding themselves. Who would have thought a sensible, logical man like Mike would have kept his mugs in a separate cupboard from all the other china? No doubt it was just to challenge my indisputably fuzzy brain.

I would have liked to blame last night's champagne, but I suspect it was both more and less than that. I hadn't drunk very much, thanks to the cautionary rumbles from my stomach, and had eaten very sparingly, it was so late when we'd finally reached the restaurant, which seemed to be populated entirely by cricket fans, each of whom wanted to add another word of congratulation. Mike dealt with everyone with courtesy, though by the end of the meal his face muscles must have been as tired as the rest of him. There had been no opportunity for the sort of conversation we really did need.

I couldn't even attribute this languor to sexual overindulgence – we'd both fallen to sleep so quickly we woke still stickily tangle-limbed at dawn. I simply felt tired. Age. That's what it must have been. The forties roaring towards me.

Mike was due for a hot day in the field, where I'd have been perfectly happy watching him. But someone had to summon the pest control people, who seemed to be in considerable demand. I'd dialled them the first time as soon as the first sip of tea was inside me, and was still trying them when Mike left for the ground.

He'd come down stretching blearily and rubbing his back. 'People forget what hard work scoring a lot quickly can be,' he said ruefully. 'No wonder tennis players are over the hill at thirty. I'd like to think there are plenty more hundreds in me, but don't go looking for many at that pace.'

'Not this week, anyway,' I said, passing him a mug of tea. 'Now, I've been thinking – I really would like to take Chris up on his offer of looking at the incident room. Just to see if it gives me any brilliant ideas. So I'll go straight to Smethwick when they've dealt with your wasps. If there's any sign of your batting today, though, you will phone me, won't you? Even if you plan no more than a slow fifty?'

Slow as the pest people, perhaps. They'd see us on Saturday morning, they said, and put down the phone before I could expostulate.

One of the most direct routes to Smethwick took me past my house, so I stopped off to water plants and check the answerphone and the post. And I'd got to collect that mysterious letter from Aggie, with good enough grace to show I wasn't offended, not really, by her advice about my love-life. Her beloved granddaughters didn't live close enough to provide her with an opportunity to practise her worrying skills, which she preferred to keep finely honed. If I found her interest in my life irritating, I had to remember that leaving my keys with her meant I didn't have to waste time whenever I wanted something mended or delivered; more important, through no fault of hers, her life had been at risk on more than one occasion.

She came to the door so slowly I wished I'd taken my key and let myself in, but that was something I'd always reserved for emergencies. There was earth under her fingernails: she'd obviously come from tinkering with the pot plants that occupied high staging along her fences.

Her granddaughters had suggested that if she couldn't get down to the garden, the garden should come up to her, an idea she'd accepted grudgingly before she'd embraced it with terrific fervour. When Aggie eventually moved down to sheltered accommodation near them, she'd made it a proviso that her plants went too.

'Here you are, me love. Nice paper, isn't it? She brought her own.'

I was clearly meant to open it on the spot. I fingered it a bit to prolong the tension. And also to check that there was indeed no more than a sheet of paper in the envelope. At last, satisfied on both counts, I tore it open and fished out a note. I didn't know the writing. It was not unlike Aggie's own – that of someone whose education was cut off early and to whom writing didn't come easily. The signature at the bottom looked like *Hank Sampson*, which wasn't especially helpful.

The contents made it clear it was Sal. She hadn't seen me for a bit, she said, so how about a nice girlie natter while the weather was so good? And I should make sure I had a nice dip this time.

Aggie was most impressed by the concept of a garden big enough to take a pool. I was interested by the implication that time had passed – it was less than a week since we'd had coffee, and most of my friendships survived on the basis of a phone call or letter every six months. It occurred to me that she'd had the upper hand in that conversation; perhaps on different territory I might formulate and ask penetrating questions.

Promising to spray Aggie's greenfly when I did mine, I made my escape and phoned Sal.

Lunch? She'd love lunch. I suggested the Bay Tree, which was roughly halfway between her house and mine. My bank balance preferred the bistro to the main restaurant.

We met in the bar, where she was perched on a chair already outside what looked like a double gin and tonic. I tossed up – did I have a glass of wine before or with the meal? I couldn't do both and drive safely. The meal won. Sal's expression quite clearly told the barman she'd never seen anyone actually choose to drink tomato juice. 'The usual for me, sweetie,' she said, shoving the glass across the counter, and displaying expanses of deeply-tanned bosom.

I'd forgotten that the bistro had a vivid blue and yellow décor which made you feel you were in the middle of an IKEA trademark. Refraining with admirable self-control from replacing my sunglasses, I addressed myself to the menu. They had a system where you could choose certain items to put together your own cheap lunch menu: you could permute a starter with a main course, a main course with a sweet, or even a starter with a sweet. To my surprise Sal suggested we did that: I'd not have associated her with the need to read a menu from right to left. I chose my usual healthy option, in this case chicken. Sal plumped for what I'd have thought comfort food – shepherd's pie and what turned out to be a huge portion of caramelised bread-and-butter pudding. So we ate out of synch. *All the better for asking you questions, my dear.*

So Art was still in France, buying all this lovely wine. And her darling boys were still abroad.

'Why don't you go out and join them?' I asked, sipping tomato and basil soup.

She stared. 'Someone has to run things over here. It's a big concern.'

'I've never known exactly what the business is.'

She jiggled her shoulders. 'This and that. Importing, mostly. I tell you, Sophie, it still gives me such a thrill to see these containers down at the base and think, "Some of those are ours!" Huge things, Sophie – have you ever been inside? And all this lovely furniture. Custom-made for conservatories. We supply garden centres all over the country. And some antiques for special customers. But that's a bit hush-hush. We don't tell people like Peter Kirby, do we?'

'I don't tell Peter Kirby anything I don't have to,' I said. After all, she might have noticed a certain hostility between us at the *ad hoc* party last Wednesday.

'Quite right,' she said. She looked round for a waiter and waved him over. 'A bottle of that nice Fleurie of yours, sweetie. Thanks. Now, where was I?'

'Telling me about Peter Kirby,' I risked. I had a contact in the Fraud Squad who might be able to fill in the details about their business, not that it was necessarily illegal but because he was *au fait* with most businesses' goings-on. He was happily amassing a wonderfully profitable share portfolio for when he retired, from time to time phoning me to tell me what to buy. I liked to think it was purely disinterested advice, but still suspected it was motivated by an as yet unfulfilled desire to get his hands into my knickers.

'Peter! Oh, Art knows him through some club or other. Him and his stroppy wife. Why he puts up with her I'll never know. He's just come up from London or somewhere – *she* wouldn't go back down there, or so it seems.'

'What sort of club?'

She shrugged. 'One of these boys' things – Lions or Masons or something. You know. He's such a moody bugger. All over you one moment, wouldn't touch you with a bargepole the next. I can't make him out. Why he bothers coming to the parties I'll never know – he certainly doesn't seem to enjoy himself very much.'

I nodded. The wine arrived. My soup dish disappeared.

The wine was outstanding. God knows how much it had added to the otherwise manageable bill.

I had to mention the women and the drugs, didn't I?

One thing at a time, Sophie. 'You seem to know lots of people – I mean, lots of different sorts of people.' Not all respectable college lecturers or solicitors or policemen. Not like me at all!

'Do we? Well, I suppose it's all Art's contacts, dear. Oooh, that looks good!' she greeted her shepherd's pie. 'And there's nothing like a bit of variety.' The wink was so huge it suggested not just social variety.

My stomach blipped painfully: *had* she and Mike—? I sipped water, not wine, and waited for the spear to remove itself. My chicken was tart in a lime and ginger sauce, wonderful on the taste-buds. I crossed my fingers and hoped it wouldn't be too hard on my stomach. Perhaps changing the topic might help.

'You're very broad-minded about who comes,' I said.

'Let 'em all come, sweetheart. More the merrier. If they don't like someone they meet, they can always talk to someone else, can't they? Or stay away next time?'

'Not if they know good wine and food,' I said, forgiving the pseudo-champagne Mike and I had discussed in our very first conversation together.

'That's right! Now, one more drop of this won't hurt you!'

I covered the glass, quite literally. Her attitude to the drink-drive laws was different from mine. 'Some of the women seemed – a bit – you know—'

She pulled back the bottle. 'Indeed I don't. Are you suggesting—'

'They just seemed a bit generous with their favours,' I said, as mildly as I could.

'Not all women are as tight-arsed as you, sweetheart.'

I mustn't bridle. I pulled a face, meant to be self-deprecatory. 'All those Sundays in chapel,' I said. 'Bound to rub off. And not just on my bum, either.'

'Well, mind you give Mike a good time. None of your net-curtain mentality for him. That's all I can say.'

I nodded, with visible humility but a stomach-stabbing fear. 'He seems to like my cooking, anyway,' I said, not quite irrelevantly.

'Hmm. He likes his food. Well, they all do, men, don't they? Way to a man's heart . . . Mind you, the heart's never troubled me, so long as the other bits are in working order!' It seemed we were friends again. 'Young Guy, now, he loved his food. He'd go for the two-course cheap meal, and then ask for pud!'

He'd eaten a big last lunch, hadn't he? Where and with whom? As far as I knew, the police still had no leads on that.

Sal fidgeted with her fork, as if she'd said something she'd rather have kept quiet. I decided to go for the all-girls-together line. My smile became very conspiratorial.

'I suppose that's why he spent so much time in the Midlands,' I said. 'To *lunch* with you!' I meant to show I was using the verb as a euphemism.

She said nothing.

'The trouble with being so tight-arsed,' I said, 'is that you only get to imagine, never to find out. And he'd got a lovely body. You must have been very upset,' I prompted.

'He was a bloody good fuck,' she agreed. 'But that was all, mind. I love my Art.'

I could easily have broken into song: '*Vissi d'arte*', for instance. But I didn't. 'Why don't you get a manager in for your business? So you two can be together more?'

'Nothing like the boss being there in person,' she said, downing the last of the Fleurie, 'as you'd know if you'd ever been in business. What line are you in? All these questions . . .'

'Just a teacher,' I said quickly. 'In a college.'

'Ah. All those long holidays.'

We'd arrived separately and would leave separately. We air-kissed, neither of us, I suspected, entirely happy with the way things had turned out. She drove off first, without bothering to open the windows: presumably the big Merc had air-conditioning. My Renault was like an oven. The trouble was, you had to get in there and turn on the ignition before the sun-roof and windows would open. I flung the doors open and waited – in vain – for a cross-breeze to work.

Chapter Twenty-Seven

Helena sat me down in her office, insisting that I must want a cup of tea, since Chris was just about to have his. I didn't argue. She busied herself with an electric kettle and a teapot – no dunking the tea bag in the mug for him.

'What I want to know,' she dropped her voice to a stage whisper, 'is who irons his shirts. He always looks so crisp and elegant, even in this weather.'

'I suppose he still does them himself,' I said. 'He always did. If he was in a good mood he'd sometimes do mine too.' I stopped. I wasn't sure how much he'd want her to know about our past relationship. As for looking elegant, I don't think I'd have chosen that particular adjective, though I couldn't have explained why. If a man is tall enough, with the right shoulders and hips, clothes will usually look good. And Chris always bought good clothes, favouring Aquascutum or Jaeger. He always looked smart. But not quite elegant. Perhaps it was because that hunch around the shoulders pulled suits out of line. I wondered what Mike would look like in more formal clothes. He might make it to elegant.

That was one drawback with being short, of course: the very best clothes always seemed to have been designed for taller people. It wasn't just a matter of turning up hems – the proportions of bust to waist to hips were wrong. Helena, now, was tall enough to buy that sort of thing, but civilian secretaries' salaries probably weren't good enough to anyway. Not that she didn't dress well. Today she was in a Marks and Sparks blouse and skirt, closely related to my college summer gear. She arranged biscuits neatly on a plate.

'He should be free in about five minutes. You'll never guess what he's got with him!' She rolled her eyes. She mouthed, 'Prostitutes!' And nodded as if to quell my disbelief. 'It's to do with the deaths, apparently. They think the police should be doing more. So they sent in a deputation. I told him, I hope your budget will stretch to fumigation.'

I smiled at her titter, but said gently, 'Think of them as any other working women, Helena. Supply and demand. That sort of thing.' I thought back to TV documentaries I'd watched on the subject. 'Most of them aren't in it by choice, after all. It's to pay off debts or whatever. And once they're in, their pimps won't let them out. Isn't that the usual scene?'

She sniffed. 'I can't understand why they should do it in the first place. And as for the pimps, well, we can all walk away from jobs, for goodness' sake. It's a free country.'

It was too hot to embark on theories of economics and entrapment. I burrowed in my bag for a mirror. So the make-up had disappeared and the hair was tired and limp – I really must get that sorted out. Another burrow produced my mobile phone and my diary. Helena shrugged that she didn't mind and returned to her word-processing, the keys rattling with impressive speed.

That was one problem almost fixed: Roy could attack my mop early next week. Praise be! I'd have to think about washing bedclothes – for both houses? – not to mention towels and everyday clothes. I was so deep into domestic trivia I didn't notice Chris open the door.

'Did I hear the rattle of tea cups?' He smiled at Helena and then at me, motioning me in.

'I'm just making a fresh pot!'

So that was why she'd dithered around. She wanted to get it just right for Chris. I was touched.

'Thanks.' He shut the door behind me.

Whoever he'd been talking to, she was sporting Opium. The residue was still overpowering. I struggled to open the window wider. Chris grinned, and went to the far door, flapping it to create a breeze.

'Someone's obviously earning good money,' I said. And then heard myself asking, 'When was the last death? Amongst the prostitutes?'

He didn't even look at a file. 'Nearly ten days ago. A week last Sunday. But—'

'The day Barkat crashed.' It wasn't a question. 'Have you and Peter Kirby got your heads together about that yet? You said you'd had an interesting conversation.'

The office door opened, and Helena manoeuvred in a tray, which she laid on that awkward low table. Chris smiled his thanks.

'The biscuits are straight from the fridge,' she said.

'I won't ask what they've been sharing it with,' he said. 'Thanks. Sophie?'

I'd have taken that as a dismissal, but Helena stood fanning her face and holding her nose. 'Nasty cheap muck they wear,' she said. If I was tight-arsed, what did that make Helena? But Chris had never admired my peculiar liberality of mind, so perhaps he wouldn't find that a problem. I did. I'd wanted so much to like her but today she was really irritating me.

A little silence grew. Chris picked up a file and flicked it open. I avoided eye contact. She left. Poor woman, she could be thinking Chris and I were getting back together again. I'd have to say something; he'd have to say something. Whichever.

'I've been sending him information on e-mail; he's been sending me ditto. The funny thing is that although all our messages have apparently been received, neither of us has received them. It looks as if someone in the CID room has been intercepting them. Unless, of course, one of us is lying, and I know I'm not.'

'He's a contact of Art's,' I said.

'Art Sampson? Yes, I know. They're both in the Moose.'

'Does that make them Meese?'

'And I didn't have to wait till last night to find that out,' he continued, studiously ignoring my interruption. 'Peter told me as soon as he met you at some do at their house. They're not like Masons, Sophie.'

'I reckon he's straight, too. Jesus, Chris, what a nasty tangle. You worked off your feet with all sorts of things that have to be done by someone but have no immediate connection with solving this crime. Your DCI with communication problems, shall we call them. The prozzies pressuring you. The Chief Superintendent no doubt on someone's back. The bees in Mike's loft not bees but wasps. Hey, where did the bees come from?'

'You don't ID bloody bees, Sophie!'

'I'll bet you could. I'll bet you could place them within – say – ten square miles on account of the pollen dust they pick up.'

Before the words were out of my mouth he'd picked up the phone. I stared at the photos of his teams which had appeared on his wall. A sprinkling of women across all disciplines but not all that many black and Asian officers of either sex in senior positions.

'They don't know yet but I'm sure we soon will,' he said. 'Peter's getting on to it. And he says to tell you there were only two cameras in the cut, very fancy jobs, he says.'

'So where on earth is Guy's? Also a fancy job, I'd say. He hadn't got some fancy hidden compartment in his car, by any chance?'

'Not a lot of space to hide anything in an MX5.'

I raised my eyebrows.

'This year's model. Nineteen grand. And I checked his earnings from Rutland – they'd hardly rise to that. Not a rich club, I gather.'

I recounted what I'd picked up at Grace Road about his contribution to fund-raising – and other – activities. 'I've also got a nasty suspicion about what brought him to the Midlands so much. I think he was bonking someone I had lunch with. Sal. Married to Art Sampson.'

'And several other women. OK. We go round and round this. All of us. Peter's throwing enormous resources and energy into tracking down all Timpson's partners. But none of them seems a possible candidate. There's got to be something else. God knows where, what, who.' He drained his cup, and poured us both refills. He looked at me sharply. 'Do you still want to see the incident room – all the photos and everything?'

'That's why I came, Chris.'

As a casual, indeed slapdash filer of information, I always marvelled at the detail and efficiency of police filing. Ask and it was there, on the desk I'd been found in the middle of the CID team, who greeted me with cordiality, whatever they might have thought of my being there. I averted my gaze from the giant blown-up photos of Timpson's face from any and every angle.

Within ten minutes I had a complete picture of his house and its contents. Nothing left to surmise about. There were his black sheets, the shower in the corner of his bedroom, even a huge Southern States brass fan over the low bed. What an obvious, unsubtle man he was. I wouldn't have expected any sexual finesse from someone like that. And yet he appeared to have given satisfaction wherever he went.

I pushed the files away and sighed – as all these men and women had no doubt been sighing. There had to be something in there. Surely.

Peter popped his head round the door. 'Any luck? Don't tell me: plenty, all bad.'

I nodded. 'It was sheer arrogance thinking I could come up with anything you people couldn't. The only thing I can contribute is that he made a habit of eating large meals. And he ate at the Bay Tree on more than one occasion. And – obviously this is *sub rosa*, Peter – he was bonking your mate Art's wife. On a regular basis, I'd guess. Is Art the jealous type?'

He shrugged. 'He always said it was an open marriage – a hangover from the seventies, if you ask me, and I never thought it was a good idea then. Well, I did – but I wasn't married at the time. He prides himself on being a bit of a ram, of course. I'm surprised he hasn't tried to have his wicked way with you.'

'My poor ego! Am I the only one in the area he hasn't? Nor Guy, neither! God, what a put-down! Actually,' I added, 'I've never met the man. Some of those women at the party, though, Peter, they were – they were prozzies, weren't they?'

I'm sure the shock was genuine. 'At a private party! Christ in heaven!'

'Well, coke at a private party for that matter. Did Chris tell you what I found in the downstairs loo?'

Peter nodded grimly. 'Once on e-mail, and again last night. It was a good job he told me last night. I don't know. Being in the police you meet all sorts. Mix with them. Well, you have to, don't you? It's like in the old days, the PC on the beat going into seedy bars to cultivate a snout. The snouts have to be graduates these days, the sort we're recruiting. Bleeding hell, all these sociologists and other bleeding ologists. I reckon we're better qualified in this nick than in the wife's bleeding college.'

'The women,' I prompted.

'I didn't realise there were any toms there. In any case, they'd see themselves as high-class call girls, wouldn't they?'

'Same difference. Tell me, is it still known as keeping a disorderly house? Having tarts on the premises?'

'Why?'

'Just wondered if it might be something people – even Sal – might not want universally known. She certainly didn't like me mentioning it.' Or should it have been *my* mentioning it?

'Fuck it all! That's all we need!' One of the team, a young man, slammed a fist on to his desk. 'Fucking computer's only gone and crashed, hasn't it! Shit and corruption!'

Hardly daring to breathe, I picked through the photographs again. I pointed. 'Peter – what's on Timpson's computer?'

'How should I know? I'm not a bleeding geek!'

The young man heaved himself from his desk and came to lean on mine. 'I thought we all were these days, sir.' He looked at me with far more interest than anyone had when I'd come in. 'What do you think – er—?'

'Sophie.' I shoved out a hand.

'Clive Rogers.'

'—by name and Rogers by nature!' someone yelled. 'Watch it, miss.'

I grinned. 'What do *you* think?'

'No idea. Well, maybe some girlie stuff off the Internet.'

'He was into so many real knickers, would he bother with virtual ones?' I asked.

'Maybe if it was an addiction. Is there a name for it in men? Like nymphomania in women?'

'Satyriasis,' I supplied.

He blinked. 'So even though he was shafting half the crumpet in the Midlands, he might have wanted still more.'

'You ought to know!' came the original helpful voice.

'Some poor bugger's gone through every cupboard and shelf in the place.' I patted the file. 'And, I dare say, through the loft and the cellar as well, if he has one.'

'Neither, actually,' Peter put in.

'And I don't see him storing stuff at his high street bank, somehow. So it's got to be there, hasn't it? On his hard disk. Did you check his floppies?'

Roger pulled a face. 'Funny thing, now you mention it. Considering the power of his system, I'd have expected him to have more. A proper back-up system. And there was room in the storage box for plenty. Games, he'd got. Copies of letters to friends. Oh, and a few CD-ROMs.'

'Tell me!'

He looked taken aback. 'Well, reference, funnily enough. Encarta. Atlas. The *Guardian* and the *Times*.'

'Yes!' I punched the air. 'That explains one thing at least! He dug up a bit of my past involving Winston Rhodes.'

He nodded. 'I saw.'

'So he could check on people he'd photographed. See if they'd got a past. Blackmail.' I'd had this conversation before, hadn't I? Why not with a detective, for goodness' sake? 'We have to get into his system. How do we get hold of it, Peter?'

He snorted. 'It's a moot point, if you ask me. Whose budget do we tap? Ours or Rutland's?'

Remembering the course Chris had been on – budgeting – I grinned. We spoke together. 'Rutland's.'

'They'll pack it up and send it over to us ASAP,' Chris said. 'I'm sure they've got plenty of resident geeks of their own, but he's our stiff, after all. Do you want to hang on?'

I shook my head. 'I'm sure you've got things to do without having to entertain me. It's only twenty minutes either way for me, and a couple of hours for them.'

'Right. I'll give you a buzz, shall I? Home or mobile?'

'If at first you don't succeed . . .' I was just about to leave when I asked, 'Any ideas about the communication breakdown yet?'

He shook his head, repressively, I thought. It was a good job he was circumspect. I was still drawing breath for the next question when the inner door opened and Helena popped her head round it.

'Chris, it's nearly six: I can hang on if you need me, but . . .'

He shook his head. 'Nothing that can't wait. I have been known to word-process my own letters in an emergency, you know.'

'Where do you live, Helena? Can I offer you a lift?' I asked.

She hesitated. 'Out by Warley Woods.'

'That's practically on my way.'

'Well, if you're sure . . .' She didn't manage to sound enthusiastic, but I took it she was reluctant to put me to any trouble. As soon as we'd encouraged some cooler air into the car, we set off.

Chapter Twenty-Eight

As we hit Waterloo Road, my mobile phone tweeted. Pulling illegally into a bus lay-by I answered. Mike.

'They're still in. I shan't be in to bat tonight, almost certainly. There's a bit of a booze-up planned – a head-wetting. But I won't be too late. Your house or mine?'

'Mine. I've promised to help Chris with something but I shouldn't be too late either. About nine? And ring me if I'm not there – it could concentrate the mind wonderfully.' My own valediction was brief, his more effusive. After all, I knew I had a pair of ears beside me; he didn't.

'Your boyfriend?' Helena prompted.

I bit back a sarcastic observation that I bade farewell to all my callers that way: it had, after all, been a long, hot day for her. And she had another motive, perhaps – reassurance that I no longer had any interest in Chris.

'That's right. He plays cricket for Warwickshire.' I eased the car into the traffic to the accompaniment of irate hoots from one of the lay-by's rightful occupants.

'Chris did say something about it.' Her voice was tight, the way mine goes when I don't know whether to be embarrassed or upset.

'Oh, Chris and I have been friends for years – you know that,' I insisted. 'We really should have stuck to that. But there you are. Anyway, we'd been back to being friends for

263

months and then I met Mike.' I indulged in a sigh. 'Love at first sight.' Well, it had been lust, really, at that stage, but there was no need to be too specific. And there was no doubt that what I felt for him now was more than lust. Just thinking about him brought a little spurt of happiness. My smile was genuine.

'You see a lot of Chris, though.' Her voice was still tight.

'Well, I would do, wouldn't I, in the circumstances?'

'But tonight – you said you were seeing him later.'

I was about to declare with breezy reassurance the purpose of our assignation when I remembered the expression on Chris's face. After all, I'd recommended caginess myself and should hardly go blabbing, however much I wanted to ease a sister's aching heart. 'Oh,' I said, waving a spare hand in the air, 'he just wants me to look at something.' I nearly added, 'Not his willy,' but thought better of it. 'What's he like to work with?' I asked, feeling it was time for her to volunteer something on her own account.

'Chris? Oh, very nice. Very nice.'

Hardly the gush of a woman in love.

'A bit of a slave-driver?' I suggested. After all, he drove himself hard enough.

'I wouldn't say that. What it is, he's a bit moody. Since he got back from that course, I've hardly had a good word from him. I wondered – that's why I wondered, you see—'

'About him and me? Come on, Helena, he's taking you to Ian's party, isn't he?' I had this lurking suspicion I still wasn't saying the right thing, and decided to shut up.

The traffic was clearing quite well, but there's always a tailback at the lights for Three Shires Oak Road, so I turned off a junction or so earlier, planning to reach the woods that way. By Thimblemill Baths I said, 'You'll have to navigate from here.'

'Oh, anywhere'll do.'

No wonder Chris had treated her more distantly: he liked women – and for that matter men – to be decisive. I outlined my proposed route, which would take me, incidentally, within spitting distance of Sal and Art's house. 'So where's the best place for you?'

'Oh. Where you turn left into Harborne Road, please.'

I presumed she would go into one of the houses opposite the golf course, or maybe down one of the roads there. But she stood for some time watching my progress, and when, on impulse, I pulled on to a verge a couple of hundred yards further on just to see what she would do, she soon appeared in my rear-view mirror. I had had the forethought to be deep in a fictitious conversation via my mobile phone, and would have happily waved. She, however, seemed to have very little excuse for toiling up a very long hill in this heat and rather obviously failed to see me. Instead she turned quickly off to the right. My natural route took me down the next right, and I didn't want to be too obvious in checking on her. If that was what I was doing. It was, wasn't it? But she'd disappeared – perhaps into what seemed to be a gully at the back of houses – by the time I'd waited for clear road and three-point-turned.

Might as well stick to this road as go back to my original choice.

I was back by the Bay Tree. On impulse, I pulled the car into their service road and headed back to the bistro. It was too early for evening business, which would probably be knocked about by the heat. The bar was empty, the barman, a different one from this lunchtime's, reading the *Evening Mail*. He was slower to close it than I'd have expected, after the swift and pleasant service I'd had earlier.

'Yes?' he asked eventually.

OK. He'd asked for it. Sophie's lecturer mode. It started

with the raising of one eyebrow. It would have progressed to a frigid riposte, had I not remembered that in fact I wanted something from him. Information. Better shift into absent-minded mode.

'I'm so sorry to bother you. Only a friend of mine left something here last week. Tuesday or Wednesday lunchtime, I should think. Mrs Sampson. I said I'd ask.'

'What was it?' He turned the pages of their reservation book. 'Nothing Tuesday. Ah. Wednesday. Table Six. For three. Would that be it? Mrs Sampson and two gentlemen. What was it you said she'd forgotten?' he repeated.

'A scarf.' There were times when I lied badly. This was one of them.

'In this weather?' He peered at me. 'What did you say your name was?'

'I didn't.'

'Well, Miss Didn't. Take it from me, if we'd have found anything of Mrs Sampson's we'd have phoned. She's a valuable client.'

'That's good to hear. Not often you get such good service these days. Thanks.' Exit, pursued by a truculent stare.

I should have danced a little jig of triumph while the car cooled down, but I found I couldn't. I liked Sal. I wanted there to be another explanation. And surely there was: if she'd been with Guy she'd have been *à deux*. They wouldn't have wanted a third person. But I'd have to tell Chris or Peter about it.

I dreaded the return to my house. It was so intruder-proof, with secondary glazing made from polycarbonate sheet, that it was like a greenhouse on an ordinary day. Today it would be stifling. I parked the car in the road and plunged into the sauna that was the hall, stabbing the burglar alarm as I went. I left the front door wide open and opened all the back ones before I could think of doing anything else.

That was better. A breath of air. A positive little gale. In fact, I slipped the catch on the front door and wedged it. It then occurred to me that there was time to strip the bed and put a load through the washing machine. In weather like this it would dry almost as soon as it was on the line.

I was measuring the liquid detergent when a roar of a motorcycle reminded me that all this emphasis on fresh air might be foolish. Setting the programme, I cantered to the front door. Balden Road shimmered, but apart from my neighbours' cars was empty. Someone further up the road was mowing what remained of his lawn. No need to panic. But no reason to invite trouble. If I wanted to leave the catch up, I'd better put the chain on before I returned – with surprising contentment – to domestic trivia.

The phone interrupted a gentle misting of the house plants. I was just on my way upstairs so I took the call in the hall.

'OK, Sophie. The computer's on its way.'

'Great – do I gather someone's fuel budget is bigger than yours?'

Chris laughed. 'If you come over now, I'll treat you at the chippie while we wait.'

'I'm on my way. No: hang on. There's something you need to know. Might be quite irrelevant. But I just have this evil suspicion about Guy's last lunch. It could have been right under our noses – hell! Hang on!'

He must have heard the blast on the bell, it was so fierce.

Whoever had rung it stood just out of my spy-hole's range, and the crack the chain permitted was too narrow. It seemed to be a woman.

'Jehovah's Witness or something,' I said.

'Don't reckon much of her chances with you, Sophie! Tell you what, call me back, eh? About this last lunch business. So I can get things moving, if needs be.'

'OK. Soon as I've proved I'm one of the damned.'

I made for the door, opening it till the chain stopped it. Sal, of all people!

'Sal! Are you all right?'

She looked very fraught, most of her face hidden behind huge sunglasses. She'd even donned a floppy hat.

'Just a second.' I closed the door enough to ease the chain. 'Come on in!'

She needed no second invitation. Once inside, the distressed old lady persona disappeared, to be replaced by a taut, alert Sal, menace crackling from every pore. With the same person-steering skills as Peter Kirby she manoeuvred me against the wall. Then she showed me her left hand: an unprotected syringe glistening – my God, what had she got in there? – told me she meant business.

'You were on the phone.'

I nodded, and found a croak. 'A neighbour. I promised I'd do her—' I stopped short. Nothing must tempt her towards Aggie.

'Proper little Goody Two-Shoes, aren't you? Except whatever you're supposed to be doing will have to wait a very long time. You're going on a trip, dear. Quite a long one. Of course, it's difficult to judge precisely but I'd say you weren't coming back. I wonder what you'll have on the way. Sweet dreams? Nightmares? Choirs of angels or a chorus of devils? Funny, once, I could have sworn I had Old Nick waiting for me in the lav. Face like Guy's as it happens.'

I'd never wet myself with fear, not yet. But what I feared would happen did. I spewed. All that expensive lunch. As I retched, she jumped back, laying tongue to all the terms of abuse I knew and a few more. I didn't blame her for being disgusted with me. I was disgusted with me. She clamped her free hand to her mouth, as if she were nauseous too.

'Get moving.' She gestured with the syringe.

I backed into the kitchen. That was the side that connected with Aggie. Screams in the living room would be wasted on a garage. The thought process was so slow I could almost watch it. I could scream. I could scream for help. At last I did. I screamed very loudly. She slapped me.

'Not in here. You wouldn't mainline in your kitchen, for Christ's sake.'

OK. The living room. The patio doors were still open. I could make a dash.

'Don't be stupid!' She grabbed me by my hair.

For all she was nearly twice my age, she was tall and strong. All that swimming, I suppose.

Steering me from behind, she flung me on to a chair. I twisted round to face her. She smiled. Then pressed me down with the flat of her hand against my chest. I retched again. Despite herself she recoiled, but only long enough for her to choose the site for that bloody needle.

'Have a good trip,' she said, plunging forward.

There was a screaming yell, and a rush that could have been footsteps. Her weight shifted, but another, heavier weight crushed across my legs. I opened my eyes. The syringe quivered in the sofa. Sal's left hand was stretching for it. And a leather-clad body was doing its damnedest to make sure it didn't get it.

Chapter Twenty-Nine

I had to make my legs work. I had to get to the sofa and retrieve the syringe. I had to. Although they were cotton-wool, I had to. There! If I could make it to the sofa, I could make it to the kitchen, and drop it into the sink. I leant against the sink, panting. Now what? There was some parcel tape in my glory-hole. If I could find it.

My body must have functioned faster than I thought. The helmeted figure nodded approval as I stuck one end round Sal's outstretched wrist. He eased his weight from her and with something like courtesy passed me her other wrist. When I was too weak to bring the two together, he used force enough to make Sal scream. OK. Time to tear it. Except my fingers were too wobbly. In the gauntlets, his hands were too clumsy. He held a hand out to me: I stripped the glove off. Then the next. I knew those hands from somewhere. Knew them: that long little finger. The hands got busy. Bound her ankles for good measure. Then stuck the lot to the sofa legs.

Then he removed his helmet.

Above the sound of our panting came another sound. A siren. Voices outside, then in my hall. Someone swore: maybe he'd slipped in my vomit.

'Police!' An unfamiliar voice, that. No Chris yet.

'She's my friend. You can't stop me!' Aggie!

271

I found a thin voice, coughed to make it stronger. 'We're in here! It's OK. I'm all right. I'm all right!'

And found myself looking down the barrel of a gun. I drew myself to my full five foot one. 'Rapid Response Unit, I presume.' I grinned at the face in the helmet. And then I passed out.

Things were much the same when I came round.

Sal now wore handcuffs and was just leaving, assisted by a couple of padded-looking officers, whose faces poured sweat.

'You stupid bitch,' she was saying. 'You think that sodding Mike's so lily-white pure. It's all his doing, this. You fucking bite on that, sweetheart. If I go down, he goes down.' Under stress, her Blackheath accent was much in evidence. Mrs Wyle, I presume.

'Shut your mouth. If you want to talk to anyone, talk to us.'

If I go down, he goes down.

I could hear someone remonstrating and Aggie's voice saying crossly, 'Well, someone's got to do it, before there's a real accident.'

'Of course they have. Only not you. Get one of the lads on to it, will you? And sort out some tea.' That was Chris. 'You come along in here, Aggie. She's OK, you know. We met on the way in,' he added, his face smiling but his eyes anxious as they scanned for damage. 'She heard you yelling and dialled nine-nine-nine.'

'So how come you're here?' She turned to him. 'You don't dash round in them striped cars.'

'Sophie gave me a message,' he said.

'And how did them lot get in here?'

'The front door had blown open. God knows why. Hey! Aggie!'

She'd lifted her walking stick and was hitting the motor-cyclist across the shoulders. 'You got the wrong one. This is the one as has been following her! Came to my door, he did. You get him. While you got the chance.'

I pulled her gently down beside me. 'It's OK. He was entitled . . .' I looked up and smiled. 'After all, he's my son.'

I hadn't even realised Mike had arrived, but he was across the room in a couple of strides, and laid an arm round Nicholas's shoulders. Was he still Nicholas? Or Nick? Or did he have some other name now? Mike released him, looked from one of us to the other and nodded. Then he moved away.

Chris stuck out a hand to shake Nicholas's, his face as white as I've seen it. Aggie patted the sofa. 'Well, you should be sitting here. With your mom. Come on, son.' She shuffled sideways.

Nick sat. 'I saw you in all the papers,' he said. 'It was like looking at my own face.' He shook his head. 'But I wasn't sure if—'

'—if you wanted a mother who went round kissing people and getting her picture in all the papers,' I said. 'Jesus, I hope you do.'

He fidgeted his hands. 'Well, I've got a mum, see. And a dad. But I sort of wondered. You know.'

'You two'll need some time on your own to sort this out,' Mike said. 'In the mean time, here.' He'd done his champagne act again. There was a plate of thickly sliced bread and butter for me. *If I go down, he goes down.*

There was a general toast. Nicholas looked totally at sea. Mike, the grand gesture over, stood uneasily beside me. Chris might have been drinking poison. I stuffed bread and butter before more than the most token sip. Aggie alone seemed to be enjoying herself, and was ready to take Nicholas on a tour of the house.

Chris coughed. 'I'm sorry to break this up,' he said,

unconvincingly, 'but there's a computer awaiting your attentions at Piddock Road, Sophie.'

I was about to cavil when I noticed Nicholas greeting the announcement with something that looked horribly like relief.

'I promised Mum I wouldn't be late, see,' he began.

I nodded. 'Look, I'll come to the door with you.' I had to have him on my own just for a moment, had to see if anything could be retrieved from the chaos.

He followed.

Someone had mopped the carpet, leaving a strong smell of disinfectant. The front door was wide open; the wedge was back.

'You saved my life. And I don't even know what you like to be called. What your name is,' I corrected myself. 'I called you Nicholas, you see. But I don't know what – what your mum and dad call you.'

He managed an embarrassed grin. 'They call me Steph. My grandad came from Poland, see. Stephan. Nick's my first name.'

'And you'll have gathered I'm Sophie. I'd love – if you and your family wouldn't mind – to meet you properly. When you feel like it.'

He nodded. I wrote my phone number on my pad and tore off the sheet. He took it. Ducking his head, he started out of the door. Then he dodged back.

Fiddling with his helmet, not lifting his eyes, he said, 'My dad. You know, the other dad. Is he – what sort of bloke? I mean, that bloke in there, he's not my dad? The fair-haired one? 'Cause he looked right pissed off.'

'No. Nor's the one with dark hair.'

'The one that was free with your bubbly?'

'That's right. He's the one I'm – I'm going out with.' I'd nearly said, *I'm going to marry*. That topic still hadn't been raised by either of us, had it? Not since that big emotional moment. *If I go down, he goes down.* There was that hour unaccounted for when I was at the dentist. The two gentlemen and the lady at the restaurant.

Nick – Steph – nodded. 'Plays cricket or something, doesn't he? Recognised him from the TV and that.'

I nodded.

'He seems OK. Look, my mum worries when I'm on my bike.' He stepped right outside.

I stood on the step. 'You've been giving her a bad time recently, then!'

He laughed. 'That's what mums are for, isn't it? Anyway, I'd best be off before that bloke has me arrested for wasting police time.'

He shifted, as awkward as I felt.

'Do you have to go far?'

'Sutton Coldfield.' He gave me his address. 'We moved down here when I was ten.'

I tried not to laugh as I scribbled it down. That Brummie accent was a fake, wasn't it? His parents lived in a very couth part of town. No doubt it irritated them to death.

'Why don't we have a pizza one day? Catch up a bit?'

'Wicked,' he said. 'Tell you what, if you do call me, and Mum answers, just tell her your first name. And if she asks, you're from college, right?'

'Right. Steph' – the name came awkwardly – 'Steph, I don't want to rock the boat at home. But she's probably worried about all this diving off on your own. You might—'

'I shall tell her. Don't worry. But – you know—'

'I know. In your own time. Well, give me a bell when you're ready. Mean time, thanks.' I reached out and hugged him. That was OK. You were entitled to hug someone who'd saved your life. After a second, he hugged me back.

'See you later.'

There was a footstep behind me. Not Mike. Chris.

'We'd better be on our way,' Chris said. 'Do you want to get your bag?'

'I'll just tell Mike—'

'He'll be coming too,' Chris said. 'Under arrest. We've just broken his alibi for that Wednesday lunchtime. His neighbour denies all knowledge of a conversation about cats.'

Chapter Thirty

I don't know how long I stood on my front doorstep. There was too much going on inside my head for my feet to move. When I finally spoke, all I managed was, 'Make sure you let him take his contact lens kit. He shouldn't wear his lenses at night. And remember he's slap in the middle of a big match.'

Whatever Chris thought, he said nothing. He propelled me down the path as if it were I he was arresting. All the way to Piddock Road, he maintained a stony silence.

I wouldn't break it. The only words I could hear were Sal's Parthian shot, and though I was sure he'd hear them soon enough from the arresting officer, he wouldn't hear them from me. Mike had promised me he hadn't killed Guy. I had to cling to that.

And the computer would prove it. Somehow I knew the computer would prove it. The only trouble was making my hands stop shaking long enough to use the keyboard.

My neck and shoulders firm, I lifted my chin and looked around the room they'd plonked the computer in. Helena's office. Marks for tact, Chris? Pretty low. At least I was on a side table: I wasn't usurping her desk.

Perhaps it was shock. What was I supposed to be doing? Had I, what seemed a long time ago but was probably only a couple of hours, volunteered to do something one of the police service's own staff could have done perfectly well? And why?

Terse as I could manage, I said, 'I could use some food. Toast. And some drinking chocolate.'

Chris nodded. No jokes about my hollow legs, this time. No anxious enquiry about my gastritis. In his place would I have been any more generous? Perhaps he thought there might be some curative value for me if I brought Mike's name up on the screen in the clear capacity of perpetrator.

I forced my chin up again: let it be curative for him when I proved Mike completely innocent!

The African-Caribbean WPC who brought a tray full of food – Chris's deeds had been more generous than his manner – set it down on Helena's desk and then sat down.

'I got my BTEC in computing,' she said. 'The Super said I could watch if you didn't mind. I'm Hazel Holt.' We shook hands. 'Clive Rogers will be along in a few minutes.'

'At this time of night?' He'd been working all day. Why couldn't Chris leave the whole enterprise till tomorrow? Was keeping me busy some obscure way of lessening the pain of knowing that Mike was in custody? No. That didn't make sense. We'd arranged it earlier. There'd been a matey offer of a visit to the chippie. What point was he trying to make with all this urgency? And was it being made to me or someone else?

'Perhaps you'll feel better when you've had something to eat,' she said, pushing the Styrofoam cup closer to my hand.

Blinking, I tried it. Machine chocolate, water at the top, goo at the bottom if I made it that far down. My hands, even when I clasped both around it, weren't sure they could keep it steady that long.

'Not surprising when someone has a go at you like that. They're still checking the contents of the syringe.'

Perhaps it was my imagination but the ham in the sandwich tasted soapy. I pushed it away.

'When Clive comes I'll get you some toast,' she said.

So I was being guarded, was I? It made sense. Chris knew I had more computer expertise than I cared to reveal. Perhaps he was afraid I'd put it to bad use. Well, I hadn't always been innocent, though the thought of expunging Mike from any records hadn't occurred to me, I'd tried so hard to believe in him.

I didn't like the news about his alibi. I smacked my hands on the desk: was it his lying to the police or lying to me that hurt so I wanted physical pain?

Hazel mopped the chocolate with tissues from Helena's desk. Neither of us broke the silence.

At last I pulled myself together. I had to start somewhere. Plugging all the bits of computer together and switching on seemed a good place. Why, I could even play a computer game. Patience, maybe. Solitaire, they called it.

Hazel gasped when I switched on, but then subsided when she saw what I was calling up. I even chose the cards where the sun intermittently stuck its tongue out. Each time I dealt there was a preponderance of royalty creating jams. I was just about to try the intellectual challenge of battleships when Roger came in.

To be honest, he did look horribly as if he'd been living up to his name, his eyes pouchy and his face distinctly unshaven. But at this hour he could simply have been asleep – again, Chris's urgency defeated me. He tipped the sandwich in the bin, stared at and moved towards me the half-empty cup, and pulled up a chair. Linking his fingers, he cracked the knuckles loudly.

'Right. Where do we start?' he demanded.

'You're the geek.'

'Chris rates you in that field,' he said, moving us back to

the home page. 'A quick run-through of these?' He poked the disks and CD-ROMs.

'Those have all been checked anyway,' Hazel said. 'Mostly games. Not the sort you'd want your kid to play.'

No doubt she meant it for Clive. But I winced. *My kid*. It meant something now, didn't it? It meant I wouldn't want Nicholas – *Steph!* – playing them.

'But he's got all these reference things,' she was saying. 'I've known libraries less well-stocked than this.'

'My theory was that he photographed people, checked them in, say, old *Guardian* files, and if they had any value would either blackmail them or sell a new story to Fleet Street. Like mine,' I added ruefully.

'The one with Winston Rhodes?'

'It could have done him a lot of harm. If it hadn't been for Chris – Superintendent Groom – acting so quickly it would have done.'

'D'you know him well? Winston Rhodes?'

I dismissed my usual factual rigmarole: I'd act on my suspicion that there was a shade of personal interest in her question. 'Well enough to introduce him to you at my next party.' My engagement party?

She lowered her eyes, then grinned. 'I'd like that. OK, I'll get you that toast. Anything else?'

'Milk, please,' I said. Nursery food. Comfort food.

'Right. Let's see what we can find in here,' Clive said.

Most of the files were straightforward enough. In his access program Guy had got an interesting set of addresses and phone numbers, which I printed out. Not everyone, after all, kept at his fingertips the numbers of the news desks of our leading tabloids. Clive wrote something on it and stowed it in a file.

Guy had been more discreet about his accounts, however. The computer demanded a password. This should have been easy but my head was still cotton-wool, and Clive's no better.

'What if it closes down if we get it wrong?' he asked.

'What if it erases itself if we get it wrong?' I added. 'What we need is a sixteen-year-old with acne and computer confidence.'

'My kid brother. Only I don't think the Super would like me to invite him to the party.'

'This is daft. There must be dozens of official police geeks. Why me?' I tapped away, using his initials, combinations of letters from his name, bits of his address.

'And why me? I'm not the expert he's cracked me up to be. There's something up, maybe. The words politics and power keep coming together in my mind. No, that won't work either.'

Nothing. Just as we feared, the computer told us it wasn't going to play with us any more if we didn't get it right next shot.

'Oh, fuck!' I spilt the now lukewarm chocolate all over my lap. As I mopped, it occurred to me that the word had more than one meaning, and that it might have summed up Guy's attitude to life. I tapped. It did.

'Fucking hell!' Clive said, as a virtual page turned, to give a set of columns.

We had a list of place names; sets of initials; another set of letters and figures; and sums of money. Large ones.

'Well,' I said, 'these meant enough to him to hide away from prying eyes. I just wish they meant something to me.' I buried my face in my hands.

'We've actually got an incident room full of officers,' Rogers said. 'Well, we will tomorrow. And there'll be a couple still around now. Why don't we print it all off and see what they can make of it?'

While the paper rolled out, I had another dab at my skirt.

I just hoped it had been ruined in a good cause. Hazel reappeared, closing the door behind her with her bottom.

She peered at me. 'Why don't I find you something to wear and I'll swill that out? You can just wait outside while she changes. He won't mind that.'

Which explains how I came to be wearing a paper suit when Chris flung open the door ten minutes later. Expecting a far from party mood, I thrust a wad of paper at him. 'Those are all the files we've got at so far. What I'd like now is a set of spare floppy disks.'

He raised an eyebrow but disappeared. Returning after five minutes, he flipped a new box at me. 'Not thinking of taking them out of the building, are you?'

'I'm thinking of your having a set of duplicates just in case the computer goes down.'

He stared.

'Well, it's not unknown. And you've been having communication problems recently, haven't you? Connected with computers? I'm not taking any risks.'

He opened his mouth, but shut it. He worried the cellophane wrapping on the box of disks – a particularly impenetrable one, apparently. Quips about tampon wrappers would not have gone down well. At last, he tore through it with his teeth.

There was another battle of wills going on. Mine and his. I was aware of Clive's attention flicking from one of us to the other. I wanted quite desperately to know how Mike was getting on. But I was equally determined not to ask Chris anything. His treatment of Nick – Steph! – had appalled me. His police conscience might justify treating a possible criminal badly but Steph had saved my life and got no more than a cold handshake for his pains. Talk about visiting the sins of the mother on to the next generation.

No conversation claiming my attention, I copied file after file, then, just as systematically, printed out those I hadn't yet explored. One recorded regular payments, apparently, and, in a parallel column, sets of figures which recurred again and again.

'Looks like bank account numbers,' Clive said.

'Be nice to know who's paying him,' I said. 'And for what. Look: ASS! I ask you!'

'I'll take them downstairs, shall I?' Clive gathered a sheaf and opened the door.

'Yes. Take yourself off home, lad. You've done well.' Chris was going to ignore my efforts, was he?

'Not me. Couldn't have done it on my own. See you later, Soph.'

We flapped tired hands in farewell.

Chris and I hadn't moved our gaze from the screen when the door opened and shut again.

'AS, and it could be Art Sampson,' said a new voice. Peter Kirby's. 'It would tie in with the picture young Teddy drew. And I haven't seen them for some time, but I'd say two of the other pictures were of the Sampsons' sons.'

'The ones in permanent exile? The ones Sal mourns as if lost for ever?'

'The very same. This is the drug-feeding business I was telling you about, Gaffer. The complaint Teddy Nkosi made against persons unknown.'

I looked him straight in the eye. 'Why didn't you say something? The other day at my house? You seemed to pooh-pooh the whole idea.'

He sat down on Helena's chair and leaned towards me. 'Because, Sophie, we weren't on our own, were we? And we all know that someone was stopping me and the boss here communicating.'

'Harvinder Mann! Surely not!' Not someone who could joke like that.

'I don't know. I hope not. He seems a good copper.'

Chris turned and left the room without speaking.

Kirby's raised eyebrows matched mine.

I owed Chris enough loyalty not to offer any explanations.

'Hey, Sophie, are you sure you should be here?' he asked at last. 'You look dead knackered. Go on, you push off home. I'll organise someone to drive you. Chris shouldn't have asked you to do this. Not tonight.'

I smiled back. 'Hazel's off somewhere with my skirt. I'm not gracing the streets of Harborne like this!'

'I'll go find her.'

The disks. And the computer. What did I do about them? In this whole chaotic business, it occurred to me that there were only two people I could trust absolutely. Me and Chris. I had to see Chris alone before I left. I didn't want to grovel. But if that were the price for seeing him, then grovel I would.

Within minutes, Hazel reappeared. She'd not only sponged my skirt, she'd stood under a hand-drier with it until it was wearable, if creased. But changing back no longer seemed a priority. I dropped it by my bag.

'D'you know where Chris is?' I asked.

'Interviewing,' she said, deadpan enough for me to understand that it was Mike who was in there with him.

'Could you give him a message for me?'

'Fire away.'

I tried to work out neutral words that wouldn't offend his professionalism or alarm Mike. In the end, it seemed easier to type something. At least Guy's machine could do something useful:

Chris,
  I need to speak to you before I leave. On our own.
  S.

I passed it to her unfolded.

And sat. And waited.

I didn't produce anything as fancy as a sunburst, but I did manage to start a list of questions, tapping away on Guy's computer. I was beginning to think as quickly directly on to the screen as I did on paper, and there was no doubting that this nice laser printer would produce more legible results than my hand.

The letters stuttered and jumbled, but at last I made them make fierce sense.

Who ate lunch with Sal the day Guy died? If one man was Guy – 'big meal' – who was the other?

Surely, surely the bare hour Mike had been away from me would not have been enough for him to have got to Warley, eaten with Guy and Sal, removed the Epipen from Guy's boot, inserted bees he'd hidden somewhere into Guy's glove and then got back to me. In any case, we'd shared a sandwich before we left his house. No, common sense, if not trust – and where was that? – told me he was too conscientious to eat twice. Distrust – almost using Chris's voice – pointed out that eating two lunches would be nothing to killing someone. And he needn't have eaten. He could have made some excuse and gone outside.

The door opened. Chris.

Without speaking he read over my shoulder.

'Well?'

'Here are the disks. It's my theory that someone will tamper with the computer, so you'll need back-ups of everything.'

He gave a short laugh but took them anyway.

'No. Don't leave them – anywhere,' I said, as he dropped them on to the corner of Helena's desk.

He pocketed them. 'The computer will go into the tamper-proof room where we store evidence. If you've finished with it, that is?' He pointed to the screen.

'If you've got the answer to the question?'

'The question's certainly on my list. We've already put it to Sal. I'm afraid she insists it was Lowden. She says he asked her to lure Guy there and keep him talking while he burgled the car. Got rid of the Epipen in a council waste bin.'

'Do you believe her?'

'What reason has she to lie?'

'Plenty. Two sons and a husband. Have you checked that they really were abroad?'

'Well, that's one thing Peter Kirby and I have established.' He sat on Helena's chair, leaning forward as if for the first time he was really talking to me. 'If you saw the man with white hair the day you said you did, and in the circumstances Kirby and Mann describe there's no reason for you to have lied, then Kirby says he's sure Art was at that party. Sal's not been very co-operative about guest lists. Maybe you could suggest a few names.'

'Apart from Mike and Barkat and Teddy?'

'Point taken. I can't see Teddy as the bravest witness under fire.'

'There's always Mike and me.'

He ignored that, very pointedly.

'No doubt someone from the restaurant will be able to tell you if the three people who ate there were all there all the time.'

'Someone's on to that now. Restaurants don't close till late,' he added, suppressing a yawn.

It was catching. 'Could you organise some transport for me?' I asked.

'Won't you be waiting for Lowden?' His smile was enigmatic.

'You arrested him, remember?'

He shook his head. 'He's been released. Without charge. After he showed us very strong evidence to suggest that he was in fact shopping in Harborne at the relevant time. Some of these computerised tills print out the time of the transaction. We'll have to verify that the person making it was indeed Lowden, but I shouldn't imagine that will be difficult. The signature on the bill is identical to his, and he's shown us what was purchased.'

'So why isn't he free to go?' I was on my feet.

Another short laugh. 'He's making a statement. About the man with white hair. As soon as he saw Teddy's sketch he ID'd it. He was a bit irritated you hadn't mentioned it to him before. Art Sampson, of course.'

Chapter Thirty-One

I'd never hit Chris before, and I wasn't about to now, but I'd certainly never been as close. He'd stretched his joke far too thin. I wouldn't indulge him by asking what Mike's receipt was for, either.

'So, just to sum up,' I said, 'it looks as if Art Sampson is at the centre of things. It was he who had the row with Barkat, and no doubt you're busily trying to connect their movements for the twenty-four hours or so before Barkat died.'

'CID are,' he corrected me.

I fished round in my brain for that literary term which means describing a part in terms of the whole. Or did I mean whole in terms of a part? On the whole it was better to give up.

'And you've established that Barkat's car – at least, the one he was driving that night – contained both drugs and hair from a dead prostitute. And the woman died of extra-pure heroin. Meanwhile you – or *CID*! – also establish that Timpson used drugs to an extraordinarily cavalier extent, considering it could have finished his career full stop. And the two men are at the same party. A party held by Art and Sal. Do you have anything useful on either of them? Or on the handsome sons? Apart from doctoring innocent burgers, that is?' I leaned back and looked up at him. 'Have you shown Mike the sketches of them?'

'Handsome sons they are. To the best of my knowledge they're all as pure as the driven snow.' Perhaps for the benefit of my neck, he sat down so that I no longer had to look up at him. 'We're talking to Customs and Excise, of course. But they've never attracted undue attention, them or their father.'

Two bad clichés in one utterance. Chris must be as knackered as I was.

'I suppose it'd be too much to hope that even as we speak' – I was at it now! – 'someone is going through the contents of all Art's containers?'

'Could take ages. But then, we've got enough to encourage us to look.'

I nodded. 'What about Sal?'

'Well, it depends what was in the syringe, doesn't it?'

'She rather implied it wasn't water.'

'She could be up on an attempted murder charge. Another drugs link. But a woman can't be made to testify against her husband.'

'Don't forget the coke at the party. There was the mirror and the razor blade.'

'Whoever had used them hadn't been too high to remember to wipe all the prints. Except for the char-lady's. May even have been her that wiped them, I suppose.'

'You'd need to talk to someone with more experience of these matters, but I'd say one or two of the guests at the party were—' I paused, delicately.

'Working women,' he mimicked me. 'Old news, Sophie. Peter Kirby's been working on that connection. We could charge her with keeping a disorderly house, just as an extra. Trouble is, until we've turned her house inside out, we can't pull the really big, life-imprisonment stunt.'

'I wouldn't bother with the house,' I said, as the door opened to admit Hazel. 'I'd go for her garden shed.'

'Mr Lowden's waiting in reception, sir,' she announced.

Chris nodded. 'Off you go, then, Sophie. I'll let you know about that syringe.'

'Thanks. I'd like to know if it was attempted murder.' I was half out of the door when I dodged back. 'Chris – remember what I said about that computer.'

His eyes narrowed. 'I won't forget.'

Mike levered himself out of one of the deplorable chairs. He made no attempt to kiss me, and did not remark on my unusual gear. The wave he gave to the officers lurking behind that high counter was no more than courteous. A taxi thrummed away, pumping diesel into Smethwick's already polluted air.

Mike gave his address.

'I've phoned Teddy. He won't be expecting us.'

I nodded.

We both fastened our seatbelts. He was so quiet I didn't know what to do. But as I turned, he reached for my hand and gripped it.

As we headed into the city, the atmosphere got steadily heavier. The driver, who'd been as quiet as us, announced they'd had a big storm over Sutton Coldfield way, with flash floods. Maybe it was moving south, he said.

Whether it was or not, Bournville was like a Turkish bath. While I opened all the windows, Mike busied himself with glasses and malt whisky. It seemed natural to move into the garden. From time to time, the distant sky lit up. The thunderclaps followed the flashes more and more closely. We sat in continued silence, sipping. I wasn't anxious or apprehensive. I could sense he was still looking for the right words, the right emotions, perhaps. But it would be all right.

The storm was certainly getting closer.

'Maybe we'd better get this lot protected.' He pushed the

chairs and table together, swathing them in a shaped plastic cover. But we stayed out, watching, listening. He topped up our drams.

At last rain started to fall: huge drops you could almost count.

I'd already slipped off my sandals, and the paper jump suit behaved like a wet T-shirt. It struck me I'd be more comfortable without it. And without the rest of my clothes. In a moment, the two of us stood naked together, letting the rain drop where it would.

It was only when we were dry and in bed, the temperature having dropped so much we were glad to close windows and pull up sheets, that we started to talk. God knows what time it was. And Mike had a day's play ahead of him, an England place to win.

'You heard about the receipt,' he asked.

'Hmm.'

'You'll want to know why I didn't mention it before.'

'It did cross my mind.'

'Chris didn't tell you?'

'I didn't ask him.'

In the darkness I could feel rather than see him smile.

'I thought I might ask you – hell! That was close!' The flash and rumble were almost simultaneous.

'Well, I might as well switch the light on and show you. With this lot raging round us we won't be able to sleep for a bit.' He swung out of bed, crossing to his clothes, folded on a chair. The trousers hung down the back.

He was back in a couple of strides. I loved the way he could be naked with me, as completely unselfconscious as I was with him.

'You remember that a woman can't be made to give evidence against her husband?'

I nodded.

'That's why – apart from that moment with Teddy – I haven't mentioned marriage. I didn't want you to think even for a second that I might want to shelter behind you.'

I shook my head in disbelief. 'It never crossed my mind.'

'Not yours. Other people's maybe. Anyway, when I saw this I thought what a wonderful engagement ring it would make. OK, we'd known each other less than a week. Now I've known you long enough to realise you'd rather have a say in your own ring when – if! – we get it. In the mean time, I'd still like you to have this.'

'This' was a big, baguette-cut emerald. Curiously it was too big for my engagement finger, but fitted the right ring finger as if it had been made for it.

The storm receded. We slept.

The rain had smashed many of his plants flat, and splashed others with earth. Apart from that, the world smelt wonderful. Risking a further soaking from the puddles which had accumulated in the hollows, we took the cover off the table and chairs – it was clearly a morning for an outside breakfast. Fortunately, since we didn't seem to have stayed at his house for some time, Mike was the sort of person who kept bread and fruit juice in his freezer.

The chairs were distinctly wobbly after their night with wet feet – no doubt they'd swollen unevenly. The table was particularly bad.

'Remind me not to go wherever you got these for my new chairs,' I said, not quite seriously.

'After last night you wouldn't want to. They were from Sal. A present from Sal. Maybe,' he looked at me sideways, 'a bribe. To lure me to her bed.'

'I wondered if she'd tried.'

'I bet you wondered if she succeeded. Well, to be honest,

she did. Not just because of the chairs. There was a point – while Sandra was with Guy – when . . . But' – at first his laugh was embarrassed, but then it became almost joyful – 'you know what? I couldn't get it up. Oh, Sophie – it was so humiliating. As a toyboy I'm a complete failure!'

'Good,' I said. Then I became serious. 'Do you suppose that was why she went for me – because she was jealous?'

'Because you'd started to ask dangerous questions, more like. No, Sal hasn't an ounce of jealousy in her body.'

There was no point in arguing.

'Was this some of the stuff Art imported?'

'Yes. What are you doing?'

I was on my knees, looking at it closely. 'Did she say anything when she gave it you?'

'Made some joke about it being an investment.'

Did people as rich as Sal make jokes about investments?

'Did it come in a flat-pack?'

'Good God, no! Exclusive ethnic stuff like this?'

'Have you ever tried to take it apart?'

He looked at me as if I was away with the fairies. At this point the doorbell rang. He disappeared.

He emerged in a moment. 'We're to go inside and shut all our windows. It's the wasp man. He says there may be the odd angry insect around. Hey, why are you bringing that? I've got chairs inside!'

It didn't take the man long to deal with Mike's unwelcome guests. I was about to repeat my crack about the hornets' nest but I stopped. Taking the chair apart had exposed something that was no laughing matter.

A phone call having established that the downpour meant that the pitch at Edgbaston wouldn't be playable till lunch at the earliest, Mike and I drove off with the whole patio set in the back of his car. In fact, the way the clouds were bubbling up over the city suggested further storms.

'Too bright, too early,' I remarked, invoking Black Country weather lore. Not that I cared much. The brilliance of the morning brought out the best in the big stone glinting on my right hand. I'd never had anything of so much value, in both intrinsic and emotional terms. Mike must have glimpsed me wiggling my finger to make the sparks fly; he removed a hand from the steering wheel to clasp mine.

We'd still not discussed the idea of marriage. There was a tacit assumption that the relationship was going to last, and I had no objections to making the public declaration that a wedding would involve. Quite the reverse. In fact, now I came to think of it, a bit of dressing up and jollification wouldn't come at all amiss. It could be glorious fun, something that would shine out in a life that had been full of mundane hard work as long as I could remember. I giggled, like a teenager. And then it became a full-blown joyous laugh.

'Hm?' Mike asked.

'It's just that – I'm so happy!'

When he could, he stopped the car and proved that he was too.

Happiness was clearly the wrong emotion for Piddock Road. A request to see any of the three men with whom we'd been dealing was denied: they were all in a meeting.

'We'd better see one of the team,' I said. 'We've got something in the car they'll want.'

The civilian receptionist pulled a face, but tapped her phone again. We sat on the brown chairs and waited.

I could feel Mike's rising irritation as time passed. At least he was wearing jeans. My skirt was short enough for more thigh than was comfortable to be sticking to the rexine. We waited.

At last Mike heaved himself to his feet. He was tall enough to lean intimidatingly on the counter, whereas I counted myself lucky I didn't have to stand on tiptoe to see over it. He leaned. 'Look, I know it's not your fault, but we have to speak to someone in CID soon. I have a car-load of evidence out there. Heads, I can tell you, will roll if anyone steals my car with that cargo in it.'

She cast her eyes up. 'I have tried to reach them.'

'Well,' he said, 'try succeeding.'

She did try again. The message was relayed that the whole of CID were in a meeting.

'Tell them to get one person out now. Or I'll go to the press.'

We sat, and resumed our wait.

Not, this time, for long.

The interior door was flung open by no less a personage than Chris, who had aged by ten years since last night. Not altogether surprising, given the amount of sleep he'd probably had. Even his voice was harsh with fatigue. Or something else. 'Yes?'

'Someone has to take delivery of what's in my car,' Mike said. 'After that we'll leave you to whatever you're engaged in. You can check the stuff at your leisure,' he added. 'I just want it out of my keeping.'

'Bring the car into the car park.' Chris disappeared.

We left through the street door.

'What the hell can be up?' Mike demanded as he opened the car door.

'Something major, I fancy. Something to do with Kirby and Chris not getting information. And it's the worst thing, isn't it, when you find a bent policeman?'

Mike nodded. 'The man looked ill. Which way?'

'Follow the road round.'

A couple of constables were waiting for us.

'*Garden furniture!* Is this right, sir? You've made all this to-do about *garden furniture?*' The elder one stood arms akimbo, not attempting to get it out.

'Garden furniture with an extra something,' I said. 'You might say, a hidden ingredient. Which is why we want it logged and then dismembered only in the presence of a senior officer. Superintendent Groom, for instance.'

'He's a bit tied up right now.'

'So I gathered. But this may help him tie up some other things. Like people wanted for murder. Careful – don't let that leg come out of its socket till he's there.'

Still grudging, one unloaded the table, the other taking a couple of chairs. Mike extricated the last two himself, and set off after the constables. I locked up and followed.

A sergeant was already issuing Mike with a receipt.

'You won't leave the stuff sitting there, will you?' I said. 'You'll have to put it somewhere very secure – the room you store your evidence, for instance.'

'You make a habit of telling people how to do their jobs, do you?' one of the coppers asked.

'I'm afraid she does,' Peter Kirby's voice declared.

I whipped round. He looked as grey and drained as Chris. Almost. And angry. But he managed a smile. 'The bugger of it is, she's usually right,' he added. 'Have you two got time for a coffee?'

'When we've seen that lot sealed,' I said.

We were back in the ugly room where we'd first met Harvinder Mann. He was nowhere to be seen. There was an ominous stain on the wall, as if last night's rain had found an unauthorised route from the roof.

Kirby laid three mugs of herbal tea on the desk, rubbing his knuckles where they'd pressed on the mugs. 'Should have used a tray,' he said. 'Hot. Now, why all this song and dance about Chris Groom being present when that stuff's looked at?'

I looked him in the eye: he wouldn't like this. 'Because of this funny communication business. I hope you're straight. I hope Harvinder's straight. But at least I know Chris is straight. He'd rather die than do anything wrong.'

'You've seen him this morning?'

'Didn't like what I saw. What is it? The computer?'

He nodded. 'Someone's fed it a bug.'

Chapter Thirty-Two

'That's no problem,' I said, refraining with admirable self-control from falling about on the floor in hysterical laughter. 'Chris has paper records and a set of floppy disks. The evidence is still intact.'

'You don't understand, do you? It means someone in here tampered with the computer.'

I glanced at Mike.

'Hence all of you being tied up in a meeting?' he prompted.

'Exactly.'

'Any idea who?' As he hesitated, I added, 'Well, it can't be you since you're here talking to us. Which leaves Harvinder or one of the other CID team. Oh my God, it also leaves Helena, doesn't it? Oh, Jesus!' I found a chair and sat. 'And there I was encouraging Chris to leave as much as he could to her.' I buried my head in my hands. 'Me and my big mouth.'

'We've no proof, of course.'

'You bloody should have. I take it leaving the computer where it was instead of stowing it somewhere safe was part of someone's grand plan? Entrapment?'

He looked shifty.

'Has she admitted it?' I pursued.

'She's not been available to deny or confirm anything. She came in at the usual time and left immediately.'

'And is now—?'

He shrugged. 'We've got all ports and airports covered,' he added, more positively.

'Couldn't someone have set up those clever surveillance things we hear about?' Mike asked. 'Seems a bit elementary, somehow.'

'Not to mention expensive.'

'Even so!' Mike appeared to hunt for words. 'You've got all these deaths. You've got Sophie put at the most terrible risk—'

'Maybe if you hadn't come up with that crazy cat alibi, if you'd come clean about what you'd really been doing . . .'

The men squared up to each other.

I intervened. 'And there I was happily suggesting she help him with his mail.'

Peter made an effort. 'I don't think you can blame yourself for the fact that she kept intercepting messages between him and me. And she got to read all his mail anyway. But there is a certain amount of anger in the air, believe me. Mostly directed at himself, of course.'

'Maybe the contents of Mike's furniture will cheer him,' I said. 'Especially if he does check it out himself.'

'Do you want to be there?'

'I'd give my teeth to see his face.'

'And it is my furniture,' Mike added.

So there we were, all dolled up in paper suits, squatting round Chris as, wearing gloves, he dismembered the furniture leg by leg. Each hollow tube was full. Chris had already laid a little trail of polythene bags from the table beside him on the floor.

Still squatting, he peered inside, exploring with his fingers.

At last he came up with something different – also in a polythene bag. A screw of paper. He opened it and without comment held it for Mike to read.

To Chris's evident chagrin, Mike threw back his head and laughed. 'Oh, show it to Sophie!'

Raising his eyebrows, Chris found a polythene bag large enough to take it now it was flat. Eventually he passed it to me.

Mike darling,
  You may not be much of a fuck but you're a real sweetie. Have this on me. It may improve your perfor-mance (won't say where!) – if not it'll certainly improve your bank balance.
  XXX

'And has it?' Chris asked, with no trace of humour in his voice.

Mike blinked. 'You've got the complete consignment.'

At least he had as soon as I returned the note.

Chris nodded, but not as if he was convinced. 'OK. This'll nail her, I suppose. And the witnesses at the restaurant are prepared to testify that you were not one of the lunch guests. Oh, Timpson and her husband, of course. Tell Teddy we used his sketch. And apparently she made some great to-do about leaving something in her car and needing it. So she had ample opportunity to filch the Epipen.'

'And plant the bees?'

'Ah. Well, there's something interesting about the bees. Not only are they not English and living in Mike's loft, they're actually French and used to live in vineyards.' Chris managed a smile. 'So well spotted, Sophie.'

I gave a modest nod. 'But how did she get them into his gloves? And persuade them to stay there?'

301

'I suppose you'd carry them in a small jar or a test-tube or something,' Mike said. 'Once they were in the fingers of the glove, all you'd have to do is fold them over. The leather's so heavy it would stay put. And Guy always used to clap his gloves together as he walked out to the middle – they'd be quite irritated by the time he shoved his hands inside. And the inner gloves would hold the stings nicely in place. My God!' He turned away.

'But how come his bag was in her car? That posh Merc we saw in the cricket club car park?'

'Right,' Chris agreed.

'But why?'

'Because he came in by train that day. We've got computer enhanced video footage. Obvious really. If your car's being serviced.'

'Eh? Serviced? I thought it was in some station car park?'

'The garage was under instruction to leave it there *after* its service. All part of their customer care. They'd already collected it from there. Like I said, obvious, really.'

'Timpson was no fool,' Mike said.

'Indeed he wasn't. All those initials and figures—'

'They'd be destinations and amounts of drugs,' I said. 'Sorry. Should have thought last night. I suppose you can get quite a lot of stuff into a cricket bag without anyone knowing. But why bump off an efficient courier?'

'The photos,' Mike said. 'Maybe he was trying his hand at blackmailing Art: more of the profit or I blow the gaff.'

'Spot on, I'd say,' Kirby said. 'Still no sign of his camera, though.'

I jumped. I'd forgotten he was there.

'I'd also say,' he continued, 'that he was trying to recruit Teddy to do the same thing. On an international level. You quite sure they never asked you, Mike?'

'Quite. But if I'd succumbed personally to that stuff' – he pointed to the bags of white crystals – 'I guess they'd have found ways of trying to persuade me.'

'There was another sketch.' Chris snapped his fingers. 'Someone we haven't placed yet. You remember: Art, Art's sons and another bloke.'

'And me.' Kirby assumed the hostile facial expression Teddy had caught. Then he grinned.

'Sophie – you know something about this guy,' Chris said. 'Your face gives you away every time,' he added dourly.

'Mike and I saw him pissing in Sal's swimming pool. You remember, Mike? Big-built man.'

'Maybe if I saw the sketch,' he said without conviction.

'OK. Get this lot sealed up, will you, Peter? We'll adjourn to my office.'

I wasn't sure about that; but he'd have to face it soon enough, and why not with us? As it was, we arrived to find a consignment of furniture, this lot in polythene sheets. Chris stared in disbelief.

'Christmas come early?' Mike suggested, starting on the sticky tape.

'No. Leave it. I didn't order it. Don't touch it till we've checked the provenance. Use the other seats. Tea? It'll have to be from the canteen.'

'I'll sort something out,' I said, heading to Helena's sanctum.

'I—' But he stopped, shrugging.

Helena's office had been transformed from the little outpost of tidy efficiency into twelve square yards of chaos. There were sheets of paper everywhere, covered with shards of the china I'd given Chris. She'd sprinkled the lot with the contents of the tea caddy and coffee tin.

'And Helena's connection with all this?' I asked, stepping back into Chris's room, dusting tiny flakes of china off my feet.

'I've no idea. I've nothing to connect her with the Sampsons, nothing at all.'

'Maybe I can help there.' I told him about the lift I'd given her. 'It'll maybe provide whoever talks to Sal with a topic of conversation.'

'Have you got a photo of this Helena woman?' Mike asked. 'Well, you must have, on her file. Maybe – I've known Sal and Art for years, remember – I could make a connection for you.'

Peter headed for the door.

'Hang on.' Flushing deeply, Chris dug in his wallet.

Mike took the little photo. He nodded curtly. 'Used to be Art's secretary. Plain Helen in those days.' He laid it face down on Chris's desk, holding it there as if keeping a lid on his anger. 'Must have left about six years ago. Maybe less.'

Harvinder interrupted a lingering silence. 'Here are the sketches, Gaffer.' He looked as if he was bringing funeral flowers.

Mike reached for them. 'Christ, I knew he was good but not this good! He's really caught you, hasn't he, Peter? So this is who you reckon was – yes! Mind you, he won't want this to get about, Chris!'

'I have reason to believe,' I said, 'that he may have been blackmailed. Remember Teddy said he'd taken no part in the burger-lacing incident?'

'And?' Chris prompted.

'I believe his solicitor is trying to persuade him to come forward.'

'For Christ's sake, give me a fucking name, won't you?'

And Chris never swore.

304

Mike looked at me. 'Sophie doesn't know his name.'

Chris turned on him. 'Let Sophie fight her own battles. She's more than capable.'

As if he hadn't spoken, Mike continued, 'Can't you wait for his solicitor to do the biz?'

'Oh, for Christ's sake—'

'OK.' Mike named a prominent local businessman, known as much for his charitable work as for his wealth, which was considerable.

Chris nodded, with no apparent gratitude. 'OK, get on the phone to Afzal, Peter. And get someone to bring some bloody tea!'

'I've got some herbal. Will that do?' Peter left.

There was a vicious silence. I was the least able to break it: six months ago a situation like this would have led me back to Chris's bed, and if ever a man needed comfort and oblivion it was now. But not from me, the woman wearing the evidence that had released Mike from arrest. The stone was so large it would have taken a much less observant man than Chris to miss it.

Harvinder coughed. 'Mike – your club have been on the phone. There's been another heavy shower over Edgbaston – play's unlikely to resume till mid-afternoon. But they'd like you to phone in as soon as possible.'

'Hell, this could cost us the match. And a win over Glamorgan would have been useful. Do you play, Harvinder?'

He shook his head. 'Badminton.'

'West Midlands champion,' Chris said, as if giving the information hurt. 'Ah! Peter!' He made an effort. 'Those are the most disgusting mugs I've ever seen!'

'My nephew gave them me. Come on, they're clean and you can't say they're not cheerful.'

'Any news of what was in Sal's syringe?' I asked, sniffing the tea. Lemon and ginger.

'The same sort of extremely pure heroin that finished the prozzies,' Peter said. 'Interesting way to die.'

'She didn't just want to get me addicted, like the guy in that movie?'

Peter shook his head. 'She wanted you dead. They haven't,' he added grimly, 'yet cultured whatever bugs the syringe might have carried.'

'For Christ's sake – d'you need to tell her that?' Mike yelled.

Chris looked at him as if he were seven. 'In my experience Sophie's always wanted to know the truth, the whole truth—'

'Even so!' Mike shuddered.

'I suppose there's a connection,' I said, thinking an interruption would be timely, largely because despite myself I preferred Chris's less chivalrous approach, 'between the dead prostitutes and the women at that party – the ones who tried to plaster themselves over Mike. You must have noticed them, Peter. Hell, they were so obvious even my butcher refuses to go to parties there.'

That was something from which my nose had, after all, been conspiciously absent.

'Tying up nicely. And tying up with Barkat. Do you know,' he demanded, getting up and kicking free of the chair, 'the bastard used to make his women pay to – to service him? Beat them up if they didn't want sex, made them pay if they did. Two of the girls were real gone on him. The rest were shit-scared.'

'Girls in the plural?'

'Nice little earner. A whole string of – of tarts. Sells them drugs. If anyone gets stroppy, make sure the stuff's extra pure. They take their usual and – whoof! End of problem. Not,' he added, managing a smile, 'cricket. I shouldn't imagine there'll be any more parties for a few years. 'And I can't say I'll be sorry. It's tricky, this job, having to mix with all sorts – being sufficiently matey to convince them and yet keeping your distance and staying clean. And my wife hated Art like poison. Never wanted to go.'

I should imagine she'd made her feelings pretty clear.

'We only went because I knew him down south. Anyway, it won't take much to tie them together. A bit of graft, a bit of patience. That's what we're good at.'

Mike rubbed his face. 'What about Barkat's accident? We know there was this chase, and that it seemed to be Barkat doing the chasing. Right? That vehicle that jumped the lights – was that part of someone's plot?'

'Seems it was just some bugger who was pissed as a newt and – well, all we can charge him with is dangerous driving and failing to stop at the scene of an accident.'

'He can kill someone and—'

'If Barkat hadn't been chasing hell for leather after someone else . . . Oh, these things are never straightforward, are they?' Chris looked as if he was drowning.

'You'll sort everything out in the end,' I said, hoping that would apply to his private life, too.

Mike was parking outside my house when I said, 'I don't need an engagement ring, Mike. It's not that I don't want to marry you, don't think that. And I quite think a big, silly wedding would be nice. But being engaged – there's something horribly naff and bourgeois about it.'

'There might be something nice and comforting about it if you're stuck in Brum and I'm swanning round Oz.'

I didn't ask who for.

'And I thought – a mate of mine had a ring specially designed for his wife. In the Jewellery Quarter they do that sort of thing. And it would be nice . . . Maybe a Christmas present? That you just happen to wear on that hand?'

All this money he was lavishing on me! I'd have to stop him, to explain that I couldn't hope to compete, dearly as I'd love to. Soon. But later. In the mean time I leaned across and kissed him. Only as we pulled apart did I realise that Aggie was standing on her front step with a grandstand view. We got out of the car.

'Only that son of yours has been round,' she said. 'Brought you some flowers – they're in my sink. Hang on.'

Mike squeezed my hand.

There was a note.

Dear Sophie,
    You did great last night. Soon as I've talked to Mum and Dad we'll have a balti, right?
    Steph (Nick!)
    PS It'll all turn out all right.

And perhaps it would.

A Coffin for Two

Quintin Jardine

After cracking their first case together as a private investigation team, Oz Blackstone and Primavera Philips find themselves simultaneously in love and in the money. And where better to lie back and contemplate life than the picturesque village of St Marti, on the rugged Costa Brava.

But is their new home quite so idyllic as it looks? Some very dark secrets begin to emerge as the inhabitants draw them into the intrigue which bubbles away beneath the surface, until suddenly, faced with a mysterious skeleton and an unauthenticated Dali masterpiece, Prim and Oz stumble across one of the century's most amazing stories . . .

'Entertaining . . . keeps you intrigued'
Carlisle News & Star

0 7472 5575 X

HEADLINE

A Word After Dying

Ann Granger

Superintendent Alan Markby and his girlfriend, civil servant Meredith Mitchell, are in need of a holiday – and the Cotswold village of Parsloe St John seems the perfect choice. Their neighbour, retired journalist Wynne Carter, is as convivial as the village itself and, over a glass of blackberry wine, indulges in her latest obsession, Olivia Smeaton, a racy old lady whose life – and death – she is convinced are not all they seem.

Markby is more interested in buying Olivia's house than the circumstances of her vacating it, but Meredith is intrigued: by the old lady, the death of a cherished horse and a dusty junk shop run by a white witch. When another fatality – of a very grisly nature – is discovered, it seems her suspicion is justified. Clearly Olivia isn't the only enigma in Parsloe St John . . .

'Probably the best current example of a crime-writer who has taken the classic English village detective story and brought it up to date' *Birmingham Post*

'Classic tale . . . a good feel for understated humour, a nice ear for dialogue' *The Times*

'Deft plotting and elegant descriptive prose . . . a delicate comic touch and endearing eccentric characters' *Publishers Weekly*

0 7472 5187 8

HEADLINE